"The action is nonstop and deadly, the details compelling, the story surefooted and satisfying."
—Rutledge Etheridge, author of
Agent of Destruction

"A blend of science fiction and martial arts with a strong element of fantasy . . . Entertaining."
—*Science Fiction Chronicle*

Iroshi
Laicy Campbell came to Earth to learn the way of the sword, and became a ronin. But it is on the planet Rune that she discovers at last the task she was meant for.

The Glaive
The Iroshi returns—and when her mentor and friend is killed, she vows to seek the truth about his death. But the truth runs deep . . .

Persea
Martin Dukane's obsession with the Iroshi knows no bounds. And rather than see her powers wane with age, he will make her legend immortal. Even if he has to kill her to do it . . .

Ace Books by Cary Osborne

DARKLOOM

CARY OSBORNE

ACE BOOKS, NEW YORK

This book is an Ace original edition,
and has never been previously published.

DARKLOOM

An Ace Book / published by arrangement with
the author

PRINTING HISTORY
Ace edition / October 1998

The Penguin Putnam Inc. World Wide Web site address is
http://www.penguinputnam.com

Check out the Ace Science Fiction/Fantasy
newsletter, and much more, at Club PPI!

ISBN: 0-441-00569-1

ACE®
Ace Books are published by The Berkley Publishing Group,
a member of Penguin Putnam Inc.,
375 Hudson Street, New York, NY 10014.
ACE and the "A" design are trademarks
belonging to Charter Communications, Inc.

PRINTED IN THE UNITED STATES OF AMERICA

10 9 8 7 6 5 4 3 2 1

DARKLOOM

PROLOGUE

Even with the heavy drapes open, the room was dark and oppressive. If the sun had been shining, there might have been some relief, but the apartment held too many dark memories. After it had been closed up for so long, light did not seem to fill the corners anymore.

Arden stood at the window watching rain fall in sheets. Grey clouds and fog shielded the world from brightness that might be too distracting, just as the drapes had once shielded Appolyona from the same thing.

Maybe it was a mistake to accept the quarters of the former seeress, but work had already started on preparing the rooms for her use. The loom was gone, that artifact of days long gone, and this room would soon be her living room. The bedroom boasted a new bed, installed for what she had thought would be temporary use. It already had memories of its own for her to fight off.

She would always remember the nights of love and passion in that room. And the long talks into the early hours of the morning. Arden stepped back and studied the floor just in front of the window. Almost on that very spot she had said goodbye to Rafe. Captain Semmes.

What a busy day that had been—just three days ago. The empress-to-be had offered her the position of Commander of the Palace Guard instead of sending her on her way as she had hoped. By agreement with Pac Terhn, her guide in the worlds she entered with lifeweave, that was the only way she could leave Jessa's service. He must be rolling with laughter. No one else but the abbot knew about that agreement. Especially not Rafe, who did not understand her determination to stay on Glory.

"Are you sure you have to stay?" he had asked just before leaving.

"As sure as you are that you have to leave" had been her answer.

"I'll be back," he said. "We salvagers get all over."

"I know."

She did know. But what if he did not come back?

So much change in so short a time. Jessa to be empress, something she had not wanted to do. Appolyona, Jessa's mother, one-time concubine to the emperor, and seeress, dead. Along with Granid Parcq, Jessa's father, whom some said died of a broken heart. She herself, Arden Grenfell, living and working in the palace, protecting the empress and all that surrounded her, instead of going off with the man she loved.

Arden stepped back into the bedroom to stand before the mirror. She adjusted the maroon tunic and put on the peaked cap. One more glance in the mirror, and she took off the hat and tossed it onto the bed. No hat for her, no matter what protocol said.

She looked at her watch and quickly snatched up her sword and strapped it on with the waist belt. She had better hurry, or she would be inexcusably late. She should be the last person to miss the coronation.

The frigid courtyard was filled with individual combat, monks against robbers, the battle not yet decided. Steel clanged against steel, both near and far. Brother Bryan faced two, a man and a woman, giving them a lesson in swordsmanship they might not live to remember.

Arden could only note his struggle in passing. She faced two adversaries of her own, both men, both bigger than she. But neither was a match for her skill, and together they only had a slim chance of beating her. It wasn't that they were bad, they had simply never dedicated themselves to learning the way of the sword. The gang's forte was to attack quickly, grab what they could, and get out. This time, their leaders had seriously miscalculated.

The man on the right collapsed from a slice across his chest. Steam rose from the cut. The one on the left backed away, seeming ready to leave the field to her. She pursued him, not letting him break off, pressing with blow after blow as he backpedaled. Off balance, he was barely able to defend himself. After five more strikes, his arms were visibly tiring, his feet tangling. She ended it by dropping to one knee, thrusting upward, the tip of her katana penetrating his abdomen just below the sternum. His own momentum dropped him on his back, where he lay still a moment from the shock of the wound. She pulled her sword free and turned to face another invader.

Those still in sight were running away as fast as they could. This band had known little of the martial arts background of the training at the monastery, if anything at all. Like so many people, they had assumed that it was a strictly religious organization with members who could scarcely protect themselves.

Although it was well known among the military, Abbot Grayson had never felt any need to broadcast their martial arts background. It would become more well known now, especially after they had repelled three such raids in the past year. This was the fourth, but the only time Arden had taken part in defending the monastery. Most of the time she was in the capital, seeing to her duties as head of the imperial guards and palace security.

She surveyed the battlefield. Some snow lay about the gardens, making the bare bushes and trees seem even more stark. Melancholy descended over her. Another battle, and still no red haze. It made her feel incomplete as always, as if that one warrior's achievement would always elude her. Bryan had told her it was because of the lifeweave, that its use had clouded her mind, and no matter how much she practiced or fought for real, she would never reach that pinnacle as long as the fiber's effects were in her system.

All she knew of it was what she had described: a red haze that clouded the eyes, bathing everything in its color, slowing movement, even sound. She had tried to reconcile herself to never achieving it, but could not.

She caught sight of Grayson across the way, holding his left arm. He was wounded, and that drove all thought of the red haze from her mind. She ran toward him, shouting for Brother Marion, the monastery's physician.

"It's all right," Grayson assured her as she ran up to him. "Only a scratch."

Blood ran down the back of his hand. It was definitely more than a scratch.

Marion appeared and cut away the sleeve of the brown robe to check the wound. Like most of the monks, Grayson was inside at the time of the attack and had not bothered to slip on a coat.

"Dammit, there are others more seriously wounded," Grayson boomed. "Tend to them first."

The physician looked up at him, then at Arden. Although worse than a scratch, the wound really did not appear serious. She nodded.

"I'll tend to it," she said.

Marion nodded and hurried off toward a monk lying very quietly on the grass. After kneeling beside him a moment, the physician helped the wounded man get to his feet. He seemed unsteady but whole. She took the severed sleeve that Grayson had held onto and gently wiped away some of the blood in order to get a better look at the actual cut. It was long but not deep.

"Come on inside so I can wash it," she said.

"Don't fuss! I can help the wounded here."

Arden looked around at monks helping each other, some checking the enemy dead.

"There are enough helping already," she said. "Come along."

Only a few of the monks appeared to be hurt, leaving the majority of the members to tend their wounded. He huffed, but in the end, he let her lead him inside. In his private bathroom, she washed his arm and dried it. She had him hold a thick towel over the cut and sent him into his study while she searched out antiseptic and bandages from the cabinet.

"The raids are getting worse," he said, then winced as she dabbed antiseptic on the cut. "These robber bands are striking all over the country."

"I know. At least they haven't hit the palace or the capital yet. That's one reason I could get away for a few days."

Two major developments had occurred after the new empress was crowned. First, she had agreed to meet with the enemies of Glory to work out a peace for the war that had gone on much too long. Second, too many of the soldiers that were called home and turned into civilians had nowhere to go. There simply had not been enough jobs to go around, and many of the soldiers had never done anything else anyway.

Some of the ex-military men were taken into the imperial guards and the home guards, in part because so many of their compatriots quickly formed roving bands of robbers. Glory was becoming an armed camp now that peace had been declared.

Grayson shook his head.

"Everything has come apart in just a year and a half," he said. "I don't think anyone knew it would get so bad."

"You did," she reminded him. "You said that Jessa should take things more slowly."

He shrugged. "I had no idea things would get this bad," he repeated.

Arden finished taping up the bandage, and he flexed his arm. Clearly it was already beginning to stiffen slightly.

"That will do you until Brother Marion can apply some nuskin," she said.

He smiled at her. "Thank you, daughter." He sat back in his chair and relaxed for the first time. "Is Don Vey still in prison?"

"Yes. And likely to stay there for a very long time."

Many of the empress's supporters thought the former prime minister was a danger to her and should be executed. A minority even believed he might be behind some of the robber bands, egging them on, but how could he do that from prison? The abbot had always argued that the man had done nothing deserving of execution. Of course, he did not believe Vey should be locked up either, since the prime minister had been acting in Glory's own interests and under orders from Jessa's father, Emperor Granid Parcq. As the two men had seen those interests. But Grayson had accepted the decision without further argument as the very least that others would accept.

"So many changes," he said. "First woman to rule Glory. The war finally over. And this." He waved his hand toward the courtyard. "I'm just too old for so much change."

"You'll never be too old," she said, and patted his shoulder.

However, she had to admit that he did look older than he had eighteen months ago. That was one of the first things she had noticed on her return two days earlier. Since the problems in the countryside had begun, he had volunteered the protection of the monastery to the farmers and other peasants. In turn, small bands of the lotus-trained monks roamed outside the monastery's precincts watching for trouble. If badly outnumbered, they could at least warn nearby farmers. If not, they drove the bands away.

Brother Bryan came in to report.

"Only a few minor wounds on our side," he said. "One concussion and several small cuts."

It was a bit of an understatement, but Bryan always did put the best light on battle. The toll was higher for the robbers: one dead and three seriously wounded. Anyone slightly wounded had managed to get away with the rest of his band.

"We may need to start locking the gates," Bryan suggested. "I know. I know," he said to forestall objections from the abbot. "How can the farmers get in if they need to? We can keep one of the brothers as lookout on the main gate to let them in when necessary. Or in the bell tower."

"I will think about it," Grayson said. "Is everything cleaned up out there?"

"Just about. As soon as the raiders are tended to, we'll get them to the constable."

The two men discussed further arrangements, and Bryan left. Arden poured two glasses of wine from the bottle on the credenza, handed one to Grayson, and sipped from the other. She stood looking out the window for a moment, then sat down in the other overstuffed chair.

"It's a good thing all of these men didn't come home with their guns," Grayson said suddenly.

The soldiers had been disarmed when they returned, and those weapons were being stored off world. However, most of the returning warriors had swords and knives in their homes on Glory. Also, such weapons were readily available from swordsmiths—whose numbers were increasing, since there were no laws governing the ownership of those types of weapons. Guns were banned except for military and police use, and the number of such weapons was thankfully low. Although any day now she expected to hear of wholesale gun-smuggling.

"I am sorry this happened while you were here," he said. "I know you were looking for a bit of peace and quiet."

She smiled. "It was good practice," she said. "I haven't raised my sword in anger since . . ."

"I know," he said, removing any need to continue.

That one night, a year and a half ago, had been the start of all the changes, and she had been at the center of it. Both as a loser and a winner. It felt as if that had happened decades ago.

That had also been one of the last times she had seen Rafe Semmes, captain of the *Starbourne* and Jessa's former boss. Although there had been messages back and forth, they had not seen each other since. She almost felt ashamed that she had not often missed him, but there had been so little time for contemplation. Her duties kept her busy seeing to palace defenses and incorporating as many of the returning soldiers into the imperial guards as possible.

All because of a promise made hastily, but with little other choice. To a man long dead, yet living within the world conjured up by the powers of lifeweave. The attraction was in the beauty, of both the fiber and the cloth woven from it. Its colors shimmered differently according to the personal chemistry of the person it touched. By weaving it, she could sometimes know future events, although her path was not as direct as Jessa's mother's had been. But then, lifeweave had killed Lyona the seeress after so many years of use, of weaving out battle plans and maps, troop placements and ship dispersements.

The warmth of a hand on her shoulder brought her back to the present.

"Daughter, you haven't been using lifeweave again, have you?" Grayson asked, clearly concerned by her distracted attitude.

"No, not since that time."

He nodded in satisfaction. He never thought using lifeweave to gather information was worth the dangers, but usually left that decision up to her. She considered herself immune to its addictive side effects, but she had stayed away from it since using it to locate Jessa after her kidnapping. No need in taking any chances.

The rest of the day, the monks worked to get everything back to normal within the monastery's precincts. The fight had lasted only a short time, but violence always leaves a mess behind. By dinnertime, they had nearly everything put to rights and had just settled down in the dining hall when a messenger appeared from a nearby village.

"Robbers are attacking Laurel," the farmer reported to Grayson as soon as he was presented.

The abbot looked stricken, but did not rise immediately. The village was nearly an hour away. The attack was probably over by now, and rushing to aid the victims would be precipitous. He ordered a meal and wine for the messenger and appointed a small group to set out as soon as they had bolted down their own meals. He and Arden helped with their weapons. It was snowing when they sent them into the night.

"You did recognize that man as coming from Laurel?" she asked as they watched the departure from the main gate.

"Yes," he answered. "It's a bad day when we question even that, isn't it?"

Arden nodded. It would be a long time before anything even near normalcy returned to Glory.

Six paces long, four paces wide. Another hour before he would be let out for exercise. He had to keep moving. For the first time in more than a year, he felt excitement, felt that there was something to look forward to.

Don Vey wondered if this might be the cell that had once confined Arden Grenfell, as he had wondered at least once a day for more than a year. Although he had never visited her in prison, it was he who had put her in that cell and he who had taken her out. Better that he had just left her, or signed the death warrant. Yes, that would have been best. If she had been executed, Waran Parcq would be alive and on the throne now instead of his half sister.

The former prime minister collapsed on the cot, one fore-

arm across his forehead to block out the bright light overhead. The days were dull, each like the last, like the next,
and so on. Meals were brought in three times a day. Occasionally there were visitors or communications from the
outside world. He read, he exercised, he even breathed, all
at someone else's whim. Their time, their pleasure.

A difficult adjustment at best, for the man who had been
the second highest official in the world. Second only to
Granid Parcq, now the late emperor, who had been a man
with delusions of grandeur and an obsession with a dead
concubine. Her obsession had been with lifeweave—may
he never see another piece of it again as long as he lived.

Must not dwell on that now. Better things were happening. A plot was brewing. It was always good to have friends
on the outside. He grinned to himself. How thoughtful of
Jessa and Arden to have made his revenge possible. If the
immediate plans went well, that is. If they went well.

The party straggled in, tired and hungry. Brother Farlow reported that the village had been robbed of much of its food and nearly everything else of value, and the thieves were long gone by the time the would-be rescuers arrived. All that was left to do was bind the wounds and comfort the victims. At least this time, no one had been killed.

Grayson had already arranged for food supplies to be taken over, but even the monastery's stores from the autumn harvest were being taxed to the limit. Arden spent the next few days helping where she could during the day and talking with the abbot about ways to counter the current problems at night.

"Have you thought any more about that supply of lifeweave you and your friends brought?" he asked one night. "It should bring quite a lot of money if you could get it sold."

"Yes, I've thought about it. Jessa has been too busy to give it much thought, though. And she would have to authorize the sale."

"Is she still going to marry that Belle fellow?"

"Next month," Arden said, and looked at him quizzically. "I told you that."

"Yes, I know. I keep thinking about him and her mother's message."

"Lyona. Yes."

One of the reasons Jessa had agreed to become empress of Glory was her mother's message. Arden did not consciously remember much of it, but had been able to report it subconsciously with the help of lifeweave, the same substance that had helped get the information in the first place. In essence, Jessa had preferred to marry Jonas Belle rather than be trapped on Glory by ascending to its throne. Once the way was cleared for her to do both, she agreed to accept her own responsibilities.

Just as Arden had accepted hers.

"You know," Grayson said. He handed her a glass of wine and took a drink from his own. "The easiest way to sell the lifeweave would probably be to contact Raphael Semmes and have him take it to one of those trading posts he knows so well. I would bet he got a good price for his share."

He sat in the overstuffed chair opposite her. Everything in the study was old-fashioned and comfortable, the overall style based on something the abbot called "Victorian."

She had figured on leaving the arrangements to someone else. However, the abbot might have a point.

"You are still in touch with him, aren't you?"

"On occasion," she answered. "He moves around a lot."

"His kind always does."

"That's a good idea, though," she said to cut off any further discussion of the captain. She stood up, stretched her arms overhead, and yawned. "Meanwhile, I had better get to bed. I want to leave early in the morning."

"All right," he said, but remained seated. "I will see you off tomorrow. Sleep well."

She leaned down, kissed his cheek, and thanked him, then padded off to her own rooms. One day, those rooms would be given over to someone else, someone who lived in the monastery instead of someone making irregular visits. The thought left her with late-night blues. She downed the last of the wine in the glass she had brought with her, undressed, and crawled into the immense bed.

In moments, the sheets warmed and the security she always felt within these walls lay over her like an extra blanket. She reached under the pillow, her fingers found the square of lifeweave, and she pulled it out. She spread it on the sheet beside her under the covers and ran her fingers over its surface. It was one of the squares she wove that led her to Jessa on Caldera. Even in the dark, she could trace Captain Semmes's features in the square. Was it because of the narcotic effects of the fiber or just the memory of the picture itself? With the demands of each day, she might not think of him often; however, she always had his likeness nearby.

She reached over to the other side of the bed, imagining the sheets warmed by his body lying there. Imagining the feel of him next to her.

The first thing she thought of when she woke the next morning was selling the lifeweave stored in the vault of the palace with Rafe's help. The reasons for selling it were good, both personally and professionally.

Grayson was waiting for her when she came to the dining room. Breakfast was simple but hot and, once it was eaten, she was ready to leave. He walked with her to the main door, where her bags had been set.

"Don't wait so long to come back," he said, and hugged her.

"There's no reason for you not to come to the city once in a while," she chided.

He chuckled, his body shaking as they parted.

"What? And leave the peace of the countryside?"

He laughed out loud, and she joined in.

"You must come for the wedding," she said.

"Not really. Jessa will have the palace chaplain and his minions to preside. I doubt that any of us will be missed."

"I'll come and get you myself," she said with a smile, and poked him in the chest with her finger.

"We'll see." His smile faded. "Be careful, daughter," he said seriously. "Everything will come right in time, but we must be wary until it does."

"I know."

She gave him another hug, shrugged into her heavy coat, picked up her bags, and passed outside. He waved as she turned toward the main gate. The cold north wind swirled inside the walls as if trapped and seeking an exit. On the other side of the wall, her car waited, all serviced and ready to go. She stowed her bags in the back. Arden sighed as she climbed in behind the wheel and started the engine. There were times when she wished she had never left the monastery and Lower Forest to see what the rest of the world was like. However, these days, the world intruded on the monks, and she could only hope they would remain safe.

The capital, she found with relief some hours later, was almost exactly the same as when she left it. She conducted a routine check of palace security and reviewed the reports on conditions in the city. Tomorrow, she and Captain Alvarez would work on the plans for the wedding. Everything was nearly set, even though the event was more than a month away, but constant review would prevent any last-minute glitches. She hoped.

She retired to her own apartments within the palace complex without seeing the empress. Jessa had taken over her father's rooms after some months of hesitation. They were the most secure within the palace, and it had only been logical that she should occupy them. Her own inclination, however, had been to clean out her mother's old apartments and live there. It had taken some doing, but Arden and others had at last convinced her that the idea of moving in there had more than a touch of morbidness about it.

That had created some grumbling, too—not the move into Granid Parcq's apartments, but the fact that Arden had so much influence over the empress. Most of the other government advisors thought it improper that the head of the imperial guards was treated as an advisor and confidante, but none of them had any appreciation of what the two women had been through together. They had heard the stories, of course, without understanding the adventures. Even Arden did not always understand the supposed bond between them, and less often, she wondered if it actually existed. Jessa was often moody and short-tempered with her, sometimes exhibiting a meanness that was surprising.

For an hour, Arden worked on the plan to sell the life-weave, writing down all the advantages for using the ser-

vices of Rafe and his crew. All except the most personal
of all: her desire to see him. A desire that grew now that
she had opened the possibility.

Even her dreams that night were filled with rehashing
their adventures, with added elements as dreams often have.
The next morning she fell into the palace routine as if she
had never been away.

Arden and Jessa and the rest of the imperial advisors sat
around the conference table. The morning meeting had
gone relatively smoothly, until Arden introduced her
scheme for selling the lifeweave.

"We should keep that for future emergencies," Con-
stance Dylan, the Minister of Finance, argued.

"What would constitute a greater emergency than what
we have now?" Arden asked. "The countryside is besieged. If we don't get control of these robber bands, they
will surely be attacking the city next."

Dylan snorted. "The city is more than they want to
tangle with."

General Hsing nodded agreement. The city's security
contingent, or home guards, along with the regular army,
came under his authority as Minister of Defense, an authority he guarded jealously. Of all the members of the
ministerial cabinet, he resented Jessa and Arden as women
the most. Agreeing with Dylan must have taken a moment's
thought.

"There is no need to panic," he said condescendingly.
A bored expression crossed his ruggedly handsome face.
He was fourteen years older than Arden and had the very
annoying habit of acting as if she were a child who always
overreacted. "The capital is perfectly safe from these ma-
rauding bands. There are few of them, each made up of
few soldiers."

"That makes them dangerous in themselves," Arden
said. "Being small and mobile, they are able to strike at
will, then be on their way before a defense can be mobi-
lized. If we had outposts in each district, they could respond
more quickly than the regional garrisons can."

"That is just not practical," Hsing said. "They will

eventually tire of the bandit's life and give up their ways."

"And if they don't?" Arden asked.

Hsing shrugged. "They will."

"Meanwhile, the farmers and villagers live in fear and lose everything they have. Eventually, they will move out of the countryside. If that happens, who will feed Glory's people?" Hsing shrugged again and smiled at her as if she were speaking nonsense. "And what if all of the bands join together one day? There are enough people in those bands to form a good-sized army. Would the city be safe then?"

"That will never happen. They have neither the discipline nor the leadership to do that."

"They're from your armies, General," Jessa spoke up. "Are you saying they are not as well trained in military matters as they should be?"

Hsing looked nonplussed, and he fussed with the papers in front of him a long moment. The rest remained quiet, waiting.

"Of course, they are well trained," he stuttered. "But they are only basic soldiers, after all."

"I understood that some of their leaders are ex-officers," the empress continued.

"Still, there is little reason for the bands to join together," he blustered.

"Perhaps they would do so for the express purpose of attacking the capital," she said, and looked from him to Arden. "I think the selling of the lifeweave, at least part of it, and using the proceeds to build and arm district outposts is worth looking into. I want a report by the end of the week."

"Of course, your majesty," Hsing said in a surly voice.

Arden nodded. The general had become her enemy from the moment she was appointed head of the imperial guards. Every time they disagreed about something in council— and they had as yet agreed on nothing—his dislike for her grew more toward hatred. That made it difficult to feel any satisfaction at this latest victory. She had hoped that for once, he would see the merits in her suggestion. It would seem that they would never agree on anything, simply because of who they were.

The door to the meeting room opened, and Jessa's personal secretary walked in. He strode to her chair, looking at no one else in the room. He leaned down and whispered to the empress for a long moment. As he spoke, her eyelids fluttered, the only sign that what he had to say was upsetting.

She nodded when he finished, then cleared her throat as he walked out.

"It seems that Arden's predictions have come true even earlier than she thought." A murmur rose around the table, and expressions ranged from surprise to curiosity. "A band of these marauders entered the city about two hours ago, attacked the prison, and freed Don Vey." A few ministers gasped. Hsing looked angrier than Arden had ever seen him. The prison came under his nominal authority as part of the home guard, although traditionally, it was independent. "They have already made their way out of the city and disappeared into the countryside."

She turned to General Hsing. "General, I will need that report even sooner. You and Arden get to work on plans right away. I also want to see plans for outposts on the perimeter of the city."

He nodded his understanding. Jessa turned to face Arden with a smile that showed both her exasperation and her hope that the situation would not get further out of hand.

"Arden, would you please get in touch with the *Starbourne* and see if Captain Semmes can get here soon? I think you're right that he would be able to sell the lifeweave more quickly and at a better price than we could."

"Of course," Arden said, making sure the tone of her voice was neutral.

"I also want a full report on this attack on the prison and what efforts are being made to find Vey and his rescuers from both of you. I especially want an investigation made into the possibility that they got help from inside the prison." Hsing started to protest. "We have suspected for some time that he was in contact with someone on the outside. I want to know if there is any truth to that. If there is, he must have had help from within the prison."

She stood, and everyone rose from their chairs. "Arden, would you come with me, please?"

Hsing favored Arden with a hateful look, then marched out with the others. Jessa waited until everyone was gone, then started out herself. Arden stepped up beside her as they walked toward the imperial apartments. She did not speak until they were in the sitting room. The fireplace, made legendary by the late emperor, who was forever chilled, was cold but showed signs of recent use. Perhaps at night when Jessa was alone, she looked into the flames and wished for another life. The new lines in her otherwise young face spoke of sleepless nights when duty weighed heavily.

The furniture was new, less ponderous than the former pieces, with her own personality showing through. Or the personality she once knew, Arden thought. Jessa sat in a large overstuffed chair, much like the ones in Abbot Grayson's study. They were made for comfort, not to impress those who only visited. Jessa motioned for Arden to take the matching chair, set near and at an angle to her own so that conversation was easy.

"Do you think I should postpone my wedding?" she asked abruptly.

"Not unless you want to. It's not going to be any safer months from now, even a year from now. Getting these things under control is going to take time."

"Maybe we should have the wedding on Weaver."

"That's not possible. You know what the law says. It's been difficult enough to get permission for Jonas Belle to be your husband rather than your consort."

Jessa sighed. Rich though he may be, Jonas was not of royal blood, and the law was quite specific about that, too. It had been Abbot Grayson's suggestion that as a son of the owner of his world, Jonas was of the ruling family of Weaver and, therefore, qualified even if they did not use royal titles. The council, other government officials, and members of the judicial system had accepted that argument, albeit reluctantly on the part of a few.

"Has he hired extra security?" Arden asked.

"Yes. He didn't like the idea but understood the neces-

sity for my sake. He is also keeping his travel plans secret.
No one here will know of his exact arrival time except you
and Hsing. Neither of you should tell anyone until the last
minute.''

Arden nodded. ''What do we do about Vey's escape?''
she asked.

''I should have listened and had him executed. But it's
too late now. We do need to get these robber bands under
control; however, I think we can do more by making jobs
for them.''

''Many of them are becoming too accustomed to the life
they're leading now. It will be difficult to change their habits.''

''Not that difficult, I hope,'' Jessa said. She rang for the
steward and ordered a cup of tea for herself and Arden. ''If
we can give them a good reason to leave that life, surely
they would do so. Some of them must have families and
would prefer living with them rather than being on the
move all the time.''

''You must remember that's the way they lived as soldiers. What they're doing now isn't that much different.''

''Anyway, we had better discuss the lifeweave,'' Jessa
said, changing the subject. ''We need to know the current
market value and decide how much it will cost to set up
these outposts. That will help determine how much of the
lifeweave to sell. I suspect you will have to do most of that
work. Hsing will be of little help.''

''More than likely. I already have much of that done.''

The steward returned with their tea. He set the tray on
the side table between them, poured, and left as quietly as
he had come.

''We will probably need to sell at least half of that old
shipment we have stored away,'' Arden continued. ''We
could sell some of the other half right here. There must still
be a market for it on Glory. I would suggest holding onto
as much as we can. We may need it to feed people if all
or most of the farmers are driven from their land.''

''That would be a better use than before,'' Jessa said
sadly. Appolyona, her own mother, had been the biggest
user of it on Glory, until it killed her.

They discussed how to handle the sale and a few other issues for a while as they drank their tea. Finally, Arden got to her feet.

"I had better see about getting in touch with the *Starbourne*," she said.

"It will be good to see them again," Jessa said.

"Yes, it will."

"Arden," Jessa called just before she reached the door.

"Yes?"

"The guns are safe on Baltha, aren't they?"

Guns had been banned from personal use for generations on Glory. And since wild game was a rarity, guns for hunting had never existed. Once the war ended, most military weapons of all kinds—but especially guns—had been gathered on the nearly airless world of Baltha, where the main military armory had existed for years. Banning swords and knives had never been attempted, in part because they were weapons for individual conflict and not mass destruction. Also, by law, citizens were entitled to weapons for self-defense, which was something of a dichotomy.

"As safe as we can make them, I believe," Arden said. "Baltha is so isolated, it would be difficult for anyone to sneak up there. We rotate the entire garrison periodically to make it more difficult for anyone to get a man in there."

"Like Vey?"

"Yes. I'm sure he has tried. He might even succeed in spite of all our efforts. But General Radieux is doing everything he can to ensure that the armory is nearly impregnable."

"If they should ever get guns . . ."

"We will have to arm all of our soldiers with them, too. It would turn into a real civil war if that happens."

"We must avoid that at all costs."

Arden agreed, and when Jessa said no more, she excused herself and headed for her office. Jessa was sounding tired, as if the burden of ruling Glory was too much for her, and already looked older than she should. She had never really wanted the responsibility, but had accepted the throne when her brother, Waran, the last of her family, had died. There had never been any blame voiced against Arden for his death, at least not yet.

The truth was that there had been no choice. He had intended to kill both Arden and Jessa that night. But the sight and feel of her sword plunging into his body still woke her at night sometimes. She suspected that Jessa thought about it too, and feared that incident would come between them one day. Their friendship was already tenuous at times, with the empress acting warm, then cool toward her.

Once in her office, Arden shook off the memories and prepared to face other, although related, ones. She called communications on the comm unit and set them to finding the *Starbourne* and establishing a link with the ship. The first voice she should hear would be that of Owen, the communications officer.

As she prepared to wait, she opened the bottom drawer of her desk and took out a pouch. She untied the drawstring and opened it, but did not take out the contents. It was important to have some idea of what Vey was going to do. Short of capturing him or one of his fellow conspirators, there was only one way to get even a hint of what that might be.

She started to turn the bag upside down and dump out the contents, but stopped. Not yet. She had stayed away from the hand loom and Pac Terhn for a year and a half, even though she was convinced she herself was immune to lifeweave's addictive properties. Using it to search the future was the last thing she wanted to do, not only for her own safety, but also for Jessa's. The guide's willingness to help find the princess, and the guarantee that Arden would serve her, possibly for the rest of their lives, indicated an interest in the princess herself. That interest had never been discussed between them, nor an explanation given.

The comm unit chimed, ending for a time, at least, contemplation of that move. Although it had come quicker than she would have expected, she thought the call must be about the connection to the *Starbourne*. Instead, the voice on the other end was that of her captain, George Alvarez.

"We've captured one of the women who attacked the prison," he said. "I thought you might like to be in on the interrogation."

As the car sped toward the prison, Arden thanked whatever gods had spared her the need to try the lifeweave, at least for the time being. The ex-soldier had been captured in a wooded area not far from the outskirts of the city. She had apparently been wounded in the attack and been abandoned by, or gotten separated from her mates as they made their way to the vehicles parked right outside the prison. She had managed to reach the woods just south of there, but had left a trail too easy to follow. Maybe being abandoned had made her mad enough to give up her friends. If not, there were ways to try to get whatever information she might have.

This might be the first time in Glorian history that a female soldier had to be persuaded to talk. Equality did have its bad side after all.

It was fortuitous that Alvarez had been with the pursuers when the woman was captured. Otherwise, Arden might not have known of the capture. Hsing would have seen to that. The captain had been at the prison on other business when the attack occurred and had joined in the pursuit. Since the imperial guard outranked all other city organizations, he had been able to use his position to insist that the questioning be delayed until both the general and his own boss were notified. Would the general be there? Or would he prefer to learn about the interrogation from his underlings? Hard to tell, but she hoped he would stay away, even though this was more his bailiwick than hers. His ego might get in the way.

She parked the car in the lot, got out, and made her way toward the administrative entrance. The door opened as she reached it, held by one of the guards who had apparently been watching for her. He led her down a long hall, then into a small room. Alvarez stood inside with Warden Hensley and two home guard officers, his maroon guard uniform contrasting sharply with the others' drab green. On the other side of a one-way window a woman sat alone in a larger, brighter room. She had brown hair and a medium build and wore a brown jumpsuit. She looked about twenty-seven, but it was difficult to tell. There was a careworn look in her eyes, and her jaws were closed tight, making her lips a thin line across her face.

Arden nodded to the men. Alvarez introduced her to Captain Case and Lieutenant Starling of the prison staff.

"Thank you for notifying me, gentlemen," Arden said.

They all nodded and turned to look at the prisoner. She sat calmly at a large table with her hands clasped on its top. Her eyes were closed, her breathing regular. As they observed, her eyes opened and she looked straight at the mirror.

"Do you have her name?"

"No ident, and she hasn't said a word," Alvarez said. His dark brown eyes were veiled, the long dark lashes nearly touching his cheek. His black hair was cut in the newest short style, and his jaw was set nearly as tightly as the prisoner's.

"We sent a blood sample and prints for identification," Captain Case said. "We should get the results any moment."

"Has anyone questioned her?"

"No," Alvarez said. "The doctor treated her leg wound. She's had a shot for pain. That's it."

"We'll wait until we get her ident information, then talk to her. That may give us some leverage." She turned to the warden. "Tell me what happened."

"Not much to tell, really," he began. "It was well planned. We're not sure how they got inside so easily."

"Someone on the inside?" Arden suggested.

He bristled slightly, but his expression was more one of embarrassment.

"Possibly. No warning went up at first. They knew exactly where Vey's cell was. They blew the door with a small amount of explosive and got out before we could respond in force. They left one of their own dead and two of ours dead and one wounded in their escape."

"How many were there?"

"At least twelve. They had four rovers parked on the west side. They drove off in different directions when they left here. The one she was in went west into the woods." He motioned toward the prisoner. "We managed to give chase pretty quickly, but they had too much of a head start on us."

"Why didn't anyone see them when they pulled into the parking lot?" Arden asked.

The warden shrugged.

"How were they dressed?"

"In brown jumpsuits, like the one she has on."

"They were all dressed alike?" Hensley nodded.

That could only mean they were organized

"We don't have anyone watching the grounds outside," Hensley added. His face was flushed, the color accented by the grey hair he wore cut short. "Never had any reason to. And we're fairly isolated here."

Arden nodded. The vehicles might have made enough noise that someone would have noticed, if anyone had been watching outside. There were no immediate neighbors who might have noticed anything.

The door opened, and a guard entered. He handed some papers to the warden and left. Hensley studied them a moment, then handed them to Arden.

"Her name is Gwynneth Morley," she read. "She was a sergeant in Griswold's Brigade, the twenty-fifth. She's twenty-seven, single, couldn't find a job when she came back from the war, and has a mother and father living in Homer."

Homer was the second largest city on Glory, located on

the west coast. It had already experienced some problems with the robber bands. Arden read over the rest of the details. She could have met this Gwynneth Morley during the war—there had been quite a bit of contact with the 25th. Starting the interrogation on that footing might lead somewhere.

"All right, gentlemen," she said, and handed the papers to Starling. "Are we ready?"

They all nodded and she, Warden Hensley, and Captain Case went into the interrogation room, leaving Alvarez and Starling to watch from the other side of the glass. Morley looked over as they entered. The room was cool, but the prisoner was sweating slightly. Was it fear or the pain from the wound? Arden felt a sudden reluctance to put her through more hardship, but they had to know why Vey had been rescued and, if possible, where he had been taken.

"Hello, Sergeant Morley," Arden said as she took a chair at the table opposite the woman. "I'm Arden Grenfell, once of the sixteenth, Harrison's Brigade. We met during the war. On Warrick II, I believe."

The tired eyes appraised her, then returned to contemplating her own hands on the table.

"The twenty-fifth saw some hard combat," Arden went on. "A lot of commendations, as I recall. You got a few yourself."

Three were listed in her records. Morley's eyes flickered.

"Most of the men you served with must have been surprised at your abilities. I had the same problem at first. Still do sometimes."

Another expression flashed across the woman's face, but was gone before Arden could decipher it. She did remember such times.

"Yes, I was one of the first women in combat, you know. After a couple of years I was transferred to the imperial guard. Had to start making a place for myself all over again."

She paused. The silence dragged out.

"I was luckier than you. Being transferred to the guard gave me a job to last me a long time. I can't imagine what it must have been like when you came home."

"Bloody awful," Morley said angrily. "By the time I got home, there were already robber bands in the countryside. Everyone at home looked at me like they expected me to start killing them any minute. Even my parents."

"That must have been rough," Arden said before the former sergeant had time to regret speaking out. "I guess Vey was helpful in giving some of you a purpose."

Morley suddenly looked sullen. The outburst was regretted and might not be repeated.

"Who was the leader of your band?"

Morley put her head down on her hands.

"We need information from you, Sergeant. We'll get it one way or another. I would rather not hurt you any more than you've already been hurt. In fact, I'd prefer finding you a job somewhere."

Morley snorted and raised her head.

"You can't find what's not there," she said.

"I can and will. We're getting ready to expand the guards: the imperial guard and the home guard. We'll need experienced military people. Like you."

"And you're just going to forgive and forget what I've been doing the past year?"

"No, not entirely. But we're more apt to if you help us now."

Morley shook her head. "I couldn't even if I wanted to. They would come back and kill me somehow, if they knew I had told you anything."

"You're going to tell us," Arden said. "If you do so willingly, we can help you after. If you don't, we will get the information we want and your friends will still come after you. But then you won't have any protection from them."

Morley looked at the two men, one standing with his back to a wall, the other close behind Arden, and seemed to dismiss them as factors in the conversation.

"I'm head of the imperial guard," Arden said. "You know I can help."

"Sorry. You could have helped a year ago, but didn't. You're right. My friends might kill me anyway, but they *did* help me a year ago. I won't tell you anything."

Arden sighed and stood. "I'm sorry."

"Sure you are," Morley said, and looked her in the eye. "About everything, I'll bet."

"Yes."

The door opened, and Lieutenant Starling came in. He carried a small case that Arden knew contained various drugs guaranteed to help make someone talk. Certain tests had been run while Morley was in the dispensary, to determine which drug would work best on her. The biggest problem was that there was no guarantee that the drug wouldn't have serious side effects, even as far as killing the subject.

She took a last look at Morley and started to ask one more time. However, the look on the woman's face did not invite the offer of another chance. The woman's voice had been without feeling, even when accusing Arden of indifference. Shaking her head, Arden left the room. This was best left to experts, in this instance Case and Starling. She and Alvarez joined Warden Hensley in the hall, and they went to his office. He offered her coffee, which she accepted gratefully.

The talk turned to who might have helped from inside. Because of the suspicions, none of the prison officers was taking part in the interrogation. Hensley printed out a list of everyone on duty that morning, what section of the prison they were assigned to, and a background on each. Nothing of interest came to light at first.

"We'll have to review the tapes from this morning," Hensley said. "Maybe something was caught by the cameras."

She glanced over the lists again, and one name suddenly caught her eye.

"I didn't realize that Prentiss was still here," she said.

Sergeant Prentiss had enjoyed tormenting her during the six years she had been locked up in one of the cells.

"I thought he was relieved of duty because of his openly expressed opposition to the empress."

"He was convinced that it was in his best interests to accept the inevitable." Hensley frowned. "I do believe that

he was in the cell block where Vey was held for the past
year.''

"Maybe we should check on him," Arden suggested.

He took the printouts and scanned a few pages. After a
moment, he ordered the tapes for certain areas to be set up
for review in the security room. Everything was ready by
the time the three of them got there. They watched in silence for a time, fast-forwarding through parts.

"This is the area Prentiss should have been in this morning," Hensley said.

The sergeant appeared for a time, but disappeared at one
point. The warden switched to another view, found the right
time on the tape, and began running it. The view included
the side door through which the attackers had entered. Prentiss appeared but did not seem to do anything compromis-
ing.

"He still should not have been there," Hensley said.

The sergeant was currently off duty. The warden ordered
the security chief to have him picked up at his home or, if
he was not there, to have him found.

"I suspect you will not find him," Arden said.

They started back to his office.

"Frankly, if it wasn't for his contact with Vey, I
wouldn't suspect Prentiss. He's always been good at his
job, never got in any trouble."

"But he doesn't like having to work with women. He
never did."

Hensley looked at her, started to speak, but thought better
of it. He probably did not like the way things were working
out in that area, either. She had almost never seen the warden when she was in his care. Prentiss was the one who
saw to her needs and discipline. Mostly the discipline. Until
now, she had thought all resentment was behind her, but
she found herself hoping he had given her reason to discipline him.

They took seats in his office again and settled down to
wait. How long might it take to break a woman's will,
especially one who had shown her courage in combat? It
could happen quickly if Morley felt guilt over what she had
done since returning home. Or if she had little natural re-

sistance to the drug. If she had strong resistance, the drug could prove dangerous.

Hensley had just poured Arden another cup of coffee when the door opened. Starling walked in, his expression perfectly bland.

"The prisoner has had an adverse reaction to the drug," he announced.

"Is she dead?" Arden asked.

"No, but she has slipped into a coma."

She tightened her hands into fists and shook her head. Dammit, she had not wanted to hurt the woman.

"Did you get any information at all?" Hensley asked.

"A little. Most of what she said seems of little use."

"Where is she?"

"In the infirmary. The doctor is seeing to her. He seems to think she might recover if given the proper treatment."

"I hope so," Arden murmured. She looked up. "How soon can you bring me a transcript of the interrogation?"

"In just a few minutes if you want to wait."

"Yes, I'll wait. Thank you."

Less than half an hour later, the lieutenant returned with his captain and copies of the transcript for everyone. Arden read through it twice.

"This mention of Baltha," she said. "It seems out of context."

Both of the officers read over that section.

"We were asking her about the places she had been in conjunction with the robber band. Maybe she was stationed on Baltha once and got her military service mixed up with this other."

"Her record, please." Starling handed it to her. She flipped through the pages until she came to the part she wanted. "Yes, she was stationed there a few years ago. At the armory."

"Do you think Vey would have set his sights on the armory?" Starling asked.

"Could be," Arden said, deep in thought. "He'd have a hard time finding a ship to take him, though. Still, anything is possible."

The comm on the warden's desk chimed. He answered it, then extended the handset toward Arden.

"It's for you," he said. "The captain of the *Starbourne*."

The last couple of months had been very lean, and Raphael Bedford Semmes was in a bad mood. His crew kept pointing out that after selling the lifeweave, they had no desperate need for money, but it was not just the money. It never had been. He enjoyed the search, the thrill of discovery, getting in and out before anyone else found out about a wreck.

True, there were occasional victims in those wrecks. He did not like that much, since it always acted as a reminder of how fragile life could be—especially on airless worlds or ones with hostile environments. People died hard in such places, and the deaths were usually ugly. Of course, if any of the crew was alive, the cargo belonged to them or the company they represented, and he and his crew only had the pleasure of rescuing survivors. That usually brought a reward from the insurance company and sometimes from the shipper.

Another bad part was the days of inactivity as the *Starbourne* made its way through jump gates and the void between worlds, searching the comm channels for emergency signals from downed ships. He had taken to roaming the ship at all hours, unable to sleep during ship's night.

Today he was more restless than usual. He nearly jumped up from his bunk and headed for the bridge, but there was nothing for him to do there, either. No more than in his own cabin. Liel had done his usual job of training the two newest members of the crew, and they had become as much a part of the team as those they replaced had been. Finding a new astronavigator had taken the longest. Jessa had been very good and was difficult to replace. Good astronavigators were never easy to find in the best of times. Most of them belonged to the guild, because that was where the money was, and he never hired guild members.

His comm unit buzzed, and he tapped the "on" button.

"Captain," Liel's voice came from the speaker. "There's an incoming call for you."

"Live?"

"Yes, sir."

It must be an important call if someone was paying the charges for a live call rather than a delayed one.

"Who is it?"

"Arden Grenfell."

He took a deep breath and exhaled quickly. It had been quite some time since he had heard from her, or she from him. Time and distance have a way of wearing down good intentions.

"Send it through," he said.

The open line clicked and crackled as his exec transferred the call. When the line cleared, he knew the connection was remade.

"This is Captain Semmes," he said, flinching at the formality.

"Hold one moment, Captain," an unfamiliar male voice said. "Commander Grenfell will be right here."

More clicks and crackles, and he realized he was holding his breath so he could be sure to hear when she spoke. It seemed to take forever, but was probably only a matter of seconds.

"Captain Semmes?" her voice said at last. She was being formal, too.

"Yes" was all he could say.

Noises came from the background, and he realized that other people were in the room with her. He waited another few seconds for her to speak again.

"There," she said almost breathlessly. "I'm alone now, Rafe. How are you?"

Now her voice had that breathy quality he loved to hear on the comm. He had missed it. All he would have had to do was call.

"I'm doing fine," he answered. "To what do I owe the honor?"

"I am calling on business," she said. "But when I heard your voice . . . Well, memories came rushing back and all that. Sometimes I forget how long it's been."

"Me too."

He felt suddenly angry at her, as if it were her fault they had not spoken or seen each other in so long—which was ridiculous. He struggled to think of something else to say, but nothing came to mind. Then she saved him from further thought.

"I know it's awkward," Arden said. "Maybe I should just get to the business."

She paused to let him respond, but he still could think of nothing to say.

"Yes, well," she said. Her voice had become business-like again, her tone more severe. "We need your help with the lifeweave we still have."

She went on to describe the problems Glory had been experiencing with the roaming bands of robbers. The plan to build regional outposts made sense. The fastest way to finance such a project was certainly the lifeweave.

"With your connections, we felt sure you could sell off the lifeweave quickly and at the best possible price. We will keep some of it back for future needs. For one thing, we don't want to flood the market and bring the price down."

"That's not a problem," Rafe said. "We can sell it in batches in different sectors, if we have to. That should help maintain the price."

"You'll do it, then? We will pay your regular commission, of course."

"The usual is thirty percent."

"All right."

"I assume you want to get this done as soon as possible," he said after another pause. "I'll check to see how quickly we can get to Glory and let you know."

"All right. And thanks, Rafe. We appreciate it."

"Anything for old friends," he said and disconnected.

"We appreciate it," she had said, using the royal plural. Or did she mean she and Jessa appreciated it? The whole of Glory appreciated it? It would be good to see Jessa again, but she, too, had probably changed a good deal.

4

The car sped through the city, back toward the palace complex. There was a lot of work to do in the next few days, plans to make, arrangements to recheck, and Arden sat in the passenger's seat filled with regrets. Her mind would not stop remembering the captain, his face, his voice, the warmth of his hand on her body.

The coolness of his voice over the comm.

It had not been the voice of a stranger, but that of a friend or lover filled with disappointment. Did he blame her for the loss of contact over such a long period of time? That was not wholly her fault. He could have called, but did not.

She sighed, and her driver cast a sideways glance at her. He probably thought her discontent was due to . . .

That poor woman. Gwynneth Morley had suffered a lot for her world, and Glory repaid her by not giving her a job and killing her because she, on her own, had found a way to live. Where was the justice in that? Further proof that no matter how just your intentions may be, radical changes have far-reaching, sometimes dire, effects.

Morley's death, which came just before Arden left the prison, would have a greater effect than even she might have imagined. What that effect might be depended on how the ex-soldier died.

With everything that had been happening, Arden knew

that trusting anyone at the prison was no longer an option. She had ordered the imperial medical staff to conduct the autopsy rather than the doctors in the prison infirmary; specifically, Doctor Lawrence, whom she knew better than the others and whom she had no reason not to trust. The results should be available within the next two or three days.

Unfortunately, there was no way to keep track of all those who might have caused Morley's death. There were just too many possibilities.

There. She had not thought of Captain Semmes for at least ten minutes. She was on a roll, and keeping it that way was important. Becoming distracted could mean that someone else might die. The biggest worries were Jessa, the wedding, and Jonas Belle. For now, Belle's safety was out of her hands. But with the wedding only five weeks away, he would be her problem more quickly than she liked.

The car turned into the palace drive. Ryan, the guard, checked to make sure who was in the vehicle, and the gate opened. The palace was becoming an armed camp, something that had not occurred during Granid Parcq's tenure in spite of the far-reaching war. Jessa was painfully aware of that, and for Arden, it was becoming difficult to even think of leaving the complex. She was afraid that something might happen while she was gone, as if she could be everywhere, or she alone could protect the empress.

Consciously, she did not think that at all. The men and women serving under her were all good at their jobs, and she trusted every one of them. She had to. Even so, it was not impossible that one of them might not be loyal to the empress. No method of checking backgrounds or interrogation could guarantee loyalty. Could she do that with lifeweave?

For more than a year Arden had stayed away from the fiber and the hand loom, just as she had told Abbot Grayson. If she had used it as often as she had thought it might be useful, she might be as addicted now as poor Appolyona had been. That possibility frightened her, in spite of her confidence in her immunity to that very thing. However, coming events, and the possibility of anyone close to the empress being disloyal, might make such a tool necessary.

The car stopped just outside the side entrance nearest her office, and Arden got out. Another guard, Sato, saluted as she moved up to the palm scanner. It read her palm, buzzed, and she input her code on the key pad. Another buzz indicated that the lock had released. Sato opened the door for her, and she went inside. It all took less than a minute, probably, and she was accustomed to the routine. However, each time she wished it was not necessary. Not only was it inconvenient, it was ammunition for Jessa's enemies.

Come to think of it, though, the side and back doors had always been secured. So, this procedure at least was not a result of the changes since the old emperor's death.

The hallway was deserted as she made her way to the far end where her office was located. She opened the door to the electronics room on the right side of the hall and stepped inside. Captain Morgan stood behind a guard at one of the consoles across the room. He looked up and she nodded to him. He patted the man on the shoulder and came to her.

"Commander Grenfell. Everything is quiet."

"I hope it stays that way."

Morgan nodded agreement. He turned to look at the banks of vidscreens showing several dozen areas of the palace complex. People went about their business, some unaware of hidden cameras, others ignoring unhidden ones.

"Where is the empress?" Arden asked.

"In her sitting room. She's been in there ever since you left late this morning."

Arden glanced at the clock on the wall. Only five in the afternoon. A lot had happened in a short time.

"I'll be in my office for a short while. Then I'll be in my quarters."

With all the surveillance equipment at his disposal, Morgan would know where she was as soon as she did. Yet, she felt a need to say the words, to tell someone what her plans were. Where to expect her and when.

She had started toward the door, but turned back.

"Where is General Hsing?"

"I believe that he has gone home," Morgan answered. "He has left the palace in any case."

"Thanks."

She went into the hall and closed the door behind her. It had been nagging at the back of her mind that the general had never shown up at the prison to check on the attack or the prisoner's interrogation. Did he hate the idea of a woman ruling Glory enough to conspire with her enemies?

She entered her office, pulled the sword over her head, placed it on the edge of her desk, and went to the dispenser for a cup of coffee. As she sat down at the desk, she told herself that she should wait until dinner in her quarters, but cutting down on everything would be too nerve-wracking. She had cut down on tea, after all.

She started shuffling through papers in the incoming tray, and her thoughts returned to Hsing. As much as she resented his attitude toward Jessa and herself, Arden could not believe that he would turn traitor. He had always been a loyal soldier, just terribly set in his ways. Still, it would probably be a good idea for Jessa to think of replacing him soon. But with whom?

General Radieux might be a good choice. She had served under him during her time as a common soldier. His instincts were good, and as far as she could remember, he had been the senior officer least prejudiced against women. She had not seen him for years, of course, but there had been no rumors that anything about him had changed. Would he stay in the army? She would have to find out. Meantime, there was work to do.

However, going through the pile of papers, she found that nothing in the incoming pile needed to be done before next morning, and decided to make an early night of it. She closed the files, picked up the katana, and locked the door after herself.

Her apartment on the third floor was the same one that had been occupied by Jessa's mother. Lyona, seeress and concubine, had left her mark on those rooms, and no one else wanted to live in them. It was difficult enough to get anyone to stay on that floor in that wing at all. That meant Arden's apartment, rebuilt to include a small kitchen, was more luxurious and quieter than it might otherwise have been. And she was not one to fear Lyona's ghost. They had talked intimately on two occasions after her death. Although not friends, they at least had a certain amount of respect for one another.

There was a ghost, though. One that on this night brought a sadness that she had been able to avoid for months. As she walked into the sitting room, the first thing she saw was the sofa where they had sat and talked for hours. The shower, the bed, places where they had enjoyed intimacy in so many ways. Saying what she missed most about him was impossible, but the sound of his voice, the sharing of ideas—those things she missed terribly. She had forgotten how much.

There it was again, the distraction. What she had tried to avoid for so long. How could she concentrate on the security of the palace when her own yearnings were so strong? Eat now, read some reports.

She went into the small kitchen that contained all of the latest appliances and found a frozen dinner in the fridge. She unwrapped it and slipped it into the oven. The timer chimed just after she finished pouring some wine. Immediately, the comm chimed. When she turned it on, Alvarez's image appeared on the screen.

"What's up?" Arden asked.

He hesitated a moment, a sure sign that there was news he did not want to tell her.

"We have a real problem," he said after clearing his throat. She waited. "Gwynneth Morley's body has disappeared."

"What?" The hair stood up on the back of her neck.

"We just got a call from the medical examiner. She had gone back to the lab to check on something and found the body gone. We're checking everyone now and the security tapes to see who came and went."

"How in the hell could anyone get a body out of the prison?" She rubbed her forehead as she considered the problem. The first rush of disbelief was dissipating, and cool logic was begining to take over. "It might still be there. Make sure all of the guards are alerted. Have them check any large packages, boxes, crates—anything and everything.'' She thought about going back to the prison and coordinating the search from there, but Alvarez could handle it. "Let me know if anything turns up. I'll be here the rest of the night.''

"Yes, Commander.''

The connection ended, and she hit the console with her fist. Dammit! Right under her nose practically. And that meant there had to be a traitor still within the prison. No great surprise, but a chilling reminder of their vulnerability.

She should have thought to set a guard in the lab. But who would have thought such a theft could take place? It did tell her one thing, however. The ex-soldier's death might be more than an accident of the interrogation. Covering up that fact had to be the only reason someone would take such a chance. She could only hope that the doctor had already taken all the necessary samples to determine cause of death.

Remembering the dinner that had probably grown cold again, Arden went into the kitchen. She reheated it, but could manage only a couple of bites. The sense of failure lay like a stone in her stomach. Somehow she knew that the body would never be found—it was probably burning up in the heat plant or incinerator by now. Hsing would have a good time with this fiasco, even though he had shirked his own responsibility.

One thing she could do, though, was make sure the lifeweave was well guarded. She turned on the comm and tapped in the code for Alvarez.

"Assign extra guards to the vaults,'' she ordered. "Particularly to the lifeweave. Our most trusted guards,'' she added.

Alvarez acknowledged the order and had turned to make the assignment before his features faded from the screen. Arden picked up the dinner tray and dumped it into the garbage chute, then put her jacket back on and started out, but remembered her sword and went back for it. She wanted to see for herself that the cases of lifeweave were safe. Right now, there was a lot riding on them.

The elevator stopped in the basement, and she made her

way along the hall into the central area. It was the most difficult to get into, although, in another adventure, Brother Bryan had made his way to the prison cells right next door with little trouble. But he was a very talented man.

She smiled at that thought. Without his intervention, she would either have been dead these past eighteen months or chained to the loom that once stood in her living room. Jessa would also occupy the suite that once belonged to her mother, or would still be in the hands of Spohn Bryce and those Glorians who had wanted to make her empress at all costs. Everything could have turned out so differently, including the relationship between her and Rafe Semmes. In spite of the passage of time, events could still turn against all of them.

She turned the last corner and faced the doors to the vault room. Two imperial guards stood on either side. They saw her, came to attention, and saluted. She almost smiled at the sight of them: Greeley, the man on the left, was at least six-foot-three while the woman on the right, Hahn, was no more than five-foot-six. Quite an incongruous pairing, but she knew them both as good warriors who would stay alert. Alvarez had not wasted any time in getting a second guard stationed. Two more would probably show up soon.

The security lock here worked the same as at the side door, and she was inside in less than a minute. She then faced the doors of three vaults, each containing imperial fortunes of different kinds. It was the one on the right that held what she sought. Two small tables, one against the wall on each side, with two chairs each, were all the furniture in the anteroom.

Pulling the sonar key from her pocket, she hesitated. There was a very large amount of lifeweave inside there—more than she had been exposed to in a long time. Would being close to it have some effect on her since she had been away from it for so long?

She pointed the key at the door, pressed the sensors on the key in sequence, and heard the lock mechanism disengage. The sound filled the nearly empty chamber even though it was a relatively quiet lock. The door swung open with no noise at all, except for a sigh of air rushing from one chamber to the other.

She walked inside slowly. The crates were stacked against each side wall and along the back. A treasure of great value, and it did not even fill the vault. Suddenly a voice called her name, and she whirled to see who was behind her. The room was empty. The vault was empty except for her. Imagination, then. Brought on by apprehension at being exposed to the fiber.

Moving to her right, Arden touched one of the crates in the first stack. Her fingertips tingled. Again, her imagination. The effects of the lifeweave could not escape the crates. They were designed to contain all of its properties. Yet she felt something.

She unlatched the lid and carefully pushed it open. Inside, two cones wrapped round and round with the shimmering fiber stood waiting for a human touch. She stroked one with fingertips that instantly tingled. It was not imagination after all. Its properties called to her as never before.

It had always been easy to walk away before the encounters with Lyona. However, the search for Jessa and the contact with the princess's mother had changed its effects somehow. It was so uncomfortable that she had never told Grayson about it. He would storm at her, telling her to stay away from it, reminding her of its effects, of Lyona's death from overusing it. But it had not only worked, it had worked without relying heavily on Pac Terhn, her guide in that world of the mind and spirit.

What that meant, exactly, was not clear. A part of Arden wanted to explore that new aspect of the fiber's effects. She thought about it often. But she was afraid of its addictive properties. Afraid that it might lure her into its world permanently, becoming her reason to live.

Deliberately recalling the last time she saw Lyona alive had helped keep her away from lifeweave altogether. But the fear that memory created seemed to be fading, overshadowed by the desire.

A sudden, disjointed noise from outside caught her attention. She dropped the lid on the crate and turned to listen, realizing that noises had been out there for some time without her noticing. Her heartbeat quickened. It sounded as if a fight was under way. She pulled the sword belt over her head, drew her katana, and laid the scabbard on the table as she moved through the anteroom.

The day had been peaceful, just like the once-upon-a-time days before Jessa took the throne, and the monastery was settling into its night quiet. Grayson rubbed his arm where the wound still ached a bit. In a day or two it would start itching as the healing progressed. These things were pesky longer than they used to be, when he was younger. Although tonight he felt like he had never been young.

Ever since Arden's visit, he had felt that something troubled her. Asking her about it was useless. She never talked about her own problems until she was ready. If it were someone else, he might guess that commanding the imperial guard might be too difficult, but he was convinced she could handle it quite well.

He could not rid himself of the feeling that lifeweave was at the root of the problem. But she said she had not used it since the fiber enabled her to find Jessa and defeat Waran Parcq. The changes brought about on that night had certainly been far-reaching.

At least there had been no local raids for a few days, although the one on the prison in the city was disturbing. The raiders were becoming bolder, and that could become a serious problem for the future. How much longer could the monastery keep from being overrun?

A knock came on his door, bringing him out of his reverie.

"Come in," he called.

Brother Jantz opened the door and stepped inside. He came close to the abbot's chair.

"There is a group of people at the main gate asking for admittance," the monk said. "They request lodging for the night."

"How many?"

"I saw more than a dozen. And I believe they are armed."

"Are they on foot or in vehicles?"

"At least three rovers."

"Tell them . . ." Grayson began. "No, I'll come."

He levered himself out of the chair with his arms and followed Brother Jantz out. This sudden appearance so late at night did not bode well, and it would be better if he was the one to turn the visitors away.

The two guards fought hard, but they had no chance against five. They kept their backs to the walls on either side, making it more difficult for the enemy to overwhelm them, almost forcing the brown-clad warriors to come at them one at a time. The clang of blade striking blade resounded from one end of the hall to the other.

All this Arden took in at a glance as she emerged from the anteroom. With her warrior's *kiai*, she launched herself into the fight. First, to the right where it was three against one. The man never saw her or heard her. Her blade sliced into his body easily, coming free as she pulled across. He dropped to the floor without a sound. His friends had heard her shout and turned to see who it was.

As they did so, Greeley found an opening and took down one of the intruders. The third and last on this side had his hands full defending against Arden's attack. As their blades found each other, Greeley moved to help Hahn, leaving her line of sight.

Her opponent was not a bad swordsman. Self-taught, probably, with a bit of formal instruction in the military. She recognized the hacking movements, the lack of concentration on the mental aspects of swordplay. However, he was strong and determined, and she kept her full attention on foiling his efforts, on finding an opening.

It came as he raised his sword, intending to bring it down on her neck or shoulder with all his strength. He could have cut her in half had the blade come down as he meant it to. But she dropped to one knee and drove her own blade from below, the tip piercing his diaphragm, driving upward to find his heart.

He stood impaled. A look of horror passed across his face, then one of amazed acceptance. Arden had never seen such a look, neither in her war experience nor in her other adventures. It brought a sadness that confused her, fortunately only for a moment.

She pulled the sword free, stood, turned to see how the others were doing, and found the fight over. The two guards stood over two more fallen enemies, breathing hard, looking from each other to the bodies on the floor.

"One of you comm the command room and get these taken away," she told them. "Get Captain Alvarez here." Hahn sped away.

She leaned down and wiped blood from her blade onto the tunic of her second adversary, as was the custom. His eyes stared up at the ceiling, his life's blood already turning dark around the edges of the pool spread about him.

How did they get inside the palace? Why had they not set off alarms at the entrances or been seen on any of the surveillance cameras? Had they somehow gotten or been given the codes? Even with the codes, they would need to somehow duplicate an authorized handprint. How?

"I know this man," Greeley said. "Albert Drew. He's a member of the imperial guard."

"When did you last see him?" Arden asked. Now that there was a name, she vaguely remembered the man. His was a face that she had rarely seen, however.

"Not long ago." He thought a moment. "Just a few days, I think."

"Recognize any of the others?"

So. A disloyal warrior had gotten into the guard. Or, maybe, someone who became disloyal while he was a guard.

"No," the young man said. "None of the others are familiar."

At that moment, Captain Alvarez arrived with a number of guards.

"We saw what happened from the cameras," he reported, panting. "At least the end of it. They were after the lifeweave?"

"If there were more of them, I'd say yes," Arden said. "But five of them couldn't carry away much of it. I would guess they were after me."

"You're probablly right," he said. "Sorry we didn't get here sooner. It's quite a jog from the center."

She nodded. Clearly, they had to set up centers in this wing, both here in the basement and on the main floor. She gave him the orders to do that while the bodies were loaded on litters and taken away.

"We'll have to enlist more into the guard," he said.

She nodded again, knowing that could prove as dangerous as it was necessary. While they were attempting to increase security, they could also be introducing more traitors. She watched the receding litters and motioned toward them.

"After they're searched, identified, and examined, see that they all get decent funerals," she said. He looked at her oddly but nodded. "Bring me all information about them. Everything." He nodded again. "They once fought for Glory," she said. "They thought they still were."

She turned on her heel to return to the vault. She laid her sword on the table. The blade would have to be fully cleaned before she would replace it in the scabbard.

She checked on the crates, afraid that, with the doors wide open, something might have happened to the treasure. However, everything was intact and as it was when she had left the vault. She opened the same crate, reached in, and touched the spool of fiber again. A thrill raced through her like an electric shock. She pulled her hand away, shaken. A thrill always came from touching it, but never anything that strong before.

Must be her heightened senses after the fight. That must be the reason.

Still shaking slightly, she lowered the lid on the crate and walked away. With great care, she closed the vault doors, making very sure that they were locked. She picked up her katana and scabbard and left the anteroom. Captain Alvarez waited for her in the corridor.

"Change the security codes and double the guard here," she told him. She thought a moment. "We need to increase security throughout the entire palace complex. We'll have to start recruiting more warriors for the guards." She repeated his earlier statement and shook her head as she led the way toward the elevators. "How do we make sure they are and remain loyal?"

Alvarez said nothing as he walked beside her. They had worked together long enough that he knew she was thinking out loud and did not expect anything from him right now. Later, they would discuss her thoughts and his thoroughly. She had come to appreciate his clear thinking.

"I'm going to my office. Report to me there when you have anything on the intruders."

"Right."

He turned back toward the end of the hall to supervise the cleanup while she turned the corner, out of sight. This night there would be little sleep. First, she needed to write up a report for the empress on everything that had happened and her recommendations for preventing further incursions. Then, she would have to study the reports the captain would no doubt be bringing her. The most important task ahead of her was finding a way to tell who was loyal and who was not.

She opened the bottom right drawer of her desk and took out the small bag, identical to the one in her apartment. Each contained a hand loom and several yards of lifeweave fiber, enough to make at least two squares on the loom. Although she had contemplated using this one earlier in the day, the reasons seemed even stronger now. She looked at her watch, reminding herself that had happened the day before.

She turned the bag up and let the contents spill out on the desktop. The ball of fiber rolled toward the edge, and she stopped it with her hand. A thrill went through her, slightly weaker than the one she had experienced in the vault. Less fiber, an ebbing of the excitement of the fight— either might be the reason.

Automatically, her fingers found the loose end and un-
wound the ball. The end wove easily around the pins of the
loom, as if the last square had been done only yesterday.
She picked up the needle and threaded it. Just as she started
to drop into the trance, or whatever it was that happened,
a knock came on the door. She paused, ready to tell whoever it was to go away, but it was probably Alvarez bringing the reports she had asked for. She scooped everything
into the center drawer.

"Come in," she called, wondering if she had just been
saved, or if the moment was only postponed.

Her second in command walked in, closing the door behind him, and handed her a data cube. While she put it into
the reader, he sat in a chair on the other side of the desk,
fingertips pressed together, mouth pursed.

The readout on the screen did not tell her anything new,
but the autopsies were not done yet. All of the warriors
were veterans of the war, including Drew, who had been a
member of the imperial guard for two years. Another man
who became disaffected because of a woman on the throne?

"Have someone check Drew's home," she told Alvarez.

"I'm going over there as soon as I finish here," he said.

She nodded and continued reading. None of the men had
much in their pockets. Their swords were ordinary, except
for Drew's, which had been issued by the guard. Ordinary
in that sense, then. Nothing out of the ordinary in their war
records. And nothing to indicate whom they had been
working with in their new careers. Drew was the one who
got them into the palace—the tapes showed him coming
in, but not the others. They did not show up until they
entered the basement corridor.

Drew had known all the blind paths, all the dark corners.
How could they fight attacks from the inside? They would
have to make sure the guards and others in the palace had
every reason to remain loyal. That was a job for someone
else. She had to work on the technical side of it, although
it did not seem as if there was much more that could be
done with locks and surveillance equipment. And winning
and maintaining loyalty took time, the one thing Jessa, and

therefore Arden, did not have, as they were besieged from all sides.

She finished the report and took the cube out of the reader.

"Not much, is there?" the captain said.

"No, not yet anyway. Let me know what you find at Drew's place." He started to frown, and she smiled. "Tell me tomorrow. Go get some sleep as soon as you finish up there."

He smiled with relief and stood to go.

"See you in the morning," he said.

She wished him goodnight and leaned back in her chair. Her eyes burned, and she rubbed them with her fingertips, then pressed against her temples. It was very late—early morning, actually—and she should go to bed. However, sleep would be long in coming, if it came at all.

She opened the center drawer and took out the secret items. In her haste to hide them, the fiber had come loose from a couple of pins on the loom. She replaced the life-weave carefully, savoring the feel against her fingertips. The room faded slightly, and she started weaving.

Abbot Grayson looked out at three figures waiting in the darkness. Behind the three he could make out at least three vehicles. It was too dark to see who was in them, and the figures standing at the door wore hats pulled down low to hide their features in shadow. He did not have a good feeling about this bunch, and even if he could accommodate them, he would not. Especially since one of the men in the background seemed familiar in shape and stance. Brother Jantz and two other monks, one on each side, stood poised for action if the need should arise.

"Father," the man in front said. "We are simply weary travelers seeking shelter for the night."

"I'm sorry, sir, but we have no room tonight," he replied. "The farmers in the nearby district have been forced from their homes and stay with us at the moment. I would suggest that you find a sheltered area in the forest and sleep in your vehicles."

The man's arms started forward. Grayson grabbed the

edge of the door and slammed it quickly. Without being told to, Brother Jantz shoved the bolt home. Someone hit the door from the outside with something, probably the butt of a rifle. Voices shouted, but the brothers moved silently to further barricade the wooden door with a bar and two more bolts. The wood was five inches thick, hardened by age, and would withstand even the heat of a laser rifle for quite some time. However, even the rock walls could not withstand explosives.

The three of them retreated toward the building, Jantz to spread the warning by ringing the large iron bell hanging in the tower just outside the entrance to the main building. One brother ran to the sleeping wing, while Grayson ran for the arms locker.

Within minutes every brother was armed and in position around the perimeter of the monastery walls. The back gate was the second weakest point, but every sector of the wall was covered, just in case. Grayson returned to the main gate to see what was happening. Everything was quiet. He looked to the tower of the main building where a lookout was posted, but there was no signal. Except for a low wind in the trees, no sound came from outside. The intruders might be gone. If so, the end of this encounter would be more peaceful than he would have expected. The brother who had stayed behind reported hearing the vehicles start up and move about, but could not say if they actually left or just changed positions.

At first light several hours later, Grayson checked the lookout again. The man spread his arms wide, indicating that he saw nothing. Five brothers who were familiar with the woods and how to track were sent outside, instructed to go in different directions and check to see if the intruders were anywhere nearby. They returned in the early afternoon and reported finding nothing. Apparently the visitors had gone on their way.

Most of the brothers went about their daily routines, a few went to bed to catch up on lost sleep, and Grayson retired to his study. He dialed Arden's private number in the capital.

"You sound like hell," he said when she answered. Exhausted was more like it.

"I've been up all night," she said. "You sound a bit tired yourself."

"I should be. Been up all night too. We had visitors last night."

"More of the marauders?"

"Maybe, but they didn't break inside. We closed the doors on them and kept watch the rest of the night."

"You didn't call just to tell me that," Arden said, her voice wary.

"No, I called to tell you that I think Don Vey was one of them."

The connection clicked off and Rafe sat back, feeling very pleased with himself. He had angered the woman of his dreams because he had not been willing to place her needs ahead of his. How could she expect him to do so? What made her needs more important than his?

True, a whole world was depending on Arden to accomplish the task she had been assigned, but dammit! His crew and he himself depended on what he did, not to mention the Astarians, who needed the shipment of precious metals now residing in his cargo hold. Finding a buyer had not been difficult—such items were always in great demand. Finding the right price had taken a little more time than he had calculated.

And damned if he was going to let Arden and the troubles on Glory deter him from his present course. Besides, with the metals on board, there was no room for the lifeweave.

Lighter and more valuable even than the metals, the lifeweave had once been all his, but half was a goodly amount. He had sold it for himself and his crew, and the proceeds had made him financially independent. His crew, too, for that matter. However, none of them had left the ship to live a life of luxury. They were all addicted to the life of a salvager, the sense of discovery and of adventure. Except for Jessa, of course, who had gone on to bigger and better things.

He could not envy her the responsibilities of ruling a whole world. A starship was difficult enough.

Finding a replacement for the astronavigator—now, that had been difficult. The first two had not worked out. This business was risky at best, the most risky in the independent field. He loved it: the independence and the chance of making a fortune. He finally found a replacement that fit into the crew as well as Jessa had. Phyilla was as pretty, although smaller and less austere, and as competent at her profession. She also had no family or other personal connections that could cause complications—something that dealing with Jessa had taught him to check out before problems arose.

The greatest outward sign of the fortune he had made on the lifeweave was the *Starbourne* itself. It was now one of the best-equipped and fastest ships operating in the sector. Maybe the whole galaxy, for all he knew. Some people, even Liel, had suggested the money might be better spent if he bought a whole new ship, but he could not bring himself to part with the one that had taken him so far. He held onto her just as he did his crew—loyally and, some said, foolishly.

Even Tahr, he thought with a smile. Constantly complaining though he was, Tahr knew his job, and everyone put up with him in their own ways.

Even Arden had learned during the short time they were all together on the great adventure. An adventure not to be repeated, he hoped. He could do without any more of that sort of danger. Oh, some people became addicted to it, but not him. No, sir. He had even come very close to turning Arden down when she asked him to sell the spools of lifeweave Glory had kept. But she had been more than a friend, and he was not one to leave a friend in the lurch when they needed his help.

He leaned forward and keyed the comm to the bridge. Liel answered.

"How much farther to Astar?" Rafe asked.

"Two days and a few hours," the exec answered.

"I want to get this trip done so we can hurry up with
the Glorian run," the captain said. "See if we can get there
in under two days."

"Yes, sir."

He disconnected and sat back again. He did not like un-
finished business, and the relationship between him and Arden definitely had that feel. It would be best to get it over
with so he could get on with his life. And a good life it
promised to be.

He leaned down from the chair and pulled out one of the
two drawers under the bunk. Neatly arranged in the bottom
of the drawer was a collection of small, fixed-blade knives
and daggers. He had always had an interest in the weapons
and had early on acquired a small collection—perhaps ten—
that he had found on various worlds. Since he had become
relatively wealthy, more opportunities for enlarging the collection had presented themselves. He had even had the
drawer modified so that the knives were fixed in place and
would not bounce around if the ride should get rough.

Dedicating a whole drawer to such a thing was a bit
unusual on a ship of the *Starbourne*'s size, but his cabin
was larger than the others on board. And this was his one
luxury. Well, that and the small store of exotic liqueurs
stashed in the closet. Small bottles, of course.

The comm buzzed, and he tapped the control button.
Liel's voice came through the speaker.

"Captain, we can reach Astar in just under two hours. It
will take some extra fuel and violating the slippage rule in
the last stargate."

"Do it," Rafe said, and tapped the button before his exec
acknowledged the order.

Liel would be seething a bit right about now. He hated
violating stargate rules. The fines could be very high, but
the chance of being caught was very low. Besides, the slippage on this occasion would be slight, and he trusted his
crew to make the right adjustments to avoid their being sent
into uninhabited space somewhere.

He turned back to his collection, admiring the gleam of
steel and other metals and materials. They were all very

old, antiques, some of them from Earth and he valued each one beyond the price he had paid for it.

He picked up one that he might have called his favorite if he could have admitted to that. It was the oldest of the lot, purchased from a dealer who swore it was from thirteenth-century Earth. He had seen one very like it once, in the possession of some planetary official—that was why it had caught his eye. And that was why he knew what it was. It was part of a set that once had included a katana, skewer, and scabbard. It was a shame that the knife had been separated from the set, but his good fortune to find it for himself.

Arden would be surprised when she saw it. It was so like her katana, and she would probably want it. He pulled up short mentally. That was a train of thought he did not want to follow. As things stood, Arden Grenfell would probably never set foot on the *Starbourne* again. The thought brought a wave of sadness. He shoved the drawer closed. Damned if he was going to let thoughts of her distract him again!

However, when he woke the next morning, the sound of her voice still rang in his ears, and the touch of her hand lingered on his body, from the dreams that had returned.

Night still hovered outside the windows when Arden jerked awake. A terrible fear gripped her. She sat up in the bed and switched on the bedside light. Lying beside her, tossed there by her sudden movement, lay the loom and skein of lifeweave that usually stayed in the dresser drawer. Sometime during the night she had moved across the room in her sleep and gotten them, lay back in bed, and had woven a square.

She pushed the covers off her, covering the loom, and went to the bathroom. She rinsed her face with cold water, then leaned on the vanity, looking at her naked body reflected in the mirror. Her gaze rose to study the face that did not look any more stupid than the day before. Such traits most often lay under the surface, showing only when they had been practiced much too long.

Dammit!

It would have been bad enough if she had done it consciously, but to do it in her sleep . . .

She strode back into the bedroom, put on her wrap robe, then pulled up the loom from under the covers. Rather than looking at the pattern she had woven, Arden got a pair of scissors out of the drawer in the bedside table, knotted the loose end, and cut the dangling thread. She sat on the edge of the bed and looked over at the clock. Still early morning, only four-thirty. She had slept less than an hour. That was probably all she would get tonight. In that case, she might as well go back to her office and get some work done.

But she continued to sit on the bed, the loom held loosely in both hands, her eyes avoiding looking at it. The pattern in the square of lifeweave would form a picture, something pertinent to her future, probably her immediate future. If she looked at it, that would give the picture more importance than she wanted it to have. If she destroyed it, would that dilute its importance in her life, make it easier to resist the temptation to weave again, even in her sleep?

Even if that were so—and she somehow knew it was so—the temptation was too great. It was a man's face, a man she knew only from afar: General Radieux.

What was his role to become? She had looked him up and confirmed that his current assignment had him on Baltha in charge of the forces guarding the weapons cache there. If those weapons should fall into the wrong hands, things on Glory could get a hell of a lot worse. The most recent lesson had been that it was almost impossible to know whom to trust. Could the general be trusted? She could go there to see how things stood.

General Hsing should be the one to check out the armory, but she definitely did not trust him. Her own responsibility was to Jessa. However, that included ensuring the safety of Glory. With so little time left until the wedding, she needed to know that the weapons were secure.

She did trust Captain Alvarez and could leave him in charge of palace security while she took a trip to Baltha. Rafe and the *Starbourne* might not arrive for another week. A trip to and from Baltha would take two days, giving her three or four days to check things out, and she would be

back in plenty of time to handle the transfer of the lifeweave.

That task she would not leave to anyone else.

Arden realized that she was still holding the loom. She
removed the square of lifeweave and returned the loom to
its drawer. Then she opened the antique trunk in the bedroom. From it she took a bundle wrapped in a more finely
woven piece of lifeweave cloth. It had been with her all
her life, or as far back as she could remember.

She unwrapped the bundle to reveal a stack of woven
squares resembling the one she had just finished. Her fingertips traced the outlines of the face woven into the one
on top that she had placed there after talking with him on
the comm. Rafe Semmes's eyes looked up at her, nearly as
alive as they were in person. They reminded her of the last
time they had seen each other, in her living room, just before he left Glory. They had spoken with hope of keeping
in touch, seeing each other occasionally, deciding where
their relationship would go. The decision had been made
by omission rather than commission.

She placed the new square under the one bearing Rafe's
likeness and rewrapped the bundle, placing it back in the
drawer. Her hands shook as she pushed the drawer closed.

Yes, she needed to get away. A trip to Baltha would be
just the thing. How to explain her leaving to Jessa? Neither
she nor anyone on the council would understand her involving herself in matters other than palace security. Citing
the weaving of the lifeweave square was out of the question. No one could know about that; it would conjure up
memories of Appolyona, and her death. Everyone would
suspect that she was not doing her job thoroughly if they
knew.

The best explanation would be the need to inventory
weapons necessary to arm a new contingent of security
guards and the warriors to be placed in the new sites around
the city and throughout the countryside. Inspecting those
weapons for serviceability would only be logical. Also,
some of the guards there might be needed on Glory before
the wedding, so the sooner she inspected them, the better.

Arden activated the comm console and sent a message

to Jessa, detailing the need for her to make the trip. The reasons why she should be the one to go seemed weak as they appeared on the screen, but the princess was accustomed to her commander of the guards doing things her own way. After eighteen months, she probably would not change now.

Instead of dressing and going down to her office, Arden fixed herself a glass of wine. She selected a book from one of the shelves in her living room, curled up on the sofa, and started reading. Her collection of books was extensive. Abbot Grayson had taught her to appreciate them along with so many other anachronistic things, such as the wine that came from the monastery. It had been months since she had taken time to just read.

The one in her hands was a collection of short stories written five hundred years earlier that she had read several times. Some of what they said made no sense because their world had disappeared or changed so radically that there was no longer a frame of reference. Or it was a different world altogether. Yet the human conditions described were not that different.

Arden woke later that morning on the sofa, the wine only half drunk, and the book lying open on the floor where it had slid off her lap. A glance at the clock showed it was still fairly early, but the sun was rising, its light brightening the large picture window. She showered quickly and checked for messages. There was one from the empress, requesting her to come to the royal apartments for breakfast.

She showered and dressed, strapping the katana across her back. A glance in the mirror ensured that all was as it should be with her uniform. She had elected to dispense with most of the paraphernalia usual for her rank. The golden cloverleaf insignia pinned to one shoulder and the royal badge on the breast of the belted tunic were enough. The maroon color added a reddish tint to her short brown hair. The slim trousers tucked into matching boots still showed off her athletic figure. A nice effect—one that she noticed on numerous occasions, but was still surprised by.

Shaking off the introspection, Arden left her apartment

and made her way to the other wing. Jessa ordered break-fast served at a small table in the sitting room. While they waited, she came right to the point.

"General Hsing is upset with your plans to visit the armory."

"You told him already?" Arden asked.

"Yes. I thought it only right that he be informed. He feels, and rightly so, that you should wait until he has the time to inspect the weapons with you."

They both grew silent as a servant entered with a large tray. He set out dishes, both hot and cold, for them to choose from, poured hot coffee and fruit juice, and departed. The whole time, Jessa seemed lost in thought, and Arden wondered if she had erred in requesting to make this trip.

"I know Hsing must be feeling pretty defensive right now after that debacle at the prison," Arden said as soon as they were alone again. "My instincts tell me that I must do this and you know how strong my instincts can be. Can't he make arrangements to go now? With the wedding so near, I just don't think we should wait much longer."

"I asked him and he said no. I did assign both of you to check all of this out, after all. When were you planning on going?"

"Tomorrow."

"You really do have a sense of urgency."

"Yes."

"May I ask why?"

"Just something that came to me last night while I was sleeping," Arden hedged. The same thing had happened before, and Jessa usually went along with such requests. She was aware of Arden's use of lifeweave, although they had never discussed it. "However, I do want to be here when the lifeweave is loaded on the *Starbourne*. After that, there might not be any time."

"Who will you put in charge while you're gone?"

"Captain Alvarez."

Jessa ate in silence, and Arden felt sure she was worried about offending the general further. He was still a force to reckon with in Glorian politics and in the military. In contrast, Radieux was strictly military. At least as far as she knew.

"Aren't you going to eat?" Jessa asked.

Arden looked down at her plate and smiled. The food would taste excellent, she knew from past experience, and she should be hungry, but she was not.

"I'll eat later," she said, wondering for a moment if she would. Or even if she could.

"All right, you can go to Baltha tomorrow. I'll tell Hsing that . . . Well, I'll think of some excuse." She set the fork down. "Don't make me regret this."

Arden nodded. "I better go prepare for the trip. Is there anything you need me for today?"

Jessa shook her head.

"Then I will brief Captain Alvarez on everything for the next week. There's a transport leaving early tomorrow morning."

"You're not taking one of the runabouts?"

"No. They can't have one ready until late tomorrow. I can be there faster with the transport in the morning."

"All right" was all Jessa said. Arden had expected an argument involving appearances. "Be careful."

"I will."

She got up from the table and went to the door. She paused there, thinking the empress might have something else to say. When nothing was said, Arden left the room and headed for her office.

Alvarez awaited her there, having received a copy of the message to the empress. He had been left in charge before and knew what to do, but Arden wanted to go over the new assignments within the palace. After last night, she did not want to take any chances.

Night lighting was on in the dome, and silence filled the spaces. The garrison on Baltha worked on a daylight/night schedule only slightly shorter than Glory's because of the difference in the planet's rotation. Even so, guards were evident everywhere. At least General Hsing had seen to that.

Arden arched her shoulders forward, trying to relieve

some of the tension. The trip had been uneventful, but she had forgotten what a transport shuttle was like: not much room and generally crowded and always a bit fragrant. And never any room to work or move around.

As late as it was, she had decided to head directly for the quarters assigned to her, take a shower, and get some sleep. General Radieux was most likely asleep himself, although he was expecting her.

A soldier dressed in green regular army fatigues approached from the main corridor, spotted her, and changed course slightly to intercept her.

"Commander Grenfell?" he asked when he was a few steps away.

"Yes."

"I'm Major Jones. I will escort you to your quarters if you like. General Radieux assumed that you would go there first."

"That's fine," she said.

"He will also be pleased to meet with you at oh-eight-hundred tomorrow, if that's convenient."

"It is."

He handed her a holo badge and motioned for one of the nearest guards to take her bags. The young man eyed the katana strapped across her back, then bent to his task.

"You've been here before, I understand," Jones said. She confirmed that. "The badge I gave you is unrestricted. It will give you access to all parts of the facility, except the general's office." He proceeded to detail some of the changes that had been made in the past few years.

Several of those changes were evident as she passed into the central atrium. During the war, that area had not been furnished so much as just plain crowded with bunks, indicative of the large number of soldiers stationed there. Often more than the barracks could accommodate. Every nook and cranny had been fitted out for living space, including the atrium. Now only a few guards watched over the open area with its evening lighting.

Arden paused in the center of the atrium and surveyed its comparative emptiness. The echo of their footsteps still bounced around the circular walls. A few sofas, chairs, and large plants were scattered around, accenting the forlorn feeling. Leaning her head back, she looked through the clear dome. The night sky was brilliant with stars, even more than she could see on a winter's night from the monastery. Baltha had almost no light pollution and not much atmosphere; hence the need for a dome to enclose a breathable space for those stationed here.

Major Jones and their escort waited patiently as she took it all in. When she started forward again, the major resumed enumerating changes that were not so apparent. For the most part, they had to do with reallocating space no longer needed for personnel. However, there had been a beefing up of security, both personnel and equipment, the decision for which she had taken part in.

The end of his report and arrival at her quarters occurred simultaneously, whether by design or accident she could not say. She was shown into the VIP suite and started to protest. Realization came swiftly, and she managed not to embarrass herself by insisting that she had no right to stay there. Old habits were definitely hard to break.

Once she and her bags were inside, the major said goodnight and he and the soldier left. Arden unpacked, put everything away, but felt too keyed up for bed. She wanted a cup of coffee, but decided against using the call button on the wall console in her sitting room. In spite of her exhaustion, she decided to move around a bit and reacquaint herself with some of the armory.

The door slid aside, keyed by the badge, and she walked out into the hall. The suite behind her was quiet, but a deeper quiet settled around her, the quiet of a place that was more normally alive with people coming and going, the sounds of their moving about suspended now, leaving a sense of anticipation. Those sounds would burst free any moment and surround her, drawing her into the life of the facility. Now, she was outside it, free to poke into night places and sense what others had left behind.

She moved back toward the atrium in order to orient herself. The four guards still stood in their places. Their eyes shifted toward her at her first appearance, but they remained otherwise motionless. They were trained to watch her every move as long as she stayed near enough, even to follow her if she wandered into a sensitive area, in spite of the badge that gave her access. It was the same for everyone who entered their area of responsibility, including the commanding officer.

Twelve corridors led away from the atrium like spokes in a wheel. The first one she faced led into a barracks section, as did the next one to the right. Directly opposite, two more corridors led to more barracks. In the center of those corridors were the mess halls, but they were for regular soldiers and were more than likely closed at this hour. A common hall lay just down one of the other corridors for those who needed something during the night and those few who worked the late hours.

She walked over to the plaque on one of the corridor walls that listed what was down that way and was gratified to see that she had chosen the right one. She fought back the urge to wave at the guards as she felt their gazes bore holes in her back. She would not have noticed them if regular activity had filled the room.

Two soldiers were sitting drinking coffee when she entered the mess hall. They looked up at her with curiosity, followed by suspicion as they realized that her face was unfamiliar. Their eyes lowered to the badge she wore and they turned back to their coffee, although they cast glances over at her every once in a while. The badge probably caused as much curiosity about her identity as anything else, unless Radieux had made a general announcement about her coming to Baltha.

Arden drew some coffee from the dispenser into a coarse cup, then found a table and sat down. The room was the same stainless steel and plastic that she remembered. Here too the silence seemed only a prelude to noise and activity. She blew on the coffee and took a sip. A substitute brew, and as bad as she remembered it. She had become spoiled by life in the palace, but she had no intention of trading what she had for this. Her stint was over, and a better life was sweet revenge. On exactly whom was a matter for consideration another time.

The two soldiers finished their coffee and left. One

looked back over his shoulder at her just before disappearing through the doorway. She would have to get used to that for a day or two. If that was as bad as it got, she could handle it.

She finished the coffee and dropped the cup into the recycler chute. The whoosh sounded very loud, the echoes following her out the door. One of the main storerooms was supposed to be at the far end of the corridor, and she turned that way. Offices and small administrative storerooms stood tightly closed on either side. Her footsteps echoed back at her from in front and behind. A single guard, standing watch near the center of the corridor, came to attention as she and her badge neared his station. She passed him, and the door sensor at the far end recognized her badge. The doors parted, sliding into the wall on either side.

Rifles stood in racks, butt down, packed so closely that only a sheet of paper could have gone between two of them. Years ago most of the racks would have been empty, the rifles in the hands of soldiers fully prepared to use them. The door closed behind her as she made her way into the warehouse. More and more racks came into view. Thousands of guns. Weapons that could fall into the wrong hands. It would be better if they were somehow destroyed, but there was not much chance of that happening. Too many people had uses for them.

Arden wandered among the racks, noting several different models of weapons. There were laser and projectile types. Handguns must be stored in another warehouse, something she had not remembered.

Toward the back stood another door. When she approached it, however, it did not respond to her badge. She took the badge off and waved it in front of the sensor. The mechanism clicked and whirred a moment, but did not open the door. It was not surprising that one door might not open to her, yet the fact worried her and she could not say why. She would have to ask General Radieux about it in the morning when they met.

7

Arden checked herself in the mirror and adjusted her tunic. She was nervous, and that surprised her. Meeting General Radieux should not be such a difficult matter, but he had been her superior and now they were not quite equals. At least not to her.

Although she worked her way up to a commission in the wartime army, she had only seen the general at a distance. Even then, he was an imposing figure. He was as tall as Abbot Grayson, but slender, muscular, always standing ramrod straight, and balanced on the balls of his feet as if constantly ready for action. With his light brown skin, black mustache and hair, and cap always set firmly on his head, he was an ideal representative of the military man.

A warmth swept through her body as the crush, long suppressed, returned with a rush. Arden waited a moment before buttoning up her maroon tunic. The hot flash subsided; she sighed and finished dressing. An observer might think she was still a teenager or something.

She sat on the end of the bed, put on the black boots, and pulled the instep straps for her trousers underneath. Retrieving her katana from the top of the nightstand, she moved to study her reflection in the full-length mirror in the bathroom. No, she decided, she would not wear the cap so she could enjoy the touch of redness that the maroon uniform lent to her hair. The insignia denoting the imperial guard gleamed on the right collar and that for her rank of commander on the left. She liked the gold metal better than having cloth insignia sewn on.

Arden wondered about wearing the sword for a moment, but it was as much a symbol of her status as the insignia. Everyone else would more than likely be armed, except possibly Radieux. He carried a saber, she knew.

Since this was a dress occasion, she wrapped the sword belt around her waist instead of draping it across her back as she would do if there was any possibility of attack. A knock came on the door to the sitting room. She took one last look in the mirror, then moved to answer it.

Major Jones stood just outside in his dress greens. He did not wear a cap either, but his sword hung at his side.

"I'll escort you to the general's office," he said.

She stepped out and closed the door behind her. They walked side by side, since she knew the way. However, protocol demanded that she be escorted into Radieux's office on this first visit. She hoped that the general understood that she was to have unlimited access to everything here.

They passed through the central atrium and into another spoke of the armory wheel. Not far down, they stopped before a door; Jones opened it, and Arden walked into the outer office. A corporal sat behind a desk—the first woman soldier she had encountered thus far. She stood and saluted. Arden returned the salute.

"The general is expecting you," the corporal announced.

Jones opened the next door and followed her inside. General Radieux stood behind his massive desk, a smile of welcome on his face. Grey streaked both his hair and mustache, and a few lines accented his eyes. He seemed even leaner, if possible, but his uniform still fit handsomely.

She was relieved when he held out his hand rather than saluting or waiting for her to do so. She shook his hand, then sat in one of two chairs placed in front of the desk. His sword, she saw, lay on the credenza behind his desk.

"I hope you slept well, Commander," he said as they both sat down.

"I did, indeed, General."

"The empress's message stated that you were coming to inspect our security, among other things."

"That's right."

"I hope you haven't been disappointed."

"No, sir, I haven't thus far," she said. "The only reason we felt obliged to make this trip is the threat from the bands of marauders plaguing Glory. I suppose you've heard that one of their leaders appears to be Don Vey."

"The former prime minister? No, I hadn't heard."

He picked up a pen from the desktop and twirled it between two fingers. Arden launched into an account of the most recent events in and around the palace complex. Radieux seemed to listen with only half of his attention. The major watched his commanding officer. In the middle of the tale, she knew that they had already heard about the events back home.

Why would they feel it necessary to lie about that? The information could have come to them from many legitimate sources. Could it be that identifying their source would raise suspicions at the very least? It might only be that they wanted another version of the events in order to decide if what they were hearing was true. However, the feeling of unease she had felt the night before returned.

"With Vey involved, we feel sure that they can gain access to a ship and leave our solar system, or even try to come here. There is also the danger of mixed loyalties."

She finished by telling them of the plan for building and manning outposts, and the need for more armed guards in the Capital for the upcoming imperial wedding. Silence fell over the room. Radieux still twirled the pencil. Jones watched his hands resting in his lap. Arden looked from one to the other, waiting for some reaction.

After what seemed like several minutes, the general looked up at her and smiled. A few years ago, that smile directed at her would have made her heart race. Now it filled her with apprehension bordering on dread.

"It's unfortunate that events have taken such a turn," he said. "I am happy that our empress has not been harmed by any of these machinations. Clearly, we must all be on the lookout for anything that might indicate a plot of some kind.''

Jones nodded his head and smiled in turn. She was beginning to feel as if she was the only one excluded from some sort of inside joke.

"I assume that you want to begin your inspection right away." He looked at his watch. "Breakfast is being served in the officers' mess. May I suggest that we have something brought in here so that we can review the itinerary I have prepared?"

Arden nodded.

"Good," Radieux said. "I will accompany you, of course."

"That won't be necessary," she said. "Having been stationed here during the war, I have a pretty good idea of where everything is. I'm sure you have much to do, and I wouldn't want to impose."

"It is true that I am a busy man, unfortunately. Major Jones could escort you, then. I can do without his services for a time."

The major had gone to the comm unit to order breakfast for the three of them. He turned at the mention of his name, put a hand over the mouthpiece, and replied that he would be glad to escort the commander.

"It's settled, then," Radieux said.

He pulled a palm comm unit out of the center desk drawer, opened it, and pressed a few keys. Jones returned to his seat.

"I have prepared this itinerary for you, keeping in mind your short stay and the urgency of your mission," the general said. "Also, there is an inventory list of everything stored here."

He started going over the plans. Before long, a female private arrived with the food. Jones supervised the setting up of the meal at a round conference table in the far corner behind the chair Arden had been sitting in. They moved to the table and reviewed the itinerary between mouthfuls of meat and egg substitutes, standard military fare. However, she was pleased to find that the coffee was real this time.

The review outlasted the meal. Finally, they sat back in their chairs, sipping fresh cups of coffee.

"That covers everything, I guess," Arden said. "I appreciate your thoroughness, General."

"It's my job, Commander. I take pride in my job."

"You have always had that reputation, sir. That and a history of loyalty to your emperor. Or empress."

She thought he winced at the last remark, but he covered it by leaning forward to put down the coffee mug. She followed suit and stood.

"If it is all right with you, I'll get started," she said. "As you said, there is a lot to cover."

Both men stood. If he had reacted negatively to her words, there was no sign of it now.

"Very well," Radieux said. "Let me or Major Jones know if there are any problems." He turned to his aide. "Major, you have your orders."

"Yes, sir."

The general handed the palm comm unit to Arden, and wished her luck while the major called for someone to retrieve the dirty dishes. Jones led the way out of the office and into the hall of the spoke.

"The first area on the itinerary is this spoke," he said. "Arms lockers for those posted here and a small storeroom at the end for grenades and other small explosives."

They started toward the outer rim.

The large caches of arms were all in the rim of the wheel that made up the armory. Items that would explode, such as the grenades and projectile ammunition, were kept in storerooms next to those holding nonexploding arms: rifles, handguns, swords, knives, and bayonets. Laser arms, both the guns and the power packs, were stored side by side.

If an explosion should occur in the rim, the rest of the wheel could be sealed off very quickly, first the spokes, then the central atrium. She had always thought that locating the commanding officer's office in a spoke that ended in an explosives storeroom was foolish bravado, but it had always been that way. His quarters, however, were in a safer spoke. Swords were stored at the end of that one, as well as she remembered.

She would probably leave that spoke until last, since it was the guns and more modern weapons that concerned her the most. Radieux had color-coded the spokes the same as the directory in the atrium and the stripe that ran along each floor: green for rifles and pistols, red for ammunition, yellow for laser guns, orange for laser packs, purple for swords, and blue for grenades and explosives.

The general had started the itinerary with the blue spoke, just as she had intended. Halfway down the tunnel was one of the arms lockers for the resident troops. Jones's badge triggered the door to open, and they stepped inside.

"There are still four of these?" Arden asked.

She started down the middle aisle of the locker, inspecting the weapons racks as she went.

"Yes, here in the blue tunnels and in the yellow tunnels. If there were any explosion or even an attack, at least one, perhaps two of the lockers should survive."

"How many soldiers on duty at this moment?"

"Ninety-nine on the day shift," Jones responded immediately. "There are forty-three guards at all times, including those on the monitors. Plus fifteen clerical, seven in the mess halls . . ."

"I meant only those carrying weapons," Arden interrupted.

"Those on guard duty, then, plus thirteen officers. All officers are armed while on duty. However, a few do not wear sidearms."

That information would give her some idea, at least, of how many arms might be missing from the lockers: no more than sixty in total. That would break down to fifteen or so from each locker. Assuming, of course, that each person carried only one gun.

The guns themselves appeared to be accounted for in this first locker. The ammunition cabinets could be locked individually, but were not, since the room was secure, Jones explained. Still, she noted that on the comm unit, then moved to check the air duct covers.

The grids were made of sturdy metal and locked in place inside the room in such a way as to make them impossible to tamper with from inside the duct itself. Not that the average person could have fit inside there comfortably, anyway.

She pulled several guns from the racks at random and inspected each. They were clean, the firing pins intact, and ready for action.

She then stood in front of the surveillance camera at the back of the room and hand-signaled for a test. The red indicator light blinked three times in response. She did the same with the second camera near the door, with the same result.

Satisfied, she led the way out into the hall. The only problem she had seen was the unlocked ammunition, but there could be good reasons for leaving it unlocked. It certainly would better enable the soldiers to get to it in case of an attack. All they would need to do was approach the door with the proper badge, and there it all was. However, if invaders got hold of that same badge, they would also have easy access to everything.

In the hallway, she performed the same test with another surveillance camera. The guard near the entrance to the storeroom at the end was alert. Inside the storeroom, she repeated the same inspections and asked Jones a few more questions. When they finished in there, it was lunchtime, and they headed for the officers' mess.

While she ate, Arden flipped through the itinerary on the comm unit. In the afternoon, it called for inspection of the red tunnels, at the ends of which were the ammunition storerooms. The green tunnels were scheduled for the next afternoon. Her curiosity about the door that would not open had grown. So far, it was the only one that had not responded to her security badge.

Maybe she was just getting paranoid. Either the sensor or the door could have been out of order. A simple explanation, yet with the underlying tension she had sensed in both Jones and Radieux, it was difficult to accept.

However, it would be best not to rouse suspicions further by deviating from the itinerary. After lunch they inspected the red tunnels, finding nothing of note. She refused Jones's offer of having dinner with him in the mess hall, opting instead to have a tray brought to her room. She explained

that she had to work on the reports daily or she might fall
behind. She also needed to check back with her staff and
review their assignments.

Back in her sitting room, she set the tray on the table
but sat for some time without eating. Going over the events
of the day and the two men's reactions, she found nothing
concrete on which to hang her suspicions. If she could
brainstorm with someone, the reasons for her feelings might
come out.

She resisted the urge to call Abbot Grayson. They both
had good scramblers, but she could not trust them here. No
telling what Radieux might have installed on the comm
lines, and scramblers were not totally reliable.

The food was nearly cold when she finally uncovered the
dishes and tried to eat something. In the end she pushed
the tray away with more than half of the food left. The
coffee had stayed hot in the insulated pitcher, and she
poured a generous mug of that. She worked on the day's
report and drank coffee until nearly ten o'clock. Standing
up, she stretched, then put her personal comm unit away in
one of the dresser drawers in the bedroom. She started to
close the drawer but, spotting the familiar cloth bag, she
stopped.

Lifeweave was the next best thing to brainstorming.
Every reason not to use it crossed her mind as she picked
up the bag. This time, Arden did not hesitate. She had to
understand what she faced.

She moved to the easy chair in the bedroom and put her
feet up on the ottoman. As she relaxed, she took the loom
out of the bag and began threading it with lifeweave. In
moments, she was in another world.

Pac Terhn appeared immediately this time. No tricks, no
games. The setting was a peaceful glen surrounded by a
forest. A slight breeze ruffled her hair.

"I thought this might be a nice change from that enclosed armory you've been cooped up in," he said.

"What makes you so nice today?"

"Am I? I hadn't noticed."

His grin showed the trickster side of him, and she knew

the unusual consideration he was showing would not last. She had better hurry.

"I need to see some things in the armory," she said. "Things that I'm sure I will not be shown on this inspection tour."

"I can do that."

"The price?"

"Hmm, this is a small request," he said, rubbing his chin with his left hand. "You are already bound to the empress by an earlier deal. And you have made use of the lifeweave several times without a fee."

"Only three times," Arden corrected.

"Whatever."

He waved a hand in dismissal of what she had said and stood thinking. Pac Terhn usually did not take long to propose a fee. This did not bode well, in spite of his statement that this request was small.

"I know," he said at last. "I will take your firstborn child."

"What?"

By then, he was bent over with laughter.

"Just kidding," he said. "I read that once in a story."

"I'm sure you did. But let's be a little sensible, shall we?"

"If you insist. You will use lifeweave more frequently to answer questions, say once a month. Is that better?"

Using it that often could increase her dependence on lifeweave. And she had promised Grayson not to use it at all. She counter offered twice a year for a period of two years, and after some haggling, they agreed on four times a year for three years. However, she was free to use it more often if she chose to.

In another moment, Arden found herself floating through the air. Many visits seemed to start this way, although she did not know why, and she was content to leave her guide in control this time.

Looking down, she recognized the surface of Baltha. The planet was far enough from the sun that it was always dark, although not totally black on the surface that faced toward the sun. She moved from the night side to the day side, where she could make out some shapes. In the distance, she spotted the armory. So far, indications were that the spirits she was to visit were probably still living on the surface.

Nearer the armory, she set down. Still no movement or sound around her. She fought against holding her breath. She was not actually on the surface, after all.

A noise behind her made her turn around sharply. A form floated there, transparent, and about a foot off the ground. Its shape changed constantly, as if it were smoke drifting in a breeze. Yet it stayed in that one place.

It was the spirit of something that had once lived on Baltha, but its form gave her no clue to what it had been when alive. So far as anyone knew, nothing had actually lived here. There had been nothing but rocks and dirt for hundreds, maybe thousands of years. Even though rocks and dirt often also had spirits, the one facing her had been neither of those. It had actually been a living thing.

"What do you seek?" it asked in a breathless whisper.

"Knowledge," she answered. "I need to know who I can trust and who I can't within that complex." She pointed at the armory.

"What makes you think you can trust anyone?"

"There must be someone."

"Not necessarily," it whispered. "But possibly. I sense, however, that you also want to know what lies behind a locked door. And what will happen within the next few days."

"Yes."

Its form fluttered, and a scene took shape within it. The door appeared, the handle turned, and it swung open.

When she woke, the square of lifeweave showed a man's face that was vaguely familiar. In the background was the depiction of a room, filled with equipment. It, too, was vaguely familiar. She only hoped there would be time to remember more fully the scenes the Balthan spirit had shown her.

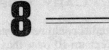

8

The final carton was offloaded and inspected. Connor O'Brien watched alongside Captain Semmes.

"Come on, Semmes," the trader said. "Right now the rate is very high on reales. You could make even more money when you convert."

"We deal only in credits, Connor. You know that."

"Yeah, I know, but you could do it just this once. It's a sweetheart deal."

Rafe did not mind O'Brien's trying to talk him into taking the local currency in payment for the precious metals. Everyone did, since it was to their advantage. However, accepting Astarian reales in payment for the precious metals would mean the payment would be less for the crew of the *Starbourne* than it would be in interstellar credits, in spite of the conversion rates.

First, they could not be converted on Astar. He would have to go to another world to make the conversion, and by the time they arrived there, the rate could have gone down. Second, there was always a fee for converting currency, and this amount would command a very large fee, since it would be figured on a percentage. Third, from Astar they were heading for Glory and probably would not have time to make the conversion. That would mean the money would have to stay in the stasis vault in his cabin. On the other hand, credits could be transferred directly to the ship's account on Centauri III once they reached Glory. No muss, no fuss.

"It's been a bad year for us here," O'Brien continued. "We sure could use the break."

"You know the drill, Connor. I especially can't change the rule on this trip. Maybe next time."

"Okay. You can't blame a guy for trying."

"No, I can't."

He did know that Connor was not lying about its having been a rough year on Astar. The monsoon season had been more violent and had lasted longer than usual. Communications systems had been badly damaged, and their repair was the main reason they needed the metals. However, the trader would not have any mercy when it came to reselling to the companies making the repairs. Therefore, any compassion Rafe showed for their plight would not transfer to those who really needed it.

O'Brien handed over the bank draft that had been in his briefcase all the time. They shook hands, and the merchant climbed into the truck. It drove away, and Rafe felt more than the usual sense of relief. For whatever reason, a feeling that he should get to Glory soon had haunted him, in spite of his earlier resolve to make Arden await the pleasure of his company. Now that the transaction was finished, they could finally be on their way.

The trip would take four days even using all the shortcuts they knew. Liel had not asked why the hurry. He probably thought he knew the reason, but it was not quite that his captain needed to see a certain head of security. Not exactly, anyway. But then, Rafe was not entirely sure of the reason himself.

He stepped inside the hatch and keyed the comm unit.

"We're done, Liel," he said when the exec answered. "Let's get the hell out of here."

He made his way to the bridge, where he found Liel readying for liftoff. With a strong sense of relief, he heard the clearance. Rafe tried to settle into the routine that would last the next four days, but found himself getting more and more worried about the delay. Sometimes Liel gave him queer looks. Maybe he too sensed that something was different about this sense of urgency.

Until now, Rafe Semmes had never believed in premonitions. Not even after working with Jessa and Arden. He still did not believe in them. Not a bit. But they still had to hurry.

At the end of the second day, the inspections had gone as planned. When they came to it, the door at the back of Green A storeroom still did not respond to her badge. Nor did it respond to Jones's badge. He promised to have maintenance check it out and was vague when she asked what was in the room beyond. The memory of her visit using the lifeweave still had not returned. Arden let Jones think she could wait, but was determined to find out on her own.

They might have expected her to try that same night she had questioned it, but waiting until the next evening might make everyone think she really had dismissed the mystery. When that time came, she openly made her way toward the door. The guard was in the tunnel, of course, but he hardly showed awareness of her presence as she passed. Once inside the storeroom, she quickly moved between the racks to the stubborn door.

It still refused to recognize her badge. She had actually thought it might have been fixed once she brought attention to it. That would have made good sense even if there was something to hide inside.

Just in case they had not fixed it, she had brought a wrench she sneaked into her pocket the day before. With it, the cover for the door mechanism came off quickly. Her training in these things was military: break in, disable it, and get through the doorway. Nothing sophisticated about it.

Crouched just within and to one side of the door, Arden found herself on the landing of a stairway that descended into darkness. Now she thought she remembered what this was: the access to an underground control center that she had only seen once when she was stationed here. Why would Jones have felt it necessary to lie about it? He must have known she would have been told about it. She fingered her badge. Why would she be denied access?

She held her breath and listened. Complete silence except for the sound of her own heartbeat. A flashlight would be a good thing to have right now. She exhaled, took a deep breath. The air was fresh. Either the passage was frequently used or currently maintained. Her soft-soled boots whispered against each step as she made her way down. Her right hand held onto the handrail. Soon darkness surrounded her.

And she descended.

The facility was deep underground and to the west of the main armory. A series of lights along the spokes, and powered by the emergency generator, was supposed to guide the soldiers into it if necessary. It had been built in case the aboveground buildings were destroyed or made uninhabitable. It had never been used under those conditions, but that it seemed to still be active was not surprising. Glory's wars might be over for now, but who knew what the future might hold?

After a time, she realized that the darkness was becoming grey. Some lights must still be on in the center itself. Emergency lights, probably. The light increased, and she stopped once again to listen. Still quiet. No. A low-pitched hum, tuned to the body more than the ears, made her skin prickle. The pitch was so low, it was impossible to tell where the sound came from except that by moving forward the effect increased until, finally, the sound was audible.

Machine noise. And there was enough light now to see that the stairs were ending.

Just below, a dim light shone above a doorway opening to the left. It did not open as she approached, and she saw a standard door latch. On close inspection, the door proved to be a high-impact safety door. Arden questioned its effectiveness. The stairway would act like a wind tunnel for any concussion and, even though the door opened outward, would probably blow it off its hinges.

She pressed an ear against the door. It hummed slightly with whatever machines were running inside. Nothing else.

Putting her hand on the door latch, she hesitated. Was anyone on the other side? If so, were they friend or foe? If it was all very innocent, she would feel foolish. However, she had to prove to herself that the facility was securely on the empress's side. If it was not, she must be able to report back at least, so that proper steps could be taken.

The latch moved downward as she pressed against it. With a slight click, the door pulled open a crack. Through it, she saw nothing but console lights glowing in twilight. She waited a moment for any movement—nothing—then opened it far enough to slip through. She pressed against the wall and let the door close silently, without letting it latch. Standing quite still, she surveyed the chamber.

Indirect lighting glowed softly from outlets overhead. Computer consoles were set up in a circle. Mounted in the open space in the center was a holo cube capable of projecting a very large image. Probably used for strategy maps. On two walls—the one directly in front and the one to her right—several surveillance screens were mounted at a comfortable eye level. They must show scenes from the surface of the planet and within the armory itself, but were black now.

Although full of equipment, the chamber appeared to be empty of people. She moved toward the nearest console, expecting to find a layer of dust on it. It was clean. She checked each one. All clean. Like the stairwell, the chamber was either being used or actively maintained. Either scenario could be true. So far, there was absolutely no reason to doubt Radieux's loyalty.

Two other doors led from the chamber. Arden opened them and peered into the empty corridors behind each. The same dim lighting and silence greeted her. There was not enough time to check them out more thoroughly, because she wanted to see if she could access any information at one of the consoles. She thought she remembered that one of the corridors would lead to quarters and the other to more quarters and offices for the staff officers.

She moved to the console nearest the door through which she had come and sat down. After turning it on, she began a search through a list of communication files. Several messages to and from Glory were listed, but before she could pull one up on the screen, voices came from one of the corridors.

She switched the console off quickly and sprinted for the exit. Just as she slipped out, another door opened and two soldiers entered the chamber. They were so engrossed in their conversation that they did not notice that the door opposite was ajar.

"Is this shutdown going to delay the project?" the short soldier asked as they moved toward the consoles.

"Of course it will delay us," the captain replied. "But a few days won't hurt us much. The general factored in the possibility."

"How much longer will the commander be here?"

"Another three days, I think."

A comm unit buzzed, and the soldier moved to answer it at the nearest console. In a moment he handed the handset toward his superior.

"It's Lieutenant Riordan, sir."

The captain took it, said hello, then listened. In a moment he disconnected and set the handset back in place.

"Get a detail and begin a search of the entire command center, including the stairwell. It seems that Commander Grenfell has decided to go walk about and may have found her way in here."

"Yes, sir."

The soldier saluted and went back through the same door by which they entered. The captain surveyed the chamber from where he stood, his gaze lighting on the exit door just as she let it cut off her view.

Quickly, Arden started up the stairs. All she could do now was make it difficult for them to take her until she could send some kind of report back to Glory. That was one of the problems with such a confined place—nowhere to run.

She had to hurry, though, before they set up an overall communications block. The hand comm strapped to her wrist was a powerful unit, but even it could not penetrate through to the surface and beyond.

By the time she reached the storeroom, she was out of breath. No time to stop and relax. The outer door opened, and she ducked behind a rifle rack, conscious now to make sure her sword did not bump against anything.

Five men moved inside, led by a sergeant. He instructed two of the men to search the storeroom; the other two he sent down the stairs. He then left, and the door closed behind him.

Since the racks had backings, Arden knew that she could sneak around the two soldiers and make it to the door without being seen. However, the opening of the door would alert them to her presence, and everyone in the armory would know her general location. She had to neutralize these two, at least for a while.

Neither of the men was being particularly quiet as they made their way up and down the rows. That made it easy to locate them and detect the direction in which they moved. Plus, any sound she made would be muffled by their noise. It would be best to move against them while they were widely separated, since they had started at opposite sides of the room.

Keeping low, she moved to the end of the row. One soldier was just starting down the row next to her. Careful not to make any noise, she lifted a rifle from the nearest rack. She moved around the end of the racks and peeked around to see exactly where the man was. He moved quickly toward the other end.

Arden had to nearly run to catch up to him. He was quite a bit bigger and she had to stand to her full height, at the same time raising the rifle. She hit him just behind the right ear with the butt of the weapon. With a cry, he collapsed to his knees. She hit him again and he fell forward without another sound except for the clatter of his own rifle as it slipped from his hand to the hard floor.

"Glenn!" his companion called out.

Crouching again, Arden listened carefully to see what the other man would do. The one before her did not have a comm unit. She would guess the other did not have one either. But there was the comm unit near the main door.

Instead of calling for help, thereby alerting his superiors, the man called out again, then started toward her. Arden slipped around the end of the row and waited. There was the crack of a knee bending as he probably checked to see if Glenn was still alive.

She slipped around the corner again, not bothering to crouch this time. She brought the rifle butt down on the back of his neck, and he crumpled onto his companion. She propped the rifle against them, whispering a silent prayer that neither man was dead.

Arden hurried to the door and stepped to one side as it hissed open. Silence followed. She looked around the doorway. The corridor was surprisingly empty, but Radieux and Jones were probably trying to keep the search for her as quiet as possible. Especially if they had not come up with a good story for putting her on a most wanted list.

Still, she expected to find the guard on duty. Unless he had been the one who reported her presence in the store-room when he was relieved and there was no one else to put in his place who was trusted by the general and . . . This was not the time for speculations.

She slipped into the corridor. Her assigned quarters was the first place they would look. What was the least likely? Actually, if they had already searched her quarters, that might be the least likely. Unless they had set a guard there.

Radieux's own office was another least likely, but he might decide to direct the search from there. If she only knew how many of the soldiers stationed here were in on the plot . . . it was the first time she had put that name to what was going on here. But she had no idea how wide-spread it was.

All of this went through her mind as she rushed down the corridor. Suddenly she saw the officer's mess. She could hide right out in the open. Even if someone was in there, they probably were not looking for her.

She slowed down, took a deep breath, hoping to give an appearance of calm, and strolled inside. It was empty. She drew a cup of coffee from one of the urns, then found a seat in the corner least visible from the entrance. Trying to look casual, she took a sip of the coffee, the hot liquid burning her tongue, then turned her attention to her comm unit. It took a moment to punch in the number back on Glory and another moment for an answer.

"Abbot, this is Arden," she said into the mike when he answered. "I don't have much time and there's much to tell."

"All right" was all he said. Even in those two words, he managed to convey concern.

She proceeded to tell him what she had learned and what she suspected.

"They know I've seen the underground command center," she concluded. "They're looking for me right now."

"Anywhere you can hide?"

"Not really. Radieux and his staff have access to every nook and cranny. And there aren't many of those in a facility like this. I'd like to find a way off this rock, but . . ."

She wondered if there was a way to sneak onto the next transport going back to Glory. Getting to the docking bay would be the difficult part.

"Anyway," she continued, "I'd better get out of here. I'm sure they're trying to trace this transmission."

"I'll get the word to Captain Alvarez as soon as I can."

"Thanks. If I'd gone direct, on a military channel, the chances of this message being picked up would have been greater."

"I know. Now, off with you. Find safety if you can."

"I will. I . . ."

At a moment like this, knowing she might never see him again, there should be much to say. Yet, she could think of nothing except . . .

"I love you, daughter," he said, and broke the connection before she could respond. At least one of them said it.

Running, finding a place to hide seemed so useless. Still, as she finished the coffee, which had cooled, she tried to think of someplace, anyplace, where she could do so safely. Frankly, she deserved to be caught. Anyone who planned so badly, or worse, did not plan at all, should be. She shook her head. She had come here because she felt uneasy about the security of the armory, yet without thinking that uneasiness might be due to Radieux's disloyalty. It was still difficult to believe.

There would be no bluffing her way out—the computer had a record of her entering that storeroom and when she had done so. Of course, the guard in the tunnel saw her, and her actions—at least some of them—had been picked up by the surveillance cameras. It had always been assumed that an enemy could not infiltrate, but no one had ever thought of the enemy as one's own people.

She had every right to be in the storeroom, when she was there, but attacking the two soldiers could not be explained away. Certainly, no one else would have done that. And they had guilty consciences. Yes, it was badly done.

Even so, someone on Glory knew what she had found, and hopefully better planning would ensue.

Right now, her only plan was to try to make it to the docking bay, find someplace to hide there, and sneak on board the next outbound transport. The one thing that might help her was Radieux's reluctance to broadcast the search for her. However, the longer she stayed at large, the greater the chance that he would forget that, and have every available man on the lookout.

Arden stood and headed for the exit. It was not quite three A.M., and the corridor was blessedly empty. She started toward the central atrium. If she was right, and Radieux had enlisted only a few of the soldiers stationed here, there was a chance that the guards there would have no reason to try to detain her.

Stepping boldly into the openness of the atrium, she strode toward the tunnel leading to the docking area. The guards reacted as usual, noting her presence without moving or speaking. Chills ran up her back and the hair on the back of her neck stood on end. She had nearly made it all the way across when a voice called her name. The sound reverberated around the great open area. She could walk on, pretending not to hear, but two figures stepped into view in the tunnel ahead. She stopped without turning.

"Commander Grenfell," Major Jones called again. "May I have a word?"

9

Abbot Grayson sat back in his comfortable chair, his mind full of worry over Arden's predicament. She had seemed positive there was no way for her to remain free on Baltha. If the general and his minions took her prisoner, what kind of treatment could she expect? How open could he be about having her a prisoner? Surely no one on Glory would believe that she had turned traitor.

Best get out of this funk and contact Alvarez. It was late evening, but the captain was probably still in his office in the palace.

Sure enough, the captain answered.

"Captain, this is Abbot Grayson."

"Commander Grenfell's friend?"

"Yes."

"What can I do for you, sir?"

"I just heard from Arden . . . Commander Grenfell . . . and she asked me to relay a message to you."

"Why didn't she call me herself, if I may ask?"

"Captain, my line here is more secure than any in the palace, and it's rarely monitored as military lines are. A call to or from the monastery is very difficult to trace. And the reason for her call was most urgent."

"Of course, Abbot. Please continue."

Grayson proceeded to retell what Arden had told him.

"And Captain," he added, "I am quite sure that she is in grave danger there. She may already have been taken prisoner by General Radieux."

Silence fell between them as Alvarez took in that part of the message and Grayson let worry settle over himself again. The captain was first to speak.

"I will forward the message to the proper people, sir. And we will do everything we can to ensure the commander's safety."

The strain in his voice came through clearly. The abbot knew that Arden trusted her second in command, and now it would seem that trust was justified. Not that there was much he could do to rescue Arden himself at this point.

Grayson assured Alvarez that he would report any further communications in return for any details the captain might have, and they said goodbye. He settled his bulk more comfortably in the chair and took a long swallow of the wine that had been waiting.

There must be something he could do other than just sit and wait. What that something might be he could not even guess. But something. There had to be.

He spent the night in the same chair, thinking and re-thinking different plans. At first light he sent for Brother Bryan, then washed up and changed his cassock while he waited. He had just finished when the martial arts expert knocked on the door. Grayson invited him in.

"Have you eaten yet?" the abbot asked.

"Yes, I have."

Grayson nodded and sent for his own breakfast while Bryan seated himself in one of the large overstuffed chairs. The abbot sat back down, momentarily surprised that the chair had cooled in spite of his all-night vigil.

"Arden is on Baltha, and she's in trouble," he began. Bryan's right eyebrow raised and he frowned, but he said nothing. Instead, he leaned forward slightly, prepared to listen.

Grayson described Arden's predicament with all the details she had imparted. Bryan's frown deepened.

"I contacted Captain Alvarez immediately and put the

problem in his hands," the abbot said just as a knock came on the door.

Bryan opened the door and let Brother Andrew in with a large tray of food and coffee. The two set out the dishes on the small, round table in one corner of the study, and Andrew left. Bryan poured coffee for himself and the abbot, who moved to sit at the table.

As he ate fresh fruit and pancakes, Grayson described the musings that had kept him awake all night. Then he admitted to having come up with nothing useful.

"It would seem that we must rely on Captain Alvarez to either find the answer or find the person who has an answer," Bryan said.

"Clearly, we can't broadly communicate her impending capture," Grayson said. "That makes finding the right people to help that much more difficult."

"True," Bryan agreed. "We can only rely on Alvarez at this point, it would seem. And be prepared to act when, or if, the moment comes."

Grayson sighed.

"Looks like that's true," he said. "We have managed to isolate ourselves on Glory, haven't we?"

Bryan nodded.

They finished their coffee and discussed affairs of the monastery. Eventually, Brother Bryan returned to the dojo and his work, and Abbot Grayson tried to settle into his tasks for the day.

It was early evening and the abbot had just returned from inspecting one of the vineyards when Brother Andrew caught him in the main corridor.

"You have a visitor, Abbot. I asked him to wait in the main reception room."

"Who is it?"

"General Hsing. And he seems terribly agitated."

"I wonder what he wants," Grayson mused. "I wonder if he's heard . . ."

"Bring us some wine," he said as he started toward the reception room. "The twenty-eight cabernet, I think."

"Yes, Abbot," Andrew said and scurried off.

Grayson approached the door of the main reception room and paused. Hsing was one of the goverment leaders Arden complained about most. His attitude toward her and the empress was openly resentful. If he knew about Arden's current predicament, which side would he be on?

He opened the door and went in. The general stood at the French doors, looking out on the gardens enclosed on three sides by the walls of the main building. From the side, his expression appeared somber in contrast to the sunshine outside. Hearing Grayson enter, he turned, his grey eyes narrowed, and he drew up to his full height of six-foot-three. The ribbons on his uniform flashed with reflected sunlight. The traditional green uniform of high-necked tunic and slacks was immaculate and well pressed. The color made his skin look pale. He removed his peaked hat and placed it under his arm.

"Abbot Grayson, I have come to learn all you know about Commander Grenfell's problems on Baltha."

No one moved, but tension filled the immense atrium. Slowly Arden turned to face Major Jones, her hands held down, palms facing him. The guards within the atrium looked puzzled, still holding to their places. Four soldiers flanked the major. If she tried to resist, they would be aided by the two behind her and the three who apparently had no part in this—except that they would follow orders from their superior.

Dammit! She had planned this as badly as everything else. And now she was their prisoner. She would not fight against soldiers who would be on her side if they only knew what was going on.

"Certainly, Major," she said in answer to his request for a word.

She started toward him, and the two men behind moved closer. The four with Jones moved closer to her, and soon she was surrounded. They moved toward General Radieux's office. Word would spread throughout the armory that something very strange was going on.

They entered the general's outer office and stopped. One of the soldiers took her sword and scabbard, and another searched her for any other weapons and took the comm unit strapped to her wrist. Satisfied, two of them escorted her and Jones into the inner office.

Radieux smiled on seeing her and stood.

"Commander Grenfell," he said.

He moved around to the front of the desk to stand directly in front of her. Arden braced herself.

"You've caused us a bit of trouble," he said, and without warning slapped her hard. Arden stumbled backward into one of the guards. He grabbed her, steadied her, then pushed her back into position.

"Some women keep forgetting their place," Radieux said. "But I know two who will soon have reason to remember."

She balled her hands into fists and began deep, slow breathing. Blood trickled from the corner of her mouth, and she concentrated on the feel of it, warm and wet, and the sweet, salty taste of it on her tongue.

"We know that you managed a transmission," he said. He moved back behind his desk. "To whom? And what did you tell them?"

If she tried to lie or tell a partial truth, they would be halfway to knowing everything. Once she started talking, it would be harder to keep from telling it all. She said nothing. Radieux nodded, and she was escorted to a room in the brig, where she was reintroduced to the captain she had seen in the underground command center.

The cell was five paces long by four paces wide. Not bad, compared to the cabin on Colin Chase's ship in which she was once held prisoner. Quite a bit smaller than either cell she had occupied on Glory.

Every step hurt, but she had to move, had to keep the muscles from stiffening more than they already had. Moving also helped her to think, get past the pain of both her body and her mind.

She could not remember much about the beating and other means of persuasion the captain had used. Worse, she could not remember what she had or had not told him. Everything was blurred by the pain and rage that still consumed her. She had become so hallucinatory, that it seemed Pac Terhn had appeared, hovering protectively, shielding her from the worst of it.

Even if she had told them what they wanted to know, it was probably too late. Back on Glory, events must be progressing toward some plan to neutralize the threat that Radieux and his cohorts represented. As for her own rescue, she hoped they understood that was the least of their concerns. Especially since she had gotten herself into this mess by being stupid.

In spite of her feelings of unease regarding the armory, it had never occurred to her that General Radieux could be at the center of those feelings. It had been inconceivable that he would be disloyal. Why? Because he was handsome and very military? Because he had not been inconsiderate when she served under him? Not reasons enough.

She moved to the cot and slowly eased herself down. She sat on the edge until the worst of the pain subsided, then pushed back until she could lean against the wall. It was cool, and she sighed at the soothing feel of it. Just as slowly, she drew her legs up to cross them in front. It hurt to breathe, enough so that she was sure they had broken a rib or two. There did not seem to be any other broken bones, but every body part hurt.

She did remember their taking her bloody and torn uniform off, letting her take a shower to rinse the blood off her body and out of her hair, and helping her put the jumpsuit on.

Her stomach growled, and she realized that it had been quite a while since she ate. After the cup of coffee in the officers' mess, there had only been water in the shower and from the sink in the corner of her cell. In how long? Hours, maybe even a day. Right after they put her in the cell, she had fallen into a stupor, but there was no way of telling for how long.

She tensed as the door opened. She bit her lip against the pain surging through her body. A soldier entered, carrying her bag. He dropped it on the floor at the foot of the cot without looking at her, turned, and left. It must be safer to keep the bag with her than where it might raise questions.

They had left her alone for quite some time. If they still needed information, they would have been back by now. Therefore, they must have gotten what they wanted.

Nausea swept through her, and she clutched her abdomen. Between the beating, no food, and deep feelings of guilt, her stomach must be swimming in acid.

Maybe they had put her toiletries in her bag. If so, there should be some tablets that would help. Getting to it in order to check seemed like the most difficult task she had ever performed. Soon, however, she managed to move from the center of the cot to the end. Holding onto the edge of it to keep from tumbling to the floor, Arden reached down until she grabbed one of the handles of the bag. Its weight made her muscles scream in protest, but she lifted it, grabbed the other handle with her right hand, and shifted it onto the cot in front of her.

The first thing she pulled out was the toiletry bag. The antacids were inside, and she popped one into her mouth and swallowed it. Everything of a personal nature had been repacked, including the small pouch with the lifeweave and loom inside. She pulled it out, frightened by the thought that had entered her mind.

Maybe she could use the lifeweave to keep from telling what she knew, if there was anything left to tell. It might also provide the means of keeping up with what was happening outside the cell. And it might help to ease the pain.

Anything was better than the way she felt at that moment.

She opened the pouch and spilled its contents into her lap. Her stomach growled again and she hesitated. Would handling the fiber be different on an empty stomach? Like the effects of alcohol? It should not make much difference, since whatever elements were in lifeweave that affected a person went into the system in a very different way.

She started threading the loom, and the cell disappeared almost immediately.

"In trouble again, I see," the familiar voice said.

Had she bothered to think about it, coming here was the last place she needed to be. Pac Terhn was definitely no friend, and right now he must be feeling gratified that she came to him so soon. What he was to her . . . now there was the mystery. Trickster, imp, even tormentor at times. He was a spirit from another world, another time, who at that moment chose not to appear in the mist that surrounded her. Yet, hearing him now convinced her that he had been there during the torture.

"What do you want this time?"

"A little peace and quiet," Arden answered.

"Hmph. A likely story."

"What do you think I want, then?"

"My help with something, as usual."

"I don't believe there is anything you can do to help me this time."

"There is always something I can do to help."

The mist cleared, and he stood before her, hands on hips. His clothes were always the same: full-cut trousers gathered at the ankles, sandals, and a shirt with full sleeves, all in brown. His auburn hair was pulled back in the usual ponytail, emphasizing his grey eyes. She had asked him often about where he came from, what he had done in life, but he refused to answer any questions about himself.

He had chosen a meadow surrounded by forest for their meeting this time. The effect was calming, and the place seemed familiar.

He squinted at her and rubbed his chin.

"You've been hurt," he said. "Now who has been abusing you?"

"I didn't ask his name."

"A lover, then?"

"No."

Maybe she was wrong and he had not shielded her after all. Even here, pain and exhaustion made it difficult to hold onto a thought. The question also brought up fantasies she had once had about General Radieux, but she shook them off. Nothing like being disappointed by a man who was worshipped from afar to shake her faith in her own powers of observation.

"An enemy," she said aloud.

"Well, you have so many it is difficult to keep up with

them all. Now, if you had as many lovers, life could be so much more interesting for you.''

Arden groaned. This conversation was not helping her pain, nor was it the least bit constructive in any other way.

"Can you show me what's happening in the armory right now?" she asked.

"Of course."

Nothing happened. Pac Terhn just stood grinning at her.

"Well?"

Silence. That was not what he thought was important, then.

"How about what's happening on Glory?"

"Of course."

Still nothing.

"Is it the price?" she asked.

"At the moment, you have nothing to bargain with and little likelihood of getting anything."

"Are you telling me that I'm not going to get out of this cell?"

"Maybe."

"Dammit! Can't you answer the questions without being so evasive?"

Once set on a path in these trances, she could often control where she went and when it ended. However, she had never learned how to set out; she needed her guide for that, and he was being more difficult than usual.

"The next few events will surprise you," he said. "I would prefer to see you surprised. And you will be when you waken and see the picture you have woven."

He turned away as if to leave, but stopped. Turning to face her again, his grin widened.

"I can show you some events elsewhere, though. For old times' sake."

She sighed. "Show me those, then."

"As you command," he said and bowed.

He waved a hand, and she floated upward, higher and higher, into darkness. Below, Baltha turned on its axis, growing smaller as she continued to move away. The coldness of vacuum pressed against her; she shivered and wrapped her arms around herself for warmth. A star brightened ahead as she moved toward it, forming into an irregular shape. A ship. The *Starbourne*. She would know it anywhere.

The hull opened up to her, took her inside so that she could observe its occupants. A woman she did not know sat at the astronavigator's console on the bridge. She was pretty, and a sudden spasm of jealousy hit her. Rafe sat in his command chair. He looked a bit haggard, she thought, and wondered if the new crew member might be the reason.

Liel moved around the bridge, always checking, overseeing, efficient. Tahr's lips were moving, so he must be complaining about something. Strange that she could not hear what was being said.

Why did Pac Terhn want her to see the bridge of the *Starbourne*? Was something going to happen to the ship and its crew? Were they in danger? If they were, it must be due to their plans to pick up the lifeweave on Glory. Which, in turn, meant that she had placed them in danger again. There might be a bomb on board, or possibly a radio transmitter set to operate when they passed through a stargate. She had experienced the effects the latter could have once, on this very ship, and it was not pleasant.

Arden floated over to the view screen set into the main console. With a start she recognized the planet shown there: Baltha. Surely, they were not coming to rescue her. They could not even know that she was being held prisoner, and could not possibly invade the armory. What the hell was Rafe doing?

The scene began to fade, and she could not hold onto it so that she could see more. In a moment she was in the cell again, Pac Terhn's farewell ringing in her ears.

The square was completed on the loom. She looked down at it. In the foreground was a man's picture. He seemed familiar, but she could not quite place him. In the background was Radieux. The two men must be working together. In one corner, a depiction of the crown of Glory, the prize at issue.

Time was passing, and there was no way to mark it. No way to know what day it was or how many hours or days she had spent in the cell. Since they had not tried their means of persuasion again, she had become convinced they must have gotten all the information from her they needed. Guilt over that had kept her prone on the cot and, when she did finally get up, out of biological necessity, she could hardly move.

Arden sat back down on the cot, trying not to breathe hard because that hurt her chest. Time might be passing, but not enough to stop any of the pain that flared not only where they had beaten her, but also rumbled in her stomach. She had never been so hungry.

The cell whirled, and she gripped the edge of the cot to keep from falling over. Part of her wanted to just lie back down and be done with the struggle. However, a tiny voice inside urged her to get up, walk, work out the stiffness and soreness that had settled over her.

She had just about decided to try to get back on her feet when a loud noise came from outside. Startled, she jerked, then moaned. When the pain passed, she listened intently. Nothing had penetrated that door since one of the guards brought her bag.

She heard more noises, but not as loud, and she wondered if she heard them at all. Sounded like scuffling, though, and blows. . . .

That had to be the sound of swords. A rescue being attempted. She laughed, not in appreciation but in derision of her own naivete. It was a dream. No one could rescue her. It was impossible.

More noises, then silence. Arden listened a little longer. Nothing. She started to sigh, but the pain in her chest cut it short. What little was left of her life would be spent in choosing between lying down and bravely trying to work out the soreness.

Tears welled up in her eyes, and she let them spill down her cheeks. She wiped them away angrily. False hope, impossible hope must be avoided in the future at all costs.

The door banged open, and she tried to jump to her feet. Her knees refused to obey, however, and with a sharp intake of air, she settled back down. A soldier appeared, someone she did not know. He wore the standard green jumpsuit issued for the armory, but was fully armed with pistol, sword, ammo pouch, and a laser rifle. He nodded to her, stepped aside as another soldier entered. He was armed identically to the first man, but wore lieutenant's insignia. Now she knew why the face in the last square was so familiar. She had seen him before, although briefly, on the transport that brought both of them to Baltha only a few days earlier.

"Can you walk, Commander?"

Stunned by his appearance and the fog that had penetrated her mind, she did not answer. He waited only a moment.

"Commander?"

"Ummm, not very well," she answered. "Walk to where?"

"Out of this cell, for starters," he said.

He had moved toward the back of the cell, and now two more men entered, both armed. Without a word, they picked her up between them, and she put her arms around their necks as she gritted her teeth.

"My bag," she said.

The sergeant who had first entered the room shoved

everything back inside and picked it up. Those carrying her moved sideways through the door, the other two following. A hundred questions raced through her mind, including "Who sent you?" but she refrained. If this was a true rescue, speed was of paramount importance. If it was not a true rescue, she was powerless to do anything about it. One question she could not hold back, though.

"Where's my sword?"

The lieutenant pointed ahead. She concentrated, looking at several soldiers. One of them held up the katana. Satisfied, Arden surveyed the scene before her.

Three guards, unconscious or dead, were being pulled out of sight into a side room. The main guard room was splattered with blood. One of her benefactors had a wound in his arm that was being tended by another. She tried to count how many there were, but the sequence of numbers just would not come. About seven, she would guess, including the two who carried her. Enough to overhwelm her guards and, hopefully, not suffer any serious injuries.

So far, so good.

Now what? The question formed in her mind but would not make its way to her tongue. Since they proceeded rapidly through the guard room and into a corridor, she guessed they had a plan. The lieutenant and two others led the way. That meant one must be following. Or had she counted right?

After just a few steps, all Arden could do was fight back the pain brought by every movement. She clenched her jaws against it, and gripped the fabric of the two men's uniforms in her fists. Once a groan passed her lips, and the lieutenant cast a worried glance back at her. She clenched her jaws harder, and closed her eyes tight against tears.

She fought blackness that swept across her vision over and over. She tried to figure out where they were and why no one challenged them. It was probably the middle of the night watch. That was the time she would choose for a rescue attempt, and Radieux must know that was when they were most vulnerable. But then, who on Baltha would want to rescue her? Who even knew that she was a prisoner?

Blackness overwhelmed her, and the next thing she

knew, she was being set down. She gasped at the pain, then bit her lip to keep from crying out. The taste of blood crept into her mouth and she relaxed her jaw.

"Commander," a voice said.

She opened her eyes and found the lieutenant bending over her.

"We have to get you into an enviro suit. To do that we may have . . ."

"An enviro suit? Why?"

"We're going outside, Commander, and getting you into the suit is gonna hurt. We brought some painkiller." Something stung her arm, and she whimpered. "It'll probably knock you out. You should start feeling the effects any minute."

She did feel sort of airy, like she was floating, and the pain was becoming distant. He kept talking to her, and she felt her body being lifted and stuffed into some sort of cocoon—first her legs, then her torso, last her arms. The cocoon was heavy, and she started to protest. Then they left her alone for a moment. Something was placed over her head, but before she could ask what it was, she passed out again.

She woke to total darkness, no movement, no sound. When she cleared her throat, the sound was muffled as if she was in a very confined space.

"Where . . . ?"

Electronic static filled the same space, then a voice.

"We're outside, Commander," it said.

Then she was not still in the cell. Darkness had never descended there. She *had* left the cell. It was not a dream.

Something shifted her position, and pain brought memory. The man who spoke was the lieutenant, whose name she had not yet asked.

"Are we on a completely closed circuit, Lieutenant?" Arden asked.

"Yes, but we must keep our transmissions to a minimum. Monitoring units are set up everywhere."

"I remember," she said. "Would you at least give me some idea of what your plan is?"

The monitors would only pick up the fact that there was

a closed transmission, not what was said. However, anyone checking those monitors could zero in on them if the transmission continued long enough.

"We have requisitioned the sled that you're sitting on," he said. "We'll work our way toward the far side of Baltha, away from the armory, avoiding patrols as much as we can. We still don't know how much information has been spread about your incarceration. Once we arrive at an appointed position, a civilian ship will meet us, take us aboard, and get us back to Glory."

"A civilian ship?"

"Those are my instructions."

Arden looked around as much as she could while in an enviro suit strapped into a seat on the sled. The others crouched around the sled, rifles held at ready, waiting. At least those that she could see. A second sled sat nearby. Another rifle had been placed near her hand. She touched its stock, wondering if the need arose, did she actually have the strength to pick it up.

"When do we start?" she asked.

"Soon. We're waiting for a patrol to finish its circuit. Once it does, we will have twenty minutes to get out of its area."

"I take it that part of the plan is to avoid contact with other soldiers stationed here as much as possible," she said.

Saying so might seem needless in normal circumstances, but it helped her injured self to get a grip on what was happening.

"Yes, ma'am."

She thought for a moment, then decided she had all the information she needed, leaving the rest of the details to her rescuers. They waited in silence until, finally, the lieutenant gave the signal to move out. He climbed into the seat beside her and took hold of the wheel. That meant four to each sled.

No matter where you went on Baltha, the terrain was bumpy at best. Lights on both corners of the front of the sled and on the individual helmets showed the way ahead. In the blackness above, stars shone steadily. Lights had been installed at the patrol stations. They were turned on when a patrol was actually there. Defensive setups were now limited largely to monitoring devices. All personnel patrols had been confined to close proximity with the armory itself since the war ended, leaving the far side in perpetual darkness.

The sled jolted along, and Arden frequently winced in pain. At least it kept her awake. From the stiffness that had seized her whole body even before leaving the cell, she knew getting off the sled would be agony.

One thing she had forgotten to ask was how long it was supposed to take to get to the far side. She dug through memories of her days stationed on Baltha, but the amount of time she came up with seemed a bit too long: thirty-six hours.

They paused periodically to get their bearings. Every so often she awakened with a start, having dozed off as a result of the mistreatment or the painkiller, or both. They traveled without stopping. The men with her seemed almost tireless. And each minute became like the last, each hour a twin of the one to come.

Once in a while, Arden sucked on the water tube mounted inside her helmet, and the lieutenant asked her once if she needed more painkiller. She declined. For the duration, the pain was the most interesting thing in her life.

Eventually, they did stop. Their leader motioned for silence. For a moment she could not imagine why, then realized they were near another outpost that might or might not be manned. Two soldiers moved off to investigate, returning only moments later to report that the way was clear. They moved off again.

The jolting of the sled no longer had much effect. Pain had become a blanket that lay over her, a bit smothering, but somehow comforting, an affirmation that she was still alive. It was becoming part of the monotony of the night in which everything blended together: silence except for occasional static, stars shining steadily above, darkness around their small pool of light that moved constantly forward, over ground that rose and fell but never really changed.

Arden was awake when the sled suddenly bucked hard.

She was thrown as the right side dropped, landing hard with her torso on the ground, but her legs dangled into emptiness, threatening to pull the rest of her after. The intercom came to life as someone shouted orders. Men breathed hard as they worked. Arden pulled herself away from the abyss with her gloved hands, instinct guiding her away from danger. Hands grabbed her arms and pulled, and in a moment solid ground lay under her whole body.

"It's a goddam sinkhole," someone shouted breathlessly. "Everyone try to grab hold of the sled, see if we can pull it back up."

Arden lay still, wanting to respond, but without the energy to even sit up.

"Where's the lieutenant?" someone asked.

"He went down," the first voice said. She thought it was the sergeant.

"Damn! Foster, grab as many of the guns in the back as you can."

There were grunts and groans as everyone used every bit of strength they had trying to keep the sled from tumbling away. Two dangers were obvious: they needed the sled to get everyone to the rendezvous on time, and if the sled fell, it could land on the lieutenant. So far, there had been nothing to indicate whether he was alive or dead.

Was there any rope? she wondered. If it was a deep hole, that would be the only way to get to the lost man.

"It's going!" someone shouted.

Other shouts and oaths filled the inside of her helmet. She raised up on all fours and turned toward the lights.

"No!" she tried to scream, but it came out a whisper.

She crawled in that direction until hands grabbed her arms and stood her up.

"We can't help him now," the sergeant said.

"You don't know that," she whispered.

"Our job is to get you safely off this rock," he said. "And that's what we're gonna do."

His accent was similar to the lieutenant's, and she wondered what part of Glory they came from. As her mind wandered around that question, she let herself be half led, half carried to the other sled. They put her in the passenger's seat in the front, gently but firmly.

"My sword."

"We have it. Let's get moving."

A fifth man lay across the back while two men ran along beside the sled. Although the somewhat low gravity made good speed possible for the runners, progress was inevitably slower. Arden cringed at every jolt, expecting to be tossed out again. They stopped every half hour, and one runner climbed on board the sled while another joined the run.

"How much longer until the rendezvous?" she asked after a while.

The sergeant looked at his watch.

"Five hours."

"Will we make it?"

"No, ma'am. We're gonna be a bit late."

Could the ship that was supposed to be picking them up wait? How soon would it be detected back at the armory? The captain of the ship would have to know how close he could safely come while he waited for the agreed-upon signal.

Meanwhile, patrols must be scouring Baltha, looking for them with faster land vehicles and a few hoverers. The only reasons they had not been found yet were the size of the search area and the fact that there were not very many vehicles. Of course, it would help if they had left no trail to show the direction they took when they left the armory. Surely the lieutenant had thought of that.

On they went, the routine the same as before. Her efforts at the sinkhole had reawakened her to the effects of the pain, and Arden wondered if the painkiller had gone into the sinkhole, too, but did not ask. Their progress slowed as time stretched ahead and behind interminably. There was no beginning and no end while both mind and body grew numb once more.

At last she fell into a deep sleep, waking only when the sled jerked to a stop.

"We're here," the sergeant said. "Foster, Greer, you two stay with me. The rest of you head off in different directions. See if you can find a spot where we can hide until the ship comes.''

Two men moved off into darkness, their helmet lamps the only means of noting their movements. Arden watched and listened through the fog of sleep and pain until all the lights disappeared.

The sergeant had said, ''Until the ship comes.'' Did he still expect it to arrive for some reason? Maybe she missed some communication. She asked him if he had heard from the ship.

''No, ma'am. We signaled as agreed, but no answer has come yet. We don't have much choice but to wait.''

''How late are we?''

''Nearly two hours,'' he answered without looking at his watch.

That was a long time. If the ship had not been challenged, it might still be up there somewhere, hiding as best it could from detection. It would have been noticed for certain if it had landed, but there was no sign of it in the immediate vicinity. Not that they could see very far.

She started to climb out of the sled.

''Are you sure?'' the sergeant asked.

Arden turned to face him and nodded affirmatively. Slowly, she stretched out her legs, placing her feet flat on the ground. Holding onto the sled, she rose slightly, but the muscles in her legs quivered and she sat back down. On the second try, the muscles quivered again but held her legs under her weight.

Damn, but she was stiff! She could only manage shuffling steps, while pain screamed in her mind. But she persisted, and soon she was taking baby steps.

One of the soldiers came rushing back.

''The nearest station is that way about a mile and a half,'' he said, pointing to her right. Arden shuffled back to the sled and leaned against it.

''Then we need to find shelter in one of the other directions,'' the sergeant said. ''Sit down and rest until the others come back.''

He checked his watch again and took a small electonic switch out of the pouch pocket on the upper leg of his enviro suit. He pushed a button. Arden assumed it was the signal to the ship. She looked at him inquiringly, but he shook his head. No answer, then. Was this rescue attempt to be in vain, after all?

Arden continued walking about, swinging her arms. Every part of her body hurt, but at least the pain now was from activity on her part. It was almost enjoyable because it meant that she was alive and able to move.

Another soldier appeared, the beam from his helmet lamp piercing the darkness first. He reported finding a rocky outcropping about a mile off. It looked large enough to hide all of them and the sled.

The sergeant quickly called in the others, using as few words as possible. He ordered the second man to wait for the others and tell them the direction, while the first soldier and he got the commander to the shelter of the rocks.

Arden started to protest as the sergeant came to help her back into the seat on the sled, but stopped herself. She wanted to walk. The exercise might do her good, but right now the most important thing was to get to cover, and fast. She must not let her pride cause these men any more harm than they had already suffered.

They were soon on their way. The little bit of movement she had managed had loosened up her muscles and joints some, but it had done nothing to help with the pain caused by each jolt of the vehicle. Once more, the pain helped to keep her awake. The distance was short and she did not want to fall asleep, especially if rescue was imminent. Once the ship was detected back at the armory, their recapture would be almost as imminent.

They reached the rocks, and the sergeant guided the sled among them. The soldiers scattered about, keeping an eye on every direction. Arden asked the sergeant to give her a rifle. It felt very heavy when he placed one in her hands.

After a while, the sergeant checked his watch again and signaled. This time there was an answering beep.

"They've got us," he said. "It should be soon."

Just then the soldier appeared who had been told to wait for the others back at their stopping point. All but one had come into the rocks.

"Farmer never came back," he reported. "I figured something might have happened to him and I should get on in here."

"All right. Keep an eye open for the ship. It should be coming in any moment."

A moment later, static arose on their headsets. Then Major Jones's voice spoke.

"Commander Grenfell. We have one of your would-be rescuers here. He says his name is Farmer. I suggest you and those with you surrender."

The sergeant signaled the men to maintain silence. Arden wondered if any of them considered Farmer a friend. She searched the surrounding area until she spotted the faint glow slightly to the right and perhaps half a mile away. It looked as if they had taken positions behind a similar but smaller group of rocks.

"Come on, Commander," Jones said. "We have enough firepower here to blast you out of those rocks and bring down whatever ship you're waiting for."

He paused, waiting for a reply. It ran through Arden's mind that she had lost some of her effectiveness—not because she was injured, but because she had been caught. They did not know how much she had learned, but they were sure to change their plans. Losing her would not mean much to either side, now. However, she hated the thought of sacrificing the men around her. Better to lose Farmer than lose him and everyone else.

"You're being unrealistic if you think all of you will leave here alive."

The sergeant patted her arm and pointed upward. An artificial glow lit a small bit of darkness, growing as it descended, and she realized there was a low hum from its engines. From the size, she judged it must be a shuttle or a lifeboat, not a full-size ship.

She plugged directly into the sergeant's receiver.

"Can you signal them of danger?" she asked.

"I already did."

The glow continued to grow.

"We have a choice," she said. "We can fire to warn it

off, or we can fire to protect it as it lands. Whatever we do, Farmer probably won't make it.''

He nodded agreement and signaled his men to be ready. Arden hesitated to give the order to fire. A man would surely die or remain a prisoner in the hands of people who would not hesitate to torture him if they felt there was a reason.

Dammit! The possibility of a man dying to rescue her was a bitter pill. Even so, it must be the pain dulling her wits that made the decision so hard to make. Her thoughts started off on another tangent, including the realization that other men's lives could be saved, but she brought herself up short. Think too long and you could die.

She unplugged from the sergeant's receiver and keyed her comm to all channels.

''Jones,'' she called. ''No one has to die here. You know that I sent word to Glory. They'll be sending a ship or two to take back the armory, so your days here are numbered. Go back . . .''

''Save your breath, Commander,'' Jones cut her off. ''I'm sure you know that not all of the troops here have been told exactly what's going on. I doubt that you or the empress would sacrifice their lives.'' He paused to let that sink in. ''Give up, and you can help spare them.''

That seemed an unrealistic appraisal of the situation, if she read him right. Her being held prisoner in the armory would certainly not deter a force sent to retake the facility. It seemed that Radieux might be depending on her friendship with Jessa far too much as a means of achieving his goals.

The engine roar overhead had grown louder, and now the ship seemed to be hovering just out of range of whatever weapons might be on the ground. How many men were in this detail led by Jones? How many separate details had been sent? And were the others converging on their location? That possibility made immediate action of utmost importance.

Chips and dust suddenly kicked up from the large rock to her right. The beam became visible for a moment in the dust. Another shot hit behind her. It looked like they weren't going to wait.

Neither was the ship overhead. It sped off behind her position, its glow disappearing into the eternal darkness.

11

The armory remained quiet as everyone went about their duties. There were some murmurings about details going outside, but everyone seemed to assume it was a drill of some kind.

General Radieux sat behind his desk, leaning back in the chair that had been made to fit him perfectly, and refrained from putting his feet on the desktop. That was not proper posture for a commanding officer, and he must always set a good example. Even for a female soldier.

Corporal Randall was a good soldier. She stayed in her place: clerical. Not like some women who clamored for combat units.

Women! Men had been trying to cope with their foolishness for centuries. On some worlds, they actually had equal rights with men. Now there was real foolishness. He did have to admit that Arden Grenfell had been a capable officer under his command, and her record in a combat unit was above average. It did not seem that she was doing quite as well commanding the palace guard, though. He took pride in having something to do with that.

She did not know that, of course, at least she had not known before coming to Baltha. He remembered how doe-eyed she would become when he entered a room in the days of the war. He had taken a certain pleasure in her crush on him. Those days seemed so long ago.

Now he relied on no more than twenty-five of the men stationed here to help him in deposing the new regime and putting a proper man back on the throne of Glory. They could not allow that businessman, Jonas Belle, to take control. Once Jessa married, there was little doubt that her new husband would do his best to take control of the crown. He was a second son, after all, and was not in line to inherit Weaver and its lifeweave business. From what Radieux had learned of the man's past, he was ambitious beyond his abilities.

Vey expected to inherit the throne himself, having been the second most powerful person in the old regime. He had wanted the general to enlist the aid of all the soldiers on Baltha to speed his takeover, but that was not practicable. Such a plan worked best when as few people as possible knew it even existed. There was also the problem of soldiers coming and going from this duty station to others. If any of them ever found out and spread the word, the cause would be lost.

However, this was one time it had proved inconvenient to have so few men in the know. It would have been so much more efficient if he could have sent out several parties—seven or eight at least—in search of the commander and her rescuers. However, keeping the uninitiated from knowing that she was his prisoner was necessary.

They had to confine her, since there was no way of knowing how much she had actually discovered in the emergency control center. How long she had been down there, they had a fair idea. She had taken nothing, since nothing was found on her. Once they got her back in their custody, the added bonus was having Grenfell out of the palace, permanently now, and that should make matters much easier when the time came for the final takeover. Having her dead would work just as well, of course.

And he had learned a very valuable lesson about her, thanks to the hidden camera in her cell. Her performance with the lifeweave had been very telling.

How long could they continue to pretend that she was confined to her suite by some kind of malady? Thank goodness Doctor Brown had been enlisted in the cause. That ruse would have been difficult to pull off otherwise. It was even more difficult now that she was on the loose.

Right now, though, he needed Major Jones to report that he had at least found her.

The comm unit on his desk buzzed, and he picked up the handset.

"General, sir," the corporal's voice said. "Security is reporting a ship in Sector G. A small one, possibly a lifeboat."

Must be a rescue ship, and not a military one. If it were military, its ident signal would have been picked up. That meant that Grenfell was in that general area. If she was taken, the ship would simply disappear, having failed in its mission. Where the hell was Jones?

"It's part of the exercise that Major Jones is leading," he told Randall. "Tell security to keep an eye on it, but leave it alone."

"Yes, sir."

He had just hung up when his direct comm unit buzzed. That should be Jones.

He answered, and almost smiled when he heard the major's voice.

"We have them pinned down in Sector G, but there's a small ship here. Looks like a lifeboat."

"Don't worry about the ship. It's not a military one, therefore it is probably only lightly armed, if at all. Take Grenfell prisoner, and it will disappear."

"They're pretty well entrenched among some boulders," Jones said. "And we don't outnumber them by that much."

"Have you contacted the other search group?"

"Yes, sir. They should be here in about two hours."

"Where is the lifeboat now?"

"It flew away toward Sector H just a moment ago."

The lifeboat would not land until its pilot could be fairly sure that he could get away with his vehicle and himself intact. Those still on the mother ship would also just watch and wait. There were advantages to the opposing side when commercial ships were used.

"Keep them pinned down until the second squad gets to

you. Surround Grenfell and her party. If the lifeboat returns, try to shoot it down. Even if you don't succeed, you should discourage it enough that it will leave.''

Jones acknowledged his orders, and Radieux disconnected. It was terribly frustrating not being able to use all the forces at his command. However, he still held the high ground, and if it took waiting them out, that was what he would do.

His desk comm unit buzzed again. Looked like it was going to be an even busier day than he had thought.

Exhaustion threatened to overcome her, except the constant firing of Jones's men was just persistent enough to keep her awake. Arden shifted positions, nearly crying out at the pain in her muscles and joints. One of the cuts on her face had opened up again, and some of the blood managed to smear on her face shield.

The soldiers kept up just enough fire to ensure that Jones and his men kept their heads down most of the time. The laser power packs were fully charged when they left the armory, but they had to conserve as much power as they could, since they had no idea how long they would be here.

Jones had not made mention of Farmer in over half an hour. He must be all right, just being held in reserve for the right moment, or when the major grew tired of the standoff.

Or until another search party arrived and made things a bit hotter for them.

Consolidating his position.

That was bad, but not as bad as things might be if Radieux could send the full force of the armory contingent against them. That was confirmation of sorts that only a small number of his soldiers were part of the general's treason.

Dirt kicked up between her and the sergeant. The shot could only have been fired from behind her. A second group had arrived. They were surrounded.

The sergeant saw it too, and signaled his men to look to all sides. They had been doing that in part anyway, but it was necessary now.

A light grew in the sky behind the major's position. Might be the lifeboat returning. No, it was different, definitely larger. And flying low.

It drew steadily nearer, and she realized with amazement that it must be the mother ship. Jones's men began firing in its direction.

"Give it cover fire," the sergeant shouted.

They fired at the flashes in the darkness in front of them, ducking when shots came from behind. They were not numerous enough to keep either group truly pinned down. And the ship came on.

Arden joined her comrades in firing at the enemy, wondering all the while where the strength came from. Actually, just sitting and firing was not difficult. Her aim was a bit off because her hands shook, but there was not much chance of hitting anything anyway. If she tried to move about, though, stiffness made it a slow process. She worked herself between two boulders that offered protection from back and front but were easy to shoot from. Mostly she concentrated on the group in front. That was the direction the ship was coming from.

That it still came on was surprising. If it was a commercial ship, someone must have offered its captain a great deal for him to endanger himself and his ship like this. Another possibility hovered in the back of her mind, but she chose to ignore it. That way lay false hope.

Sparks flew off the ship's hull where one of the lasers hit. Several hits like that in a vulnerable spot could cause them some serious problems. The sergeant signaled his men to concentrate on keeping those in front down as the ship closed in. If it was damaged or driven off, there was no hope of rescue for any of them.

Arden turned her attention to the group behind them, firing randomly, hoping to make them keep their heads down as much as possible. Everyone had turned their helmet lamps off, and there was no way to see an individual. Stone chips and dirt kept spiking up where hits were made along her shelter. Only once did she detect a hit on one of the soldiers, when a white wisp of oxygen mix curled up from his leg. Someone patched the suit quickly, all relatively soundless.

Suddenly, the ship fired some kind of rocket launcher. The rocket exploded very close to the front of the enemy's position. The flash blinded her for a few seconds. A great commotion came over the comm units, hushed in only a moment. Commercial ships were not supposed to have rocket launchers, only small laser cannon, used mostly to deflect or destroy debris that might get in the way.

Another rocket exploded, at the edge of the boulder outcrop, lighting it up momentarily. Quickly, the ship settled to the right of Arden's position, and the main hatch opened to one side. Three or four figures rushed out.

"Let's go!" the sergeant shouted. "Run for it."

She got the sword belt over her head and gripped the rifle tightly. He and another soldier came to her, helped her to her feet and, crouching low, started for the ship. Dirt kicked up sporadically all around them as each figure from the ship went down on one knee and began a covering fire. One of her rescuers reached their line and took a position with them.

On her left, the sergeant jerked, nearly pulling her down as his left leg crumpled under him. He let go of her, but she dropped beside him.

"Go on!" he yelled.

"Not without you," she said tightly.

The other soldier went down on all fours and began crawling toward the ship. A small white cloud of oxygen mix rose from the sergeant's leg.

"Help me!" she hollered at the retreating soldier, but he kept going.

She plugged her comm into the sergeant's receiver, then pulled out a tube of patch adhesive.

"Can you walk at all?" she asked as she broke the tube and applied the paste to the hole in the leg of his enviro suit.

"The leg's not gonna carry me."

"We'll crawl, then."

She helped him get his rifle draped over his shoulder by the strap, did the same with hers, then raised up on all fours.

Every movement was in slow motion as muscles and joints reminded her how abused they had been. She gritted her teeth and got her arm under the sergeant's. He pushed up to a three-point stance, and when they moved forward, his wounded leg dragged behind.

The face shield of his helmet fogged up within two feet. As much as she hurt, she knew he was in greater pain. Still, he kept moving forward with her help. Would the ship leave without them? Its crew was in danger itself. They could not wait much longer.

Arden concentrated on the ground in front of her and on the man beside her. Occasionally, she had to look up to be sure they were headed in the right direction, and the ship was there each time. Human figures still crouched before the opening, firing a covering barrage.

His breathing came rapidly, its rhythm broken only by occasional gasps. He could not see through the fogged face plate and relied on her to keep him going in the right direction.

With a gasp, the sergeant collapsed to the ground, unwilling or unable to go farther, not even responding verbally to her urgings. Had he passed out? If so, she could not carry him the rest of the way.

Dirt kicked up nearby, and Arden put both arms over her helmet. Her own breathing, already fast, quickened. She heard heavy footsteps, running, nearby. She turned away from her companion, letting her arm slip through the strap of the rifle until she could grasp the weapon in her hand. Raising it at the same time, she spotted a suited soldier running up from behind. Shots peppered the ground around him now, but he kept coming. She raised the rifle, certain that he was too near, too ready, and fired without aiming.

The figure stopped, one hand pressed to his chest where part of his life was escaping into the night. His own rifle fired wildly into the air. His knees gave way, and he slowly fell toward her. She tried to roll aside, but moved even more slowly than he did. His body sprawled across her at an angle. The impact forced the air from her lungs, and everything went black.

•　•　•

Rafe considered firing another rocket, but it was dangerous business from the ground. No one had reported seeing Arden yet, either, and he was getting antsy. The *Starbourne* could not stay on the ground much longer without endangering everyone.

Dammit! Here he was risking his ship and crew again on her account. He would never learn.

"Keep ready for liftoff," he ordered Liel, then went aft.

He found his enviro suit, got into it quickly, grabbed a rifle, and stepped into the airlock. In another moment he walked down the ramp to the ground. The ship was turned away from the action for safety of egress.

Very carefully, he turned the corner. With the night scan turned on, the face plate allowed him to detect the bodies and figures of people. Still, it was more than a little difficult to tell friend from foe, except by position.

He stared a little harder. Who was that lying about one hundred feet away? It looked like two of them.

He started toward where his own crew was firing away at the rock outcroppings. Just when he came up beside Tahr, another figure stepped into view, approaching the two on the ground. One of the prone figures turned over, raising a rifle just as the standing figure raised his.

"Who . . . ?" he started to ask, but the upright figure suddenly toppled over, hit by a laser beam, landing right on top of his supposed target.

"It's the commander," someone yelled.

Arden! Rafe knew now why no one had reported her being found. He pointed at two of the newcomers.

"You two come with me," he ordered. "We have to get them inside."

He took off, sure that the others would follow. When he reached the prone figures, he rolled the one off what proved to be Arden. Her eyes were closed behind the face plate, and he could not tell if she was breathing. The face plate of the man beside her was all fogged up, and he could not tell anything.

With the other men's help, he got Arden over his shoulder in a fireman's carry then hurried toward the ship. Laser hits peppered the ground around him.

He raced toward the ship, looking back once to make sure the two had picked up the man with sergeant's insignia on the top of his helmet. They raced into the airlock, put the injured man down, and left him with Arden and the sergeant to enter the ship first. Once out of the airlock and with his helmet off, Rafe punched the button on the comm unit just inside.

"Liel, get everyone on board and get the hell out of here."

He took the helmets off the two just rescued. Both were unconscious. By then, Tahr and two others had come in from outside. They quickly got their helmets off, then helped him carry the wounded to one of the cabins and out of the way. Rafe left for the bridge to see how things were going outside.

Seven were still outside and the exchange of fire had increased, making it more difficult for them to get inside.

"Tell them to get down and not worry," the captain said. "Get the rocket launcher ready."

"It's been ready," Liel said, but looked at Rafe nervously. "You aren't planning on firing from here?"

"Not quite. Just raise us up a little."

The word went out over the comm, and Liel and Phyilla revved the engines. Slowly, they lifted from the surface. Liel called off the changing altitude. Finally, they were thirty feet up. Rafe gave the order to target the group on the right as he watched on the view screen.

"Fire," he said calmly.

The *Starbourne* lurched slightly, and by the time it settled, the rocket had exploded among the rocks. Several figures ran away in as many directions illuminated by remnants of light from the explosion. He gave the order to target the second position, then fire. The result was the same.

Rafe started breathing again. Firing the rockets so close to the surface was not a good idea, but it had worked. In part, they had succeeded because they were too close to miss.

Liel and Phyilla lowered the ship back to the ground, and soon everyone was working to get the last of their people on board. The captain made his way to the cabin where Arden and the sergeant, now out of the enviro suits, lay on the bunks, both seeming to be still unconscious.

Tahr was tending to the wound in the sergeant's leg. It looked like a bad one. One look at Arden made his heart sink. She lay with her eyes closed, and he took time to stare at the wounds on her face, neck, and arms. She had been put through a real wringer, from the looks of it.

Her eyes opened, then widened when she recognized him.

"My lord," she said. "You do seem to show up at the most auspicious moments."

She laughed, ending in a gasp, and he realized if that had caused her pain, his running with her over his shoulder must have been excruciating. She smiled.

"I was conscious when you picked me up," she said, as if she had read his thoughts. "But I thought it was a dream." She turned her head to look at the other bunk. "How's the sergeant?"

Tahr looked over at her and started grumbling about not being a bleeding doctor.

"How is he, Tahr?" Rafe asked sharply.

The pilot, who also served as the ship's medic, looked down at the leg and shook his head.

"It's a bad wound," he said. "The bone is really messed up. He'll need a proper doctor."

"We'll get him one on Glory," Arden said. "That is where we're going, isn't it?"

Rafe nodded. "As soon as we have everyone on board."

She relaxed and closed her eyes for a moment. The ship shuddered, then rose into the air. Since Arden seemed to be sleeping, he started to leave, but her eyes reopened.

"Who sent you?" she asked.

"General Hsing and your abbot friend."

"Hsing?"

"Yes. He contacted us not long after we offloaded our last cargo. Said we could get through the defenses here better than a military ship and that no one would know who we were until it was too late. Then the abbot confirmed that you were a prisoner here and asked us to help."

"I'll have to thank him when I get back," she said,

meaning the general. She looked back over at the sergeant. "I never did get his name," she said softly. "Nor the lieutenant's."

Her eyelids drooped, then closed. When he was sure she had fallen asleep this time, Rafe went to the bridge. He contacted Hsing to let him know that the rescue had been made and they were on their way.

He sat in the command chair thinking back over the short conversation with Arden. He had wanted to take her hand, to reassure her that she was safe and that he cared. But he had not even been able to bring himself to take hold of her hand. He cared, and her pain made him hurt. Yet something held him back, kept him from showing those feelings.

Just afraid to get wrapped up in that situation again, he guessed. Too much time had passed.

The flurry of activity in the docking bay continued into the next morning. Cases and cases of ammunition and guns filled the transport ship. Most of the men worked as always, asking no questions, probably not even wondering what the hell was going on, just as soldiers had done for millennia. Rumors were rampant, however, about the training exercise. Some had heard that Major Jones had been killed in some kind of accident.

The survivors of the incident had straggled into the armory, and General Radieux had confined them to their quarters to keep them from confirming the rumors. Those trusted few who had remained with him throughout were off seeing to their own assignments in the facility, including preventing any communication between Baltha and Glory. As soon as everything was ready, all of his men would be ordered aboard the transport and they would leave this godforsaken rock.

General Hsing had already ordered two more transport ships to Baltha, their purpose obviously to take control of the armory. In this, too, timing was everything.

Captain Djinn approached, stopping just in front of his commanding officer, and saluted.

"Everything is loaded, General," he said when Radieux returned the salute.

"Good, Captain. Would you please congratulate the men on a job well done and order them to stand down."

"Yes, sir."

They exchanged salutes, and Djinn turned away.

"Oh, and Captain." The man turned back with a questioning look. "Give everyone the day off. They've earned it."

"They'll appreciate that, sir."

They had better, since it would be their last, Radieux thought. After sending two of his men to summon his select few, he made his way onto the ship.

12

"General Hsing, thank you for your prompt action. I made a mistake in going off to Baltha so hastily, but an even bigger mistake in misjudging you."

Arden held out her hand, and the general took it without hesitation. They stood in one of the smaller conference rooms in the palace, just the two of them. She had returned the evening before and, after a thorough going-over by Doctor Branard, had gotten a relatively good night's sleep in her own bed. That in spite of the fact that she had slept most of the two days of the return trip. After wrapping her chest tightly, Tahr had given her enough painkillers to knock out a good-sized man.

She had managed to talk with Grayson and the empress, however, and vaguely remembered a visit with Rafe. Soon, she would also have to talk with Alvarez and get his report.

Hsing had graciously agreed to meet with her in the palace instead of at his own home elsewhere in the city. He had to come in anyway, for a strategy meeting later in the morning, but it was understanding of him.

"Did you suspect General Radieux of being a traitor?" she asked.

"No, but in these times, it is best not to trust anyone too well."

He did not smile when he said that, but she suspected it

was his way of letting her know that he had not trusted her.
Maybe he still did not. Arden motioned toward two comfortable chairs, and they sat down.

"The men who rescued me," she said. "They were on
the same transport ship that I took." Hsing nodded. "And
you sent them." He nodded again. "What made you decide
to do that?"

He pushed back against the chair and pressed his fingertips together. He seemed to consider his reply, and Arden
suddenly wondered if he worked on intuition sometimes
too.

"I suppose it was largely due to the suddenness of your
decision to go," he said at last. "At times, you exhibit a
very strong sixth sense about some things, even if you do
go off half-cocked. And it was just not a good idea for you
to go alone."

"It never occurred to me that Radieux could be a traitor.
I served under him for a while, right there on Baltha during
the war."

She shook her head, a sense of sorrow washing through
her. It was still hard to believe.

"Yet you were quite willing to believe that I might be
a traitor," Hsing said quietly.

The directness of his comment flustered her for a moment, and she bit her lip to keep from stammering something inane. He was right, of course, and after believing
that for some time, she felt slightly hesitant to change her
opinion completely.

"You've never been shy about voicing your dissatisfac-
tion with having a woman ruling. Or with a woman heading
palace security."

"If I was going to support some sort of coup, do you
think I would be so vocal in my opposition?"

She had considered that, knowing the general was no
fool, but had not thought that to be proof of his overall
loyalty. Nor did his assistance in this latest event disarm
her suspicions entirely, no matter how much she wished it
did.

"It is true that I am not a supporter of women's rights
in government or the military," Hsing was saying. "Or in

most others, for that matter. I am an old soldier who believes women are too precious to risk in dangerous occupations. Nor do I believe that they have the training or experience to rule a world such as ours.''

He crossed his legs and placed both hands on the arms of the chair. He was not comfortable talking about this.

''Waran Parcq was raised to be emperor of Glory. Jessa Parcq was raised to take her mother's place at the loom. Or some other pursuit that might have seemed suitable.''

''Women will never have the experience or training unless someone lets them try,'' Arden pointed out.

He shrugged.

''That's true.'' He sighed and looked across the room for a moment. ''I am too old to be comfortable with it,'' he said. ''I will never like it. But I will do whatever I must in support of my empress and Glory. I am a soldier, Commander. Politics don't interest me.''

She realized with a start that she did believe General Hsing did not care who ruled Glory as long as he could serve the best interest of his world himself. What bothered him about Jessa was simply that he did not believe her ruling was in that best interest. However, she was the legitimate heir of the Parcq dynasty, and Arden finally believed he would serve her as long as she sat on the throne.

''What we need to figure out now is what Radieux is going to do,'' he said in a businesslike tone. ''He is still the second biggest threat to Glory right now.''

''The first being Don Vey?'' Hsing nodded. ''Agreed. The reinforcements were sent from here the day I was freed?'' He nodded again. ''Then Radieux has had nearly two days to plan and act. Are we getting any reports from Baltha right now?''

''Just the usual. Since we had no idea who was working with him and who was not, we issued no direct orders to anyone already there once we reestablished communications. Oh, there has been some mention of special maneuvers and of Major Jones, Radieux's adjutant, being killed. There were a couple of other deaths, apparently.''

''We know how those happened,'' she said.

She had learned that one soldier was killed in the final

firefight as everyone tried to get aboard the *Starbourne*. It was a miracle that he and Lieutenant Moore were the only two deaths among her rescuers. Others had been injured, Sergeant Howard having received the most serious wound of the survivors.

"And a transport ship left Baltha a full day after you did."

"Wasn't an order issued that no one was to leave?"

"Yes, but there would have been no way to keep it from Radieux," he said.

"What do you want to bet that the general and his followers were on that transport?" she said, hitting the arm of the chair with her fist.

"And if he's left . . ." She paused, letting the sudden thought grow. "If he is gone, and in a transport ship at that, he's probably taken as many of the guns and as much ammunition as he could get on board. He certainly cannot have had a whole lot of men left to take with him. There weren't many to start with, as far as I could tell."

She stood and paced for a moment. She moved behind her chair and hit the back of it.

"Dammit!" she said. "I was worried about his fighting off our soldiers if they tried to land. What if he took everything he could, then planned to destroy what was left so that we could not use them?"

"A bomb?" Hsing said.

"Probably more than one. Are there any explosives experts on their way there?"

"Maybe. We picked combat soldiers experienced in occupying towns and fortifications."

"There are certainly some experts already there. And if we're right about his leaving and taking his people with him, those left behind should be loyal."

Arden moved back around the chair and sat down. She leaned forward intently.

"We can't let those soldiers land and risk their being blown up," she said. "We need to identify any explosives experts already there or among those newcomers."

Hsing called Major Peebles on his wrist comm and instructed him to check the M.O.s of the soldiers on their way to Baltha and those already there, in order to identify explosives experts. He also had an order sent to the transport ships to hold off landing until they received further orders.

While they waited, they speculated on what kind of device might have been used. It could be one connected to a timer, set to explode after the soldiers had landed. It was entirely possible that Radieux was lurking somewhere near Baltha, watching for that same landing, and intending to blow the armory with a detonator once he was sure of achieving maximum carnage.

If there was a timer, it was possible there would be little time for the incoming soldiers to find the bombs. Either way, those soldiers already in the armory were at greatest risk. That might be enough to make them trustworthy, no matter which side they were on.

Word came that there were at least two explosives experts among the incoming troops. That would certainly not be enough if there were multiple bombs.

"General, I would suggest that we rely on those experts already there," Arden said. "Let's tell them what they may be up against. Have them start a thorough search, concentrating on the underground control area. If they can sweep that clean, most of them will be safe there."

"Unless Radieux is watching," Hsing pointed out. "If he sees that the landing isn't happening, he may blow it anyway."

"I know."

After a little more discussion, they decided that first clearing the underground control center was the best hope they had. It could then be used as a safe retreat as the aboveground facilities were searched. General Hsing issued the appropriate orders, making sure that word spread in the armory. That would help prevent anyone from sacrificing himself and all the others. That done, they notified Jessa that they needed to see her as soon as possible.

The empress was so solicitous of her injuries that the meeting was very difficult for Arden. She entered the sitting room limping and holding one hand against bandaged ribs. The cuts and bruises on her face would not heal for days.

A couple of them might even leave scars, the doctor had said, but he would do everything to ensure they were small.

After making sure she was comfortable, Jessa listened quietly to their joint report of what had happened and what was planned.

"I would like for you to accompany Captain Semmes to sell the lifeweave," she said after some thought.

"It will take at least a couple of weeks," Arden protested. "With the wedding so close, I don't think . . ."

Jessa shook her head. "You know him and his crew, and you know Miga, if that's where he chooses to go. I think someone from Glory should go with them. You're the logical choice."

Arden started to protest again, but thought better of it. Jessa was not really giving her much choice, and frankly the idea appealed to her. Poor Alvarez would be left to cope with the wedding security until she got back. If things went smoothly, that should not be very long.

As soon as she got Arden's acquiescence, Jessa sent the two of them on their way, promising to inform the other council members. They in return promised to keep her informed as things progressed.

"I can't imagine why the empress wants to send you away right now," Hsing muttered as they made their way to the elevators. "Going to Baltha was one thing. A lot can happen in two weeks."

"She's right that someone should be there in case any decisions need to be made regarding the sale," Arden said. "I just don't think it should be me, either."

Even as she said that, a part of her repeated that she wanted to go. The desire was not just to be close to Rafe for an extended period, but rather a need to be more active. Then, too, if the armory blew up, the value of the spools of fine yarn was more important than ever. The funds might be needed to replace those arms in order to defend the empress against Vey and Radieux. She could make that decision on the spot if she was in on the negotiations.

"I'll help Alvarez as much as I can while you're gone," the general offered.

Arden thanked him on her own behalf as well as the

captain's. As they rode down in the elevator, they discussed what might be happening on Baltha, both wishing they were there rather than in the palace, waiting to hear what was or was not going on. They parted company when they reached the lower level with promises to keep each other informed of events within their own spheres, and she strode toward her office.

Once inside, Arden contacted Raphael Semmes, setting up a meeting to discuss disposition of the lifeweave. She started to ask Rafe to come to her apartment, but thought better of it. He might be uncomfortable there, since the rooms were intimately familiar to him. It might also be best not to presume on the feelings he had shown during the rescue. They had both been under stress and unable to be objective. Best to choose a neutral location, and she decided on the same small conference room in which she had met with Hsing.

For the hour until the meeting, she stayed in her office. Alvarez came in to finish some reports. It was her first opportunity to talk with him since her return. First she thanked him for his role in her rescue. He filled in a few details of what had happened, and she informed him of the new plans that had just been set in motion.

"I will need for you to handle a lot of things in the palace for a time," she told him. "We have to resolve the situation on Baltha and get the sale of this lifeweave taken care of. General Hsing has offered any help you might need while I'm gone."

"And the empress's wedding?" the captain reminded her.

"I should be back before that. It's five weeks from now."

She should have plenty of time, but time was conspiring against her. One moment it moved too slowly, the next too fast. She glanced at the screen showing the entry to the conference room and saw Rafe approaching with Liel.

"I have to meet with Captain Semmes right now," she said, getting up from her desk.

After giving her second in command a few more instructions, she left the office and made her way to the second floor. A guard outside the conference room opened the door for her. Both men stood when she entered. She took the chair at the head of the small rectangular table.

"Gentlemen, I hope your rooms are comfortable enough," she said.

"Better than the first ones we had here," Liel said, referring to their imprisonment in a basement cell a year and a half earlier.

"For me too," she said, and smiled.

Liel nodded. Rafe remained stoic. This had to be difficult for him, but dammit, it was for her too.

"I do want to thank you and your crew for helping us, Rafe," she said. "The rescue team and I would probably be dead by now if you hadn't come."

"I'm just glad we got there in time," he said.

The words were spoken in a rather neutral tone. Clearly, he also thought they should not let the emotions they had felt take over. Not just yet. Maybe he thought they never should. If that was the case, then, it was over between them, and she felt an immense sadness at that thought. But she was sure that he would not have been so willing to risk everything to save her if he did not still care.

She looked down at the top of the table, using the moment to regain her composure. This was not the time to worry about their love affair.

She raised her head and looked straight at Rafe.

"Do you have an idea of how the market stands on lifeweave right now?"

His left eyebrow arched for a moment; then he began relating what he knew. The price of lifeweave was very high because of the impending marriage of the second son of Weaver to the empress of Glory. Several heads of state who were planning on attending the nuptials wanted elaborate garments made of the stuff. He understood the bride's gown was to be made of lifeweave also.

That last bit of information surprised Arden. She had no idea that Jessa had made that decision and wondered for a moment if it was supposed to be some sort of tribute to Lyona. Or perhaps it was a bit of a sick joke, since her mother had died from addiction to the fiber.

"Right now is a particularly good time to unload what you have on hand," he finished.

"Where is the best place to sell it?"

"Miga is still the best," Rafe said. "And the easiest."

"After what happened there the last time?"

"That's where I sold my half of that shipment."

"Twice, as I recall," she said.

Arden still remembered the sinking feeling of betrayal when it turned out the officials on Miga had made a deal with Waran Parcq to help capture everyone on the *Starbourne* and turn over the lifeweave to him. Returning there would be unpleasant at best.

At that moment a thought occurred to her that made it a good idea to go with Rafe to sell the lifeweave. Not because she did not trust him. In spite of the tension between them, she still trusted him as much as anyone she knew.

"Rafe," she said, placing her forearms on the table and leaning forward. "Would that also be the best place for General Radieux to sell weapons?"

Captain Case sat behind the desk in Radieux's office. *Former office*, he reminded himself. The plans for the armory were spread all over the desk. The handset of the communicator stayed warm from being in his hand constantly.

After the fiasco at the prison and the escape of Don Vey, he had asked for a reassignment, only to find himself placed in charge of the new troops sent to take over Baltha. When the order came not to land because of the possibility of bombs within the facility, he had asked for and received permission from General Hsing himself to land in one of the escape pods. The only reason permission was given was that he was an explosives expert and had served on Baltha once before.

Now the transport ship was in synchronous orbit, ready to report back to Glory if or when the whole facility was blown away. The one transport ship that had remained on Baltha had been sabotaged; otherwise a lot of the soldiers would have been taken off. Another ship was on its way to evacuate soldiers, but by the time it arrived, there might not be many left to worry about.

By the time Case landed, a disposal team had been sent to the underground facility to make sure it was safe. Others were busy moving guns and the ammunition and power packs outside. Those few with explosives experience, including two already on Baltha, led other teams in search of bombs. When they started the search before he arrived, no one had quite believed there were any. However, one was found in the officers' mess, and they soon took their task more seriously.

It was amazing that even that one had been found. The search was haphazard at best. Case's first task was to better organize the operation. He concentrated first on the spoke that led to the underground facility, since that was their last line of retreat.

A second bomb was found right in Radieux's office. It was probably meant to destroy any records left behind.

He looked at the clock on the far wall. If the time set on the two bombs was the same on any others, they had two and a half hours left.

The comm buzzed, and he picked up the handset.

"We've found another one," Sergeant Joyce said. "In the bursar's office in tunnel seven. It's like the others."

"Let me know when you've finished disarming it."

While he waited for word, he studied the plans again, marking the location of the new discovery. This bomb, the third, was placed in nearly the same position in one of the spokes as the second here in the office. A pattern was emerging, but with so little evidence, could he proceed with it as a guideline? So far, it seemed that two bombs might be set in each tunnel: one near the opening from the central atrium, and one in each storeroom. If they went off, only one place would be safe: the underground facility. All of the tunnels would be ruptured as well as the storage rooms, and the security doors would not be enough to save the atrium. That is, if they even worked.

The amazing thing was that so many could have been placed in so short a time without anyone noticing. Given that and the details of the captivity of Commander Grenfell, it would seem that Radieux had been followed blindly by those in his command. More than he deserved, obviously.

Case communicated a general order that all search patterns should concentrate on offices and rooms located near the entrances of the spokes, and in the storerooms that still contained arms. Those storerooms that had been emptied were sealed off for the time being, with the hope that there would be time to search them later.

Joyce called soon after. He had managed to disarm the new bomb with little trouble. At least they were simple devices, so far, but Case suspected that somewhere they would find two or three really complicated ones.

Half an hour later, the call came. A more complicated bomb had been found in the laser pack storeroom.

"I'm on my way."

He picked up his tool pouch and left the office. When he got to the storeroom, everyone on the search team had left except one corporal. He had volunteered to stay to show where the bomb was and to help the captain in disarming it, he said. The paleness of his face was a clear sign that he wished he had not, but the tight set of his mouth showed that he would do what was necessary. His hands shook only a little as he took the tool pouch.

The bomb was on the floor behind one of the storage racks, found when the last of the packs were loaded up. The corporal helped Case gently pull the rack away from the wall. The captain stooped down and took a look.

The timer, a simple clock from an enviro suit, sat on top of a fairly simple combination of wires and C35 explosive in a small metal box. No booby trap was attached to the rack. What had caught Sergeant Joyce's eye was the overall size—about twice that of the others—and several wires on the outside. They went under the box, probably meaning there was a pressure fuse on the bottom. If someone just lifted the box, allowing the button to pop out, the whole thing would explode immediately.

Case asked for a pick, and the corporal handed one over. Carefully, the captain moved wires and checked connections. Another booby trap. If he simply cut the wires to the pressure fuse, loss of the connection would also set it off.

"Get me a flat piece of metal or plastic," he said. "Something thin but slightly larger than the box."

The corporal disappeared, then returned a moment later with the lid from a box that had held power packs. Three edges were turned down at a forty-five-degree angle, and one was straight. A perfect shelf for the bomb since, once on the lid, it could not slide right off the other end.

Carefully, Case laid the lid right next to the bomb. Just as carefully, he slid it slowly up to the box. He placed his left hand against the other end of the box to steady it. Slowly, he pushed the lid until it slipped under the edge, then kept it sliding. It hung up about halfway under. Probably on the button.

He stopped and wiped a film of sweat from his forehead with his left hand. Behind him, the corporal took short, quick breaths.

He tried again with the lid. This time, after shifting it from one side to the other, it finally slid farther. In moments, the entire bomb sat on the lid.

"What time is it?" he asked.

"It's seventeen twenty-one, sir."

It would take at least half an hour to disarm this one. If there were others like it, there would not be enough time to get everything clear.

"Call Sergeant Joyce. Have him get one of the guys in an enviro suit," he ordered. "Someone with good hands. We'll have to get this outside, away from the armory, and let it go off."

Case walked carefully to the nearest airlock, where a soldier waited in an enviro suit. Behind the face shield, he looked none too happy about his assignment, but he took the bomb in hand, after being warned to walk off at least half a mile in the opposite direction of where the arms were being piled.

"Just set it down someplace level and get back in here as fast as you can," Case ordered.

Two other men went with the soldier to open doors and clear his path as much as possible. Case let out a sigh of relief as they disappeared down the tunnel.

At 1900 hours, several more bombs had been disarmed or taken outside. He ordered all those outside the armory to come in and get down into the underground center. After that, he cleared the soldiers from each area in five-minute increments. At 1920, Sergeant Joyce called.

"I found another one, sir, in tunnel eleven."

"Leave it and get below," the captain ordered.

"I can get it done, sir."

"Forget it, Sergeant."

No answer.

"Sergeant, that's an order!"

He tried several more times to raise the sergeant with no luck. He considered going to get him away, even if he had to drag him. An explosion rocked the building. Sirens sounded. Red emergency lights came on, some flashing. Case ran out of the office. Doors slammed shut everywhere as the computer started sealing off every tunnel, starting with those closest to the explosion.

Dammit! It went off earlier than expected.

He took off running toward the tunnel leading to the underground facility. He just might make it before the door closed.

The door slammed across the entrance to the tunnel. He slid to a stop, hesitated, then ran back to the office. There had to be an override in the computer. He hoped there was enough time left to find it. He squinted down the tunnel at the sound of someone running down the hall. A soldier sprinted past. The captain shouted to him and he reappeared. The man looked at the captain, then back at the door closed at the end of the tunnel. A look of doom crossed his face and for a fleeting moment the captain wondered where the man had come from.

"You know anything about the computer?" Case shouted at him.

"A little."

The captain grabbed the man's arm and pulled him into the office.

"Can you pull up the security system?" he asked, pointing at the console.

"Sure, but I don't have any of the security codes."

"Get me in there and I'll worry about the codes."

He ran into the inner office and opened his briefcase. He was given the security codes as a matter of course when given the assignment. The book he had written them in was tucked inside a pocket.

He raced back to the computer in the outer office.

"Any luck?"

"Yes, sir. It's ready now."

He flipped through the pages until he found what he wanted. A glance at the clock showed four minutes left before the rest of the bombs should go off. He entered the first code that got him into the database. It took a moment to find the right option.

"Go watch down the tunnel and tell me if I get the right door open."

He wended his way through selection after selection, and entered the code at the one he thought was correct.

"It's opening!"

"Go check the door into the other tunnel. Let me know if it's open."

The man disappeared and shouted a moment later, "It's open."

Case sprinted from the room. The soldier was nowhere in sight, but his footsteps echoed across the atrium. The captain followed as fast as he could run. Once inside the tunnel, he pushed the emergency close button, then raced on.

Another explosion rocked the building. Closer, this time, knocking him off his feet. He got back up and ran into the nearly empty storeroom. The soldier stood just inside the door leading down into the underground sanctuary.

"Thanks," Casc said as he passed through.

They closed and locked the door, then raced down the stairs. Behind them came another explosion. Dust fell on their heads.

13

The last crate had been stowed aboard the *Starbourne* and everything locked up. Guards were placed around the ship, several sleeping on board, and everyone else had made their way back to the palace. They were to lift off early next morning, and Arden and the crew needed to get some sleep. The past two days had been hectic, and she had gotten little rest in that time.

So far, though, the most difficult battle had been fought between General Hsing and Jessa. For some reason, he had decided that Arden should not be sent to Miga with the lifeweave. He argued that her wounds were not fully healed and that she should be in the palace complex to ensure security for the wedding. The empress held to her argument that Arden was the best choice for someone to accompany Captain Semmes. Meanwhile, Arden had continued with arrangements to leave.

What she had finally admitted to herself was that she did not want to go back to the administrative aspects of her position. The events on Baltha had revived her appetite for action.

However, she kept that desire to herself and talked long and hard to convince the general that someone should go, adding the new argument that General Radieux might go to Miga and try to sell the arms he had stolen from Baltha.

Neither the general nor the empress agreed with that. Why would he trade arms that would help in his takeover of the government? For a scout ship, or something like it, she said, that would help him move his troops around on Glory.

A large force could not be sent by Glory because of the neutrality of that trading world. The someone who should go was she. In the end, he relented, but forced her to listen to his advice on what to do and what not to do. Then she left them, feeling almost like a child sent on an errand by her reluctant parents.

She had invited Rafe Semmes to her office for a last-minute talk. It was time to tell him she was making the trip, too. Something she had dreaded, telling herself that a last minute problem would keep her on Glory. When told of her plans to go with him to Miga, he had made it quite clear that he did not approve. Probably it brought too many memories of their earlier trip to the same place on almost exactly the same errand. Again, they were faced with the possibility of the enemy getting there ahead of them, although she did not bring that up again. If they thought of that too much, the captain might opt for another trading world, farther away. That would prevent her from going, since she could not hope to get there and back in time to oversee the final preparations for the wedding.

The discussion with him had been short, and he left her office in a very bad mood. In spite of that, he had accepted the argument that she had seen the lifeweave come to Glory and it was her responsibility to see it sold and the money returned. He did not once voice the idea that she did not trust him. He knew better than that.

Now, in her apartment, she took a long shower and, wrapped in a wonderfully soft and warm robe, she poured herself a glass of wine and curled up on the sofa. She was tired but not yet sleepy, and there was one last thing to do.

She entered the code on the comm unit and waited for the answer. The voice was sleepy, but she knew she would be forgiven.

"Grayson, sorry to wake you."

"Ah, that's quite all right. I was wondering when you'd get around to calling."

"I know. I would have called sooner, but things have been pretty hectic."

"I'm sure they have. We hear rumors and gossip here too, you know."

She could hear the smile in his voice.

"At least you did call after you got back from Baltha and let me know you were alive. A very short call, I might add."

"I know," she said again. "By rumor, I suppose you've heard that I'm going to Miga with the lifeweave."

"With Captain Semmes, you mean."

"Well, he is carrying the stuff on his ship."

"Yes, I have heard that rumor," he said with a yawn at the end. "When do you leave?"

"In the morning. We should be back in ten days or so," she added, anticipating the next question. "I can't be much longer than that because of the wedding. I expect you to stay here in the palace when you come, by the way."

"What you expect and what happens might be two different things."

"Not this time," she said, trying to sound confident. "In the meantime, what's been going on out there?"

He told her of more raids on villages, but that nothing had been heard directly about Don Vey since his nocturnal visit to the monastery. If there was some kind of major encampment or site being built, no one was talking about it.

He asked how her injuries were healing, and she told him what the doctors were still saying. The limp was slightly improved, and her face did not hurt all the time. As for the ribs, they were coming along. She paused, hesitant to talk about the emotional effects.

"What is it, daughter?"

Abbot Grayson knew her too well, she decided for at least the thousandth time.

"I feel discontented since I got back," she said with a sigh. She went on to describe how sitting behind the desk and administering palace security no longer seemed satisfying.

"Have you yet told anyone about the pledge that keeps you there?"

He referred to the promise she had made to Pac Terhn that she would serve Jessa until the empress either died or dismissed her. It had been made in return for his help in finding the then-princess after Lyona became so ill and the emperor wanted his daughter to come home. Not to see her mother, but to take her place at the loom, weaving predictions of coming events with lifeweave.

"There's no use in doing that," she answered. She picked up the glass from the side table and sipped the wine. It was sweet on her tongue and warm going down. "It would only make Jessa feel guilty and . . ."

"And make Semmes want to find some way to get you out of it?" He paused, but she did not answer. "Or perhaps you fear that he would not do that."

Exactly, she thought. If he made no effort to persuade her to go with him, then he probably did not love her as much as she hoped. The fact that he left Glory once Jessa was safe and her ascent to the throne more or less assured had done nothing to confirm his love. He had accepted Arden's reasons for staying so easily: she needed to ensure Jessa's safety as empress after fighting so hard to get her there. And to assuage the guilt over her part in getting Jessa home.

He could have stayed, after all, at least for a while. Since then, she had been so busy revamping palace security and helping to strengthen Jessa's position, that there had been no time for romance.

Maybe his leaving had been wise, after all. He could not have helped feeling neglected by her in the past eighteen months had he stayed.

"I need to get some sleep," she said, avoiding answering his question. "I'll be in touch when I get back, I guess."

"Be safe, daughter. I'll be here if you need me."

"You always are. Thank you. Goodnight."

It flashed through her mind how much she missed the simplicity of life in the monastery. Missed evening talks with Grayson about anything and everything.

She drained the glass and cleaned it carefully. It was one

of a set of antique crystal glasses her mentor had given her.
At least she still had those and the pleasure of wine and food
from the monastery's vineyards and fields. While growing
up, she had taken products of the monks' labors for granted.
Now, she not only took solace in the things themselves, but
also in the thoughtfulness of those who now sent her the bottles of wine, cheeses, and fresh vegetables.

Sounds of the early morning were not so much different
from any other part of the day on the *Starbourne*. It was a
quiet ship, something Arden had not remembered. Perhaps
the constant buzz of noise in the palace during the day had
simply made her more conscious of the silence. It had not
helped that, once on their way, she and Rafe had avoided
each other as much as was possible in such crowded quarters.

Today—in just over five hours, as a matter of fact—they
would land on Miga. Memories of the last visit had kept
Arden from sleeping all night. Thinking of what they might
find filled her with apprehension.

After she had overseen the loading of half of the lifeweave, the vault had seemed so empty that a sudden panic
had gripped her. The cache of lifeweave was their greatest
single treasure. Converting it into credit was a great risk.

Building the defense facilities was also a risk, but one
that should yield more than one dividend. There was, of
course, the defense of the capital city and the countryside.
Plus, the amount of work in the construction alone would
employ several hundred men and women for perhaps a year
or more. Then soldiers would be needed to man them.
Those two employment opportunities should bring many of
the raiders back into lawful pursuits.

She dressed and ate a light breakfast, avoiding the coffee
substitute. Nowadays, if she could not have the real thing,
she preferred nothing at all. Afterward, she made her way
to the bridge. Rafe and she needed to discuss one more
thing before they landed, but he was not there. Liel suggested she look for him in his cabin.

She knocked and walked in at his invitation. He sat at
the small table, the ship's log recorder in front of him. The

captain's cabin was slightly larger than the others, but it had only one bunk, which added to the roominess. Arden had managed to talk him into removing the second bunk from the cabin she occupied on this trip so that she could practice with her sword and work out the stiffness in her legs. The extra space was minimal, but if she used a short shinai, the accommodation almost worked. The cost for that work was coming out of Glory's share.

He must have thought it was one of the crew who knocked because he looked surprised when she entered. He hid it quickly and motioned for her to sit down in the other chair.

"What can I do for you?" he asked as she sat.

"We need to talk about what we might find once we get to Miga."

"You mean the real reason you came along?"

His voice took on the old bantering tone she remembered, and she smiled.

"Something like that," she answered. "There is a chance that General Radieux might have come here with the arms he stole from Baltha."

"I still don't understand why you think he would sell them," Rafe said, repeating his argument from their first discussion. "Why would he do that? Those guns would be best used by his forces on Glory, wouldn't they?"

"Getting them to Glory himself would be risky. It's possible he would rather rely on professional smugglers to do it for him, but that would be costly. Plus, he could sell some of the guns in order to buy other things he needs and still keep a large portion of what he stole. He might even be interested in selling the transport ship. It's not as useful to him as a small fighter or scout ship would be."

Rafe nodded. "So you came along to see if Radieux was indeed visiting Miga, or had visited Miga, and then what? Maybe I lose my ship again, thanks to your machinations?"

"No, I don't plan to put you or your ship in jeopardy . . ."

"You never do."

". . . but it's possible he knew of our plans to sell the lifeweave. He was still in the information loop. We had no reason to keep it from him until recently," she went on, ignoring the jibe. "He'll be expecting you to show up here, and he doesn't know that we expect him to."

"How?"

"Excuse me?"

"How do we know he may come here?"

"Several things," she said patiently. "Not the least of which was the route he took when he left the solar system."

"How did you know that? You didn't send any fighters after him."

"From the emissions of his engines. We were able to trace those part of the way. And, before you ask, we didn't send any fighters because many of them have been mothballed on Pellen and the rest were on maneuvers on the other side of the solar system. Or most of the active ones."

"And what else?"

"Huh?"

"You said you were able to trace the emissions part of the way. What else told you that Radieux might be heading for Miga?"

Rafe looked at her intently as she hesitated. Arden dropped her gaze to the tabletop.

"A hunch, Rafe. Just a hunch."

"Whose?"

"Mine."

"You mean a lifeweave hunch."

"Yes, maybe," she admitted, although her memory relating to that was vague. "It did show me that you would be the one who rescued me from Baltha, but I didn't understand at the time."

He shook his head.

"I know you don't want to believe it, but it's true. People like me and Lyona can use the fiber in that way. You know it works."

"I'd rather depend on facts, Arden. Not some magical fiber."

He started to stand, but there was no room to get by her and reach the door. He lowered himself back into the chair. Silence continued between them for several heartbeats.

"Dammit, Arden," he said angrily. "You've done it

again. With the head start this general of yours had, he's probably conducted his business on Miga and is ready to leave. Hell, he may have left already. If he did buy a fighter, he could be lying in wait for us somewhere. Probably waiting until we sell the lifeweave—then he'll have lots more credits to get the things he needs.''

"Rafe, you know that we couldn't prevent his getting whatever he wanted on Miga. You said yourself they do not recognize the rights or laws of any other world. Only the laws of salvage, and we know too well that they don't honor those at all times. We couldn't come here with a shipload of soldiers. We couldn't even come here with a military ship. You were the best we had on such short notice.''

He did stand then and looked down at her.

"I'll have to tell my crew that we may be running into trouble,'' he said tightly.

She stood up, opened the door and stepped through the opening. She turned to face him.

"I'm sorry for putting you into possible danger again, but we have to know what Radieux may have accomplished on Miga.''

"I know, but maybe one day you'll tell me everything in advance and give me a choice.''

She nodded and stepped aside. He strode down the corridor toward the bridge. In a moment, she returned to her cabin to get her sword. The uniform had been left behind, but she could not leave the sword. With it slung across her back, she headed for the bridge, sure that Rafe had enough time to tell everyone what they had discussed.

Everyone except the captain looked up at her when she stepped inside. No one looked friendly. Only Phyilla's expression showed little anger; she looked more curious.

One step forward and two back, Arden thought. They might never trust her again, but that was something she could not worry about now.

She nodded to Liel and moved to stand where she could see Rafe's face.

"One thing I didn't mention, Captain,'' she said. He looked up at her, something like a look of resignation on his face. "You've probably already thought of it.''

"Probably," he said.

"There is a chance that Radieux has not made it here yet, since the transport ship is slower than the *Starbourne*. He could arrive after us. Either way, there's a good chance of a fight."

"I thought of that," he said, then looked back down at the controls on the main board. "How many men did he take with him from the armory?"

"At least twelve, we think."

He shook his head.

"We don't know how many of his men were killed in that little skirmish between them and your ship. And when the bombs blew, a few more men disappeared. We can only guess the number of personnel he had enlisted into his plans for treason."

Rafe looked around at those of his crew on the bridge. One was missing—Johns, his cook, who was in the galley, preparing it for the landing.

"Six of us against twelve," Liel said.

"Or more," Rafe added.

"There are seven of us," Arden reminded them.

"Johns doesn't fight," Liel said. "He's taken some kind of vow."

It surprised her that Rafe would have hired someone who would not fight, but said nothing. He would remind her, of course, that this was a salvage ship, not a military ship. He would probably go on about how the only time they had to fight anyone was when she was around. Which was true enough, but not something she gladly admitted to.

And there she was doing both sides of the conversation in her head.

"A salvage ship against a transport," Tahr muttered.

"Not quite," Rafe said. "They may be here to buy a fighter."

The pilot looked around, muttering under his breath. Everyone was used to his complaining like that and had turned to their own contemplations of what might lie ahead.

Planetfall was almost an hour away, but Arden decided to remain on the bridge. She sat in the one empty chair behind the captain's. It was placed out of the way, yet gave a full view of the activity. She raised up and pulled the sword belt over her head, wedging the weapon beside the chair so that it would not be thrown around. She should probably have left it in her cabin, but it was too late now.

She watched the crew work, noting subtle differences. The overall picture was one of greater sophistication than on her first trip. In upgrading the ship, Rafe must have paid a great deal of attention to the bridge. The more she looked, the less it seemed to retain from before.

Even the seats, she realized. The chair she was in certainly was more comfortable than the one she had used the first time.

Everyone effectively ignored her presence, and in the silence, her thoughts turned to the possible scenarios between them and Radieux. She had become more and more convinced that some sort of confrontation was inevitable. In spite of the hints in the lifeweave square, the idea of having to fight the general seemed almost preposterous. That was a danger of hero worship.

Reluctance aside, she preferred the idea of fighting one on one versus the possibility of a fight in space between two ships. If it came to the latter, she had no possible role in the battle. The only reason Radieux would choose that venue would have to be his actual purchase of a fighter of some kind, a ship he would logically consider superior to a salvage ship.

More reasons could be counted against that. He had a greater force in manpower. Plus, he surely would not jeopardize a newly acquired ship that was very expensive and would be key in whatever plans he and Vey had cooked up.

Once back on Glory, the fighter could be used effectively against imperial forces, yet be small enough to be hidden easily. It could be used to ferry both men and arms anywhere, even harass the armory again if they wanted to—all that in spite of the reactivation of a fighter squadron currently in progress on Glory.

So, there it was. Most likely it would be a fight on Miga, where his superiority in numbers would be his greatest advantage. It would also be the best time to take the credits gained from the sale of the lifeweave, meaning he would probably wait until the *Starbourne* had been unloaded and the transaction completed. They must be on their guard the whole time they were planetside.

They landed in mid-afternoon to find that all the dealers were tied up until the next morning. Arden tried to convince the authorities to let Rafe and the crew stay on board the ship, but that was against the rules. The crew themselves looked forward to sleeping somewhere else; it was a rare treat for them, but she resolved to sneak back on board and sleep there. Before that, however, they all enjoyed a good dinner together in one of the port restaurants.

Afterward, everyone went for a tour of the town except the captain, Liel, and Arden. The three stayed at the table. She started to order another glass of wine, having found it surprisingly good, but decided to try a Drambuie, which Rafe was drinking. It was a very old liqueur from Earth which she found much to her liking. Liel stuck to a bourbon of doubtful authenticity, which he seemed to enjoy immensely.

For a time, they drank quietly. After three rounds, however, they started to reminisce about their first visit together to Miga and how Chase and his cohorts sent by Jessa's father surprised them. They jumped over some things, remembering instead the separate escapes from the palace dungeon.

Again, they skipped over events, especially the final fight in the hangar at the port. Rafe asked Arden how being head of palace security was going, and she talked awhile about what her life had been like since Jessa gave her that appointment. She talked of not being able to visit the monastery as often as she would like, which led to describing the attack on her last visit. She skipped any mention of the occasional tension between her and the empress. That tale finished, silence descended for a little while.

"You really made a lot of improvements on the ship," she commented.

"Yes, we did," Rafe said. "It was expensive, but after selling our half of the lifeweave, we could afford it. Each of the crew chipped in some, since it's their home as much as mine.''

"Can I ask if the guns are legal?'' she said in a lowered voice.

"Perfectly legal,'' Liel said, his voice slightly slurred and a bit loud.

He grinned at both of them, more relaxed than she had ever seen him.

"I think I'd better get him to the hotel,'' Rafe said and stood. She and Liel got to their feet, too.

"Rafe, I . . .''

"Oh, here's the access card for the ship,'' he said, taking the card out of his pocket and handing it to her. "If you're found out, I'll disavow any knowledge that you were there. Sleep well.''

She took hold of the card, and for a moment they held it between them. Their eyes met, and she wanted desperately to think of the right thing to say. He let go suddenly, and their eye contact broke off.

"Thanks,'' she said. "You, too. Be careful getting him to the hotel.'' She pointed at Liel, who was unsteady on his feet.

"I will,'' he said, grinning up at his exec. "You're a good drunk, aren't you, Liel?''

"Of course I am. I'm good at everything I do.'' His grin broadened.

Rafe took his arm and led him toward the door. Arden followed behind. Outside, they said goodnight and turned in opposite directions.

The hour was very late, and the port facilities were closed for the most part. She met only one person as she made her way to the *Starbourne*. On board, the silence was deeper than she thought possible. She drank a large glass of water in hopes of countering the effects of the wine and liqueur, undressed, and climbed into the bunk. She picked up the book she had brought with her, intending to read, but the words held no interest.

Thoughts of Raphael Bedford Semmes invaded her mind, and she could not push them away. She had wished to be near him so many nights after he first left, then less and less often as she became busy and he rarely got in touch. One night, she realized that she had not thought of him in nearly a week, and that made her cry harder than she had in a very long time. Still, for a time, thoughts of him had almost disappeared.

She turned out the lamp over the bed and pulled the covers up to her chin. She wished she could recapture that time when thoughts of him had stopped keeping her awake nights.

With a sigh, she turned onto her side, prepared to lie awake for a while in spite of the effects of the alcohol. Instead, though, she found herself awakening a short time later, surprised that she had actually fallen asleep, and wondering what had wakened her.

She listened to the dark silence for several minutes. Just before she relaxed to fall asleep again, the door to her cabin began to open.

14

A shaft of light pierced the darkness as the door cracked open. Arden's hand clasped the hilt of her sword and she waited, holding her breath, listening. The door continued to open slowly, and she wondered if that perception was a product of the adrenaline rush.

"Arden," someone whispered.

She waited while a man's figure was silhouetted in the doorway. No doubt that this person either meant her no harm, or was not very good at this.

"Arden," he whispered again.

This time she recognized his voice and raised up on one elbow.

"What are you doing here, Rafe? And why in the hell are you whispering?" She let go of the sword.

"I wanted to make sure you were awake."

"And if I weren't?"

"I'd go back to the hotel."

"Well, then, I'm asleep," she said, trying to sound as firm as possible.

"Can we talk for a minute?"

"About what?"

He stepped into the cabin.

"May I turn on the lights?"

"Yes, I guess so." She sighed and put a hand over her eyes.

The light came on dimly, filtering through her fingers. She took her hand away, blinking a moment while her eyes adjusted. Rafe shut the door and sat down in the one straight-backed chair. His face was flushed, and he did not seem to know what to do with his hands.

"Are you drunk, Rafe?"

The index and middle fingers on his left hand fluttered the way they did when he was nervous or thinking. It was a motion often made by musicians. She had never found out what kind of musical instrument he had played. Maybe he still did.

"No. I had a couple more drinks. But no, I'm not drunk."

His eyes traced the outline of her body under the bed-covers. Her robe lay across the foot of the bed, and she realized that she should have sent him out in the corridor while she put it—or something—on. Now, it would just seem too self-conscious to do it. When she looked up, his eyes were focused on her face. She propped the pillow against the wall so she could sit up, and pulled the covers up under her chin.

"Sorry, I didn't mean to make you uncomfortable," he said. "You never were before and I didn't think . . ."

"It's all right," she said into the silence that fell between them. "When things change between two people, it's bound to be awkward at first."

"Have things changed so much?"

"Well, yes. We used to trust each other. Now, we're not sure."

"I never trusted you," he said and chuckled. "You were trouble from the start."

Arden laughed and relaxed more.

"I guess that's true, now that I think back."

The silence that now fell between them was less tense. Until the very end of their first adventure, they had been at odds in spite of the attraction they had felt for each other. Now, she wondered if she had made more of it than there

was. Had they fallen in love? Or was it a passion born out
of loneliness and the excitement of the moment?

She had been so sure that she loved him. However, if
that was true, wouldn't she have thought of him more in
the following months?

"I have missed you," he said.

She tensed again.

"Oh? And are you wanting to start where we left off?"

"That's not what I was trying to do." His voice turned
angry.

"What do you want here, then?"

He spread his hands as if unsure what to say.

"I don't know," he said finally. "I don't like the tension
that exists between us. I find it very uncomfortable. I don't
know if we can be lovers again, but I would like to be
friends."

The words, and the thought behind them, made her feel
terribly sad. But if friendship was all he could offer, then
it would have to be enough.

"I guess we can do that," she said. "I just wish . . ."

"What?" he prompted.

"That we had been willing to work harder at what we
had. That we had both thought it was worth the effort."

He smiled sadly.

"I suppose the time just wasn't right for us," he said.
"Maybe it never will be." He looked down at the floor. "I
did love you. I still do."

Her heart quickened and she gasped. He looked into her
eyes, and she wanted to look away so that he could not see
the effect of his words. She could not. Their eyes locked
on each other, and all of the longing was there.

Rafe stood up, walked over to the bunk, and sat down
on the edge. Their eyes did not waver. His left hand rose,
and he touched the scar on her right cheek with his fingertips. She closed her eyes at the thrill of his touch, and a
moan nearly escaped her lips.

This was not right or sensible or smart. She should tell
him to leave right now, before anything happened. Put
everything back into its former perspective.

His fingers brushed her short hair back. She opened her eyes, now moist with tears. They gazed at each other. His other hand came up, and he held her face between both. He leaned down and kissed her, softly, slowly, with all the tenderness that was part of his lovemaking.

Her own hand reached up around the back of his neck, and she ran her fingers through the hair on the back of his head. Feeling its softness, the warmth of his skin.

He shivered slightly. A sense of pleasure rushed through her.

The kiss ended, only to be resumed but more passionately. His mouth opened wider, his tongue probed into her mouth. His left hand dropped to her side, tracing the length of her body. Both hands went under her, raised her, pressing her against him.

Then she did moan.

"That's a hell of a lot of the stuff for one sale," McPherson said.

Rafe and Arden sat in his office, having just inspected the crates of lifeweave with the dealer. He was the same man Rafe had sold his own lifeweave to.

"I can take it for maybe six hundred thousand each crate," the dealer continued.

"Don't give me that," Rafe said. "You know it's worth at least twice that."

"But it's like flooding the market again."

"It's no different than our first deal eighteen months ago. In fact, the market should be even better. You and I both know Weaver has not been producing as much of the fiber as it was. We also know that a lot of people have been buying the stuff for finery to wear to the wedding on Glory. There's actually a scarcity."

"Not so fast," McPherson said, pulling his chair up closer to the desk. "Glory is part of the problem, you know. They aren't buying as much lifeweave as they did when Appolyona was alive and the war was going on."

"So maybe the market is exactly the same as it was eighteen months ago," Rafe said and grinned. "So we should deal for the same amount."

They haggled on, each stating reasons why the price should be different than the other man thought. Arden had never really seen this side of Rafe, and she found it both amusing and fascinating. He talked calmly, making his points rationally. This was what he knew, more than anything. Even more than salvage or commanding a ship. He was always sure of himself, but here that sureness was stronger, to the point of near arrogance. McPherson did not seem to be put off by it.

"Done," Rafe said at last.

He had gotten a bit over a million for each crate. The two men stood and shook hands. They made arrangements for the crates to be offloaded and the credits paid in the afternoon. Rafe bemoaned the fact that Migans still could not do simple fund transfers, and they discussed that for a moment. He and Arden stood, shook hands all around, and then left.

"That was impressive," she said as they started walking back toward the port.

"What?"

"You. I enjoyed watching you wheeling and dealing in there."

"Oh, that was nothing. McPherson is generally reasonable to deal with. Some of the others aren't so easy."

"What is it, then?" she asked. "Some kind of ritual?"

"Guess you could call it that. It's like dueling, but managing to leave with your manhood intact."

She laughed. "Well, I'm certainly glad of that."

She hooked her arm in his, and they strolled down the sidewalk in silence for a while. Once more, she was reminded of how little she actually knew about him and how much she wanted to know. She wanted to feel like she had always had a place in his life, always been part of him, and vice versa. But it was a lifetime project. There was so much to know, so many things that had made him the man he was. Learning about those things should take a long time.

They stopped in a small cafe for lunch. Silence fell between them, the comfortable kind that surrounds two people who don't need to fill the emptiness with words. However, she forced herself to bring up the subject of General Radieux and the dangers they might be facing once the credits were turned over.

"Liel should know pretty soon if he's here or been here," Rafe said when she brought up the subject. "You're sure he knows that we'll be coming here to sell the life-weave?"

"I'm sure he must have had some contact in the palace who could have told him, and it wasn't exactly a secret among the military. But, no, I haven't any information that *says* he knows we were coming to Miga."

"Can't your friend tell you if he's here and how much he knows?"

"Who?"

"You know," Rafe said.

"Pac Terhn?" Rafe nodded. "He might, but . . . well, it's just not that easy. A lot of the information I get from him and from the lifeweave isn't that straightforward. And it sometimes takes a long time to get anything at all."

"Well, I think I would just as soon you didn't use the lifeweave, anyway. Not after what happened to Jessa's mother."

Arden realized that she was blushing, not from embarrassment, but from the warm glow his concern gave her. That he cared had been shown in many ways and each time filled her with happiness. Even so, a small shred of doubt always lurked in the back of her mind. Not about his caring, but about his being around to show it.

"There you two are," Liel's voice said from behind her. He quickly took a seat at the table.

"What's the word?" Rafe asked.

"Everyone's pretty tight-lipped as usual," the exec said. He did not seem to be suffering any ill effects from the night before. "There have been at least three groups here recently that match what we're looking for. One left several days ago; a second left just yesterday; the third is either still here or left this morning. *But*," he said, then paused for effect. "I did find the transport ship from Baltha. It and some guns were traded for two almost new, high-speed scout ships. Its new owner is taking it away later this week."

"We still don't know where Radieux and his men are, then," Arden said.

"You're welcome," Liel said, sounding peeved. "You have more information now than you did."

"Thanks, Liel," Rafe said and slapped him on the shoulder. "That was good work."

"Yes, it was," Arden added.

"That's better," Liel said with a grin. "Now, how soon can we get out of here? I want to live long enough to spend my percentage."

He was always the pragmatist. However, he was right. They were too late to prevent Radieux's selling or trading the transport ship. And if he now had two well-armed ships that could be used both in an atmosphere and in the vacuum of space, he was definitely more dangerous than ever. Arden wondered how many of the guns he had taken from the armory had been included in the trade. It must have been quite a few, they decided when she voiced her question. Even used, the scout ships had to have been very expensive.

"What else would he have had to trade?" Arden mused. "We have a pretty good idea what he took from Baltha, and there was nothing else of value."

"I couldn't find out what the actual deal was," Liel said.

"Do you have any enemies here?" she asked Rafe.

He shrugged. "Not really. Any enemies I have would just come after me directly." He looked at his watch. "It's time to get back to McPherson's. He must have the credits by now."

He paid the check, and the three of them walked together to the dealer's office. No one answered when Rafe knocked on the door, and he suggested they wait downstairs where there were some chairs.

"No," Arden said. Things were not as they should be behind that door. "See if the door is locked."

Rafe touched the "open" button on the keypad and the door slid into the wall. Arden drew her sword and the two men drew guns. She slipped inside. The smell of death was in the air, the sweet smell of blood and the acrid smell of burned flesh.

No one but the three of them was visible. She lowered the katana slightly and moved around the desk. McPherson lay on the floor, his body contorted and quite still in death, a burn mark in the center of his shirt. His head was turned to one side, and the eyes were partially open. Arden stooped down and checked his pulse. The skin was only slightly cool.

"Dead?" Rafe asked from behind her as he holstered his gun.

"Yes. Not very long, though." She stood and sheathed her sword. "They probably got the credits. We have to find them."

She started toward the door. Rafe called to Liel to check the office and make sure the credits were not there.

"Where do you suggest we look?" he asked Arden as he raced after her.

"The next ship leaving the port. It's probably a scout ship."

They had made the mistake of assuming Radieux and his men had left too soon to be around to interfere with their own transaction. Maybe too soon to even know they had arrived. The possibility they would take a chance and go for the credits after their own business was finished had not occurred to her.

She rushed to the curb and started running in the direction of the port. Within a few minutes, a cab came down the street and Rafe hailed it. They jumped in, and the driver gunned it when offered twenty extra credits if he got them there fast. They paid as he drove up and jumped out the moment he stopped. Arden took off running, followed closely by the captain. Like most spacers, he had little endurance and was just able to keep up. She did not stop until forced to. She had no idea where the scout ship might be berthed.

She looked around for a computer terminal while Rafe stood panting beside her. "Over there," she said, and took off again. By the time he caught up, she had keyed in what little information she thought she knew and the computer was searching. Three scout ships were listed, but only one was scheduled for imminent liftoff. It had been berthed in hangar nine.

They found the ground shuttle and headed for the hangar. It let them off at the east side, and the berth was on the north. They hurried around the perimeter, keeping to shadows. The scout ship still sat in its place, but activity around it indicated it was being prepared for liftoff. They stopped behind a maintenance generator and peered around it.

"Do you recognize any of those men outside?"

"No, but that doesn't mean they can't be from Baltha. I have no idea who was working with Radieux." She watched for another moment. "I want to get on board. There must be a way to do it without being seen."

"Let's get closer," Rafe said. Both of them knew they somehow must make sure it was Radieux's men who were in control of the ship.

They worked their way around other equipment, trying to keep the target in sight. Workmen who saw them largely ignored their progress, probably accustomed to strange goings-on in their workplace. Very near the ship, there was a moment when the workmen were all on the other side of the ramp. They dashed across the open space and ran inside, stopping on either side of the opening.

They stayed still, catching their breath. Noises came from inside and outside. She drew her sword and motioned in the direction of the bridge, and Rafe nodded. Stepping as quietly as they could, they hurried forward. A part of her hoped that this was the right ship and another part kept praying that the general was not on board, that he had been on the scout ship that had already departed Miga. She did not want to have to face him. Not yet.

The voices grew louder as they moved closer. She could feel Rafe's tension behind her. They reached the doorway to the bridge. She stopped, took a deep breath, exhaled, and leaned around to look inside. One man sat in the exec's position at the console. A second one stood close to his right, both facing away, studying the console, making adjustments, and discussing whatever the problem was. They were both dressed in dark brown jumpsuits. Arden raised her foot to step in.

"Hey! Who the hell are you two?" A man shouted from behind them.

Rafe spun around to face him, and Arden continued onto the bridge. The two men there whirled around. The one standing was the sergeant she had seen in the underground control room on Baltha. He reached for the pistol holstered under his arm. The seated one whirled the chair around and put his hands on the arms of the chair, intending to stand.

She rushed the one standing, swinging the sword in a practice pattern to distract them for a moment. His hand grasped the handle of the pistol. Her *kiai* filled the air as she swung the sword in an arc to her right with one hand, grabbed the handle with both hands at the height of the arc, and slashed downward. The pistol came free of the holster. The blade caught the man in the throat, nearly severing his head from his body. He dropped to his knees and wobbled as blood gushed from the wound. He sprawled to the deck as the second man reached his feet.

His holster was at his waist, and his hand was already on the handle of the pistol. Behind her, Arden heard the sounds of hand-to-hand fighting in the corridor. She blocked them from her mind, concentrating again on the threat before her.

The pistol was rising at the end of the man's arm. Her own weapon was held low and to her right. She dropped to one knee, reversed the edge of the blade, and thrust forward and to her left. The tip of the blade penetrated the man's lower abdomen, moving upward. The pistol fired a charge past her head. He tried to step back, but the chair was behind him, and he sat down heavily, nearly pulling the katana from Arden's hands. She stood and pulled it free, ready to strike again if necessary.

From the look in his eyes, it was not necessary. Still, he tried once more to raise the gun. She stepped up to him and took the weapon from his hand. She bent down and wiped the blood from the blade of her katana on his jumpsuit. He kicked out, catching her shin with the toe of his boot. She yelped in pain and limped out of his reach. She leaned against the bulkhead near the door, rubbing the wounded shin, and looked out into the corridor just in time to see Rafe flatten his opponent with a right uppercut.

He leaned against the bulkhead with his back to her, looking down at his opponent sprawled on the deck. His shoulders rose and fell with his hard breathing.

"You think that's all of them?" she asked. She sheathed her sword and massaged her shin again.

He turned slowly. "I hope the hell it is."

He started toward her when a shot was fired from the corridor behind. Rafe grabbed for his left shoulder and cried out. Arden caught a glimpse of a figure running away and fired over Rafe's head as he eased himself to the deck. She ran to him.

"How bad is it?" she asked, and started to kneel down in front of him.

"I'm all right. Don't let him get away."

"Call the others," she said, and sprang to her feet.

She raced down the corridor and down the ramp. Off to the left, a figure in a dark brown jumpsuit ran away. She stuck the gun in her belt and took off after him.

At first, the bruised shin slowed her a bit. However, in moments, the pain subsided and she ran freely. The pain would return tonight or tomorrow, in spades, but right then she had no time for it.

Near the exit to the terminal, she lost him. She stood up on pieces of equipment and scanned the hangar. Did he go into the terminal, or was he hiding among the pieces of equipment gathered near that wall?

Just down the wall from the terminal entrance was another door. She remembered the port on Caldera. There had been a separate door leading to offices of the port authority, immigration, and whatever other officials were necessary to a busy port. She looked for another moment and pulled the gun from under her belt. She jumped down and headed for the door to the right, hoping that her instincts were still good.

She slammed open the door, dropped and rolled into a silent corridor. A laser shot ricocheted off the wall next to the door. She ducked and fired in the direction from which the shot came. Running footsteps sped away, and she followed at top speed.

The corridor was long, curved to the right, and semidark. Doors broke the monotony of the wall on the right every thirty feet. On the left were also doors, but only about a third as many. Soon her quarry was in constant sight as she got closer. Once, he fired over his shoulder but the shot went wild.

He was slowing, and she pushed with every ounce of strength remaining to catch up. He fired again, but she ignored it completely. His ragged breathing echoed along the corridor almost as loudly as his footsteps.

The corridor curved to the right, and the sound stopped. She could no longer see him. Her own panting drowned out the sound of his breathing, and she held her breath a moment. She heard him faintly. He must be lying in wait just around the curve, fighting to hold his breath, too. She flattened against the right wall and started edging forward.

A laser shot pitted the wall, closer to her this time. She fired in his general direction, dropped and rolled again. She crouched against the far wall just as he fired at where she had been in the middle of her roll. She fired and heard a satisfying sizzle and a cry of pain.

Still crouching, she ran in a zigzag route toward him. When she at last stood beside him, he had turned onto his stomach and was trying to crawl to the gun that lay out of reach. Arden went to the gun, stooped to pick it up, and then moved back to him. He continued trying to crawl away, and she took hold of his shoulder. He crumpled to the floor as if all the air had gone out of him.

Gently, she rolled him onto his back. Her shot had caught him in the lower abdomen. The smell of burned flesh became stronger. Both of his hands moved to cover the wound. She recognized him as Glenn, the soldier she had knocked out in the rifle storage room.

"Damn you!" he barely managed to say.

"Where are the credits?" He tried to glare at her, but pain made it impossible. "Look, I can get a med team here in moments and they might save your life. Just tell me where the credits are."

"The general will be waiting for you," he said. "You'll never get back."

"Did you radio him?"

"Yes. From the scout ship. While you fought the others."

He moaned and closed his eyes.

"Tell me where the credits are and I'll get you help," she repeated.

"Go to hell," he said, but the curse came out weakly.

His skin had paled to grey; sweat beaded on his forehead and upper lip.

"You're going to die."

"I die in a just cause," he said, and a sneer twisted his mouth for a moment. "Go away and let me die in peace."

Arden shrugged. "If that's the way you want it," she said.

Slowly she stood and looked down at him. "I'll tell Radieux that you died like a fool. He should be proud of that."

"You . . ." A coughing fit stopped him. He groaned and writhed weakly.

Before he could catch his breath and finish what he wanted to say, Arden turned on her heel and started away. He tried to shout something at her retreating back, but another fit of coughing stopped him. She caught Jessa's and Jonas Belle's names, but she forced herself to think about the scout ship. The credits had to be there, but where? Maybe Rafe had already found them.

Even the largest cabin on the scout ship was small. No room to pace; hardly enough room to think.

General Radieux, wearing his stars on the standup collar of his brown jumpsuit, fiddled with a pen. Waiting was not his strong suit, and the news he hoped to hear was more important than usual. The message from Glenn Surratt that Arden and her paramour were aboard the other scout ship had angered him. Surratt had hoped—and the general shared that hope—that he could eliminate the two of them. However, it had been hours since that message had come, and hope was dying.

The comm buzzed, and he jumped. He poked the "on" button, angry that he had become so tense.

"Yes," he growled.

"General, there is still no word from Surratt," Captain Foxhall reported. "Do you want to start for Glory now?"

"I'll let you know when, Captain," he said coldly.

"Yes, sir."

The connection closed, and Radieux leaned back in the chair. Foxhall was right. The likelihood now that Surratt had accomplished the deaths of Commander Grenfell and her companion was quite low. Therefore, the enemy was in control of the scout ship and the credits.

Damn! He had counted on getting those credits so he could replace the arms he had traded for the scout ships. And now he had only one of the ships. It did not seem wise to go back for the second one now, both in time wasted and in running the risk of being arrested for stealing the credits in the first place. Miga might be wide open, but its officials were also unpredictable.

Surratt had expressed the hope that the credits were well enough hidden that no one else could find them. They were not only well hidden, Radieux had made sure they would never fall into anyone else's hands.

His thoughts turned to Don Vey and the forces who were waiting on Glory for the scout ships and weapons he was supposed to bring them. They could probably accomplish taking over the government without them, but more arms would certainly make the task easier.

Maybe he should wait. The *Starbourne* and its crew would be heading back to Glory soon. They had to if Grenfell was going to be there to oversee preparations for the wedding.

He keyed the comm and ordered Foxhall to contact Vey for him. His own return to Glory was going to be delayed a bit.

15

The man had regained consciousness, but so far had refused to say anything. He would not even give them his name.

The bridge was still a mess, what with two bodies and blood all over the place. Rafe had made arrangements to have it cleaned up by someone he knew to be discreet, and when they arrived they went right to work. Where they disposed of the two bodies, they did not say, and no one asked. Owen had stayed with the *Starbourne*. Everyone else had come to help with the search, but they were now aft in the small salon where they sat drinking various beverages and considering their prisoner.

They had all agreed that the credits must be on the scout ship and that they must find them. What they had not agreed on was what they should do with the last of Radieux's men. Arden had resisted the urge to call for help for Glenn, and her companions had accepted that he was among the dead, without asking details. There was little flap when his body was discovered and the rumor was he had been dead for a while.

"We can leave him here, tied up someplace," Phyilla said, meaning their prisoner. "Where no one would find him for days."

"I think we should just take him with us," Johns said.

"That way we can keep an eye on him. Then turn him over to the law on Glory."

"You're just asking for trouble," Tahr said in his best whiney voice. "I say kill him. That way we can be absolutely sure he won't be a problem."

"Oh?" Rafe said. "Here's a gun." He extended one of the pistols they had confiscated toward his pilot. "Go ahead."

Tahr looked at the gun, muttered something under his breath, and folded his arms across his chest.

"I guess that settles it," Liel said. "We take him with us."

"What about leaving him here?" Johns said. "I think Phyilla is right."

"I don't think we can do that," Arden said. "He might be willing to help us locate the credits later. He might also have some idea of what General Radieux or Don Vey plans to do back on Glory."

"All right," Rafe said. "We don't have time for any more discussion. Or time to search any longer. Once the bridge is cleaned up, we're getting out of here. I don't want to leave any trace of our having been involved in the deaths of these three men."

Everyone nodded, and the discussion turned to getting everything ready for the trip back to Glory.

Radieux rolled the pen between his hands, took a deep breath, and exhaled. This was the kind of waiting he was more accustomed to. Lying in wait, knowing that the enemy would be here sooner or later. Probably sooner in this case. In war, however, he usually had a better idea of timing than this. But he could live with it. He looked forward to this upcoming fight more than any he could remember. It would be a pleasure to show this Grenfell woman what a true warrior was.

How she could have the audacity to think she was equal to a man in any way was a mystery. Even her escape from Baltha was engineered by men.

The comm chimed, and he keyed the speaker.

"General," the captain said. "If the *Starbourne* left as

reported, it should be coming through the jump gate in about fifteen minutes."

"Thank you, Captain. I'll be up there in a moment."

He intended being on the bridge for this fight. He wanted to witness every moment, every nuance of this, the first battle to retake Glory. He did wish that it could be a land battle, though. Face to face and all that. Of course, his seventeen men would make quick work of the smaller civilian force, but it would still be quite satisfying.

He straightened his uniform tunic and traded the pen for a swagger stick. He had seen them in old military pictures and had one made for himself. This was a military operation, and he was leading it as the head of the army of Glory. He had told all his men to put on their uniforms, too. No one had a better right to wear them.

Without a mirror, it was impossible to be sure that everything about him was in its proper place, but he had worn the uniform for so many years that he dressed by rote. The way it felt when he stood and when he walked told him that all was as it should be.

He opened the door of his cabin and walked into the corridor. He could feel the tension in the air even there. His men were ready, eager even, for this fight. Damn, he would love to give them a chance to face the enemy. But not this time. They would get their opportunity on Glory in a very short time.

He stepped through the door, and one of the men called out, "Ten-hut." The five controlling the scout ship jumped to their feet and snapped to attention.

"At ease," Radieux ordered.

They immediately returned to their seats and the controls in front of them.

"How long now, Captain?"

"Eight minutes, sir."

"Are the guns ready?"

They had tested them again earlier in the day. The dealer on Miga might have sold them damaged or defective goods and he wanted to be sure that was not the case. Much of the proceeds from the sale of the arms he had carried in the transport ship had gone for the shells, power packs, and torpedoes for the scout ships.

Regret at losing the other ship returned, but at least he had the satisfaction of knowing that most of the arms they had bought were aboard this ship. It had always been in the back of his mind that the second one might be used as a decoy in this project, and in some ways that had proved to be true. But time was running out. The empress and her minions were getting ready to reactivate some of the ships that had been mothballed after the war ended. The scout ships were supposed to give his side an immediate edge, and planning the assault around the wedding would not only have a detrimental effect on Jessa's supporters, it would teach her husband-to-be a valuable lesson. He must be stopped from having any control over the government of Glory. It was bad enough that a woman sat on the throne.

"Someone's coming through," Little announced from the communications console.

"Looks like they may be a bit early," Radieux said.

Captain Foxhall punched the alert button. Klaxons sounded and red lights flashed. There was no rushing to guns or other battle posts. They had all been at their places for half an hour at least, due to the captain's caution and their own eagerness.

The general concentrated on the forward view screen as the gate dilated for the ship coming through. It had the effect of giving the blackness and the stars beyond a shimmer. Then the ship appeared. It was sideways to them as the scout ship sat off to one side.

"It's the *Starbourne*," Little announced.

Yes, Radieux thought. *Come to meet your fate.*

"Get it over with," he ordered.

"Fire!" Foxhall shouted into the comm.

The plan was to use laser cannon first to try to disable the firing pods at the rear of the ship. He wanted to take them alive if at all possible, but he figured on reducing them to helpless shadows of their former selves first.

As the lasers fired, Foxhall maneuvered the scout ship behind the *Starbourne*. He kept a distance behind, which was wise, because the salvage ship fired some sort of projectile cannon in response. The distance gave the captain maneuvering room, and the projectile missed.

"Captain!" Little shouted. "Something else coming through the gate!"

"What is it?"

The scout ship bucked as something hit it. New alarms sounded.

"We have impact on the tubes," someone shouted.

"Seal it up," the captain ordered in a loud, yet calm voice.

"It's another scout ship," Little said.

"They brought our scout ship," Radieux said too low for anyone to hear.

He had not even considered that Semmes would divide his crew and bring the scout ship. It was within their grasp to recoup that loss. If they could recover the ship without damaging it too much. Semmes and his crew could not know much about military tactics, and they would be stretched pretty thinly between the two ships. Except they did have his ship in a vise of sorts, he realized as the salvage ship turned to face them.

"I don't think we can take both of them, General," Foxhall said.

"You give up too easily."

The ship bucked again and again. They dodged and bobbed, trying to avoid being hit, but every time they dodged a shot from one, they were hit by a shot from the other. All the time they had been firing their own weapons, all of them now in both directions, but the *Starbourne* was faster than expected and both enemy ships kept skipping out of range or dodging shots fired at them, even though barely at times.

"General," the captain shouted. "Our engines are still whole, but they won't be much longer. We have to get out of here!"

Damn! As much as it galled him, the captain was right. He had been outmaneuvered, but not by that damnable woman. This had to be Semmes's doing. He would get even one day. He promised.

"Get us out of here, Captain," he said as calmly as he could. "We'll fight them another day."

As soon as the ship burst through the gate, Rafe saw the other scout ship and ordered the guns fired. With Radieux caught between the two ships, they scored with regularity several times. Then his pilot maneuvered out of range with a sudden burst from the engines.

Tahr was a good pilot in his own right, but he could not match the military expertise of the other pilot. Radieux's ship was soon lost, thanks to the pilot's having gotten a quick jump on them and knowing how to utilize various phenomena to camouflage his ship.

Arden felt particular disappointment at the general's escape, on both a personal and a professional level. Once the fight started, she had hoped to take him here, in the depths of space, where the fight could be more impersonal. She had also hoped to neutralize him before he could be a factor back on Glory. Now, she might have to meet him face to face, in battle. Whether it was their swords that would cross, or their forces that would meet, she could not say. Perhaps both.

The rest of the return trip was a lesson for Arden. They were shorthanded from operating two ships: Liel, Owen, Phyilla, and Johns were aboard the *Starbourne* with the prisoner, while she, Rafe, and Tahr crewed the scout ship. Phyilla transmitted coordinates and other necessary information from their computer, which made it easier. However, it was the first time Arden had an opportunity to learn directly how a ship operates.

Even Tahr needed sleep. Rafe spelled him every four hours, although much of the time there were few operations that needed doing. Still, someone must monitor the dials and other readings.

Because they didn't want to take any chances on getting home alive, their progress was a bit slower. There would still be enough time before the wedding for her to review the security arrangements and make it to the wedding herself, though.

In the first two days, Arden spent what free time she had

searching the ship for the credits. At the end of that time, she was convinced that the credits were not on board the scout ship. Yet that was quite impossible, since there was no other way for the thieves to get them off Miga in the few hours they had possessed them. But what else could explain their absence?

Perhaps those men had had time to sell or trade the credits for something else of value. Something that could be right in front of her all the time without her recognizing it.

She was sitting in the salon at the time, eating her meal alone on the second night. Rafe was asleep and Tahr was on the bridge. She put her fork down and looked around the salon. There was nothing on the walls or furniture of any particular interest. Nor had she noticed anything in any of the other cabins or spaces. Of course, if it had been very noticeable, it would have been discovered by now. Rafe and Tahr were certainly thinking along similar lines.

So where could it be?

In the salon were two small tables, eight chairs, and a counter for preparing meals. There was the hot and cold drink dispenser, the food storage locker, and two refrigerator units, one large and one small.

Two refrigerator units?

The large one would be enough for such a ship as this, with its usual crew of no more than ten and its usually short voyages. So far, the three of them had never opened the smaller one set farther from the counter. She moved to stand in front of it. It was about three feet high and a foot and a half wide. She stooped down and started to open it, but drew her hand back.

It might be booby-trapped. Explosives were something she had little experience with. She felt around the door with fingertips, but detected nothing. Still, it was possible any wires were hidden, possibly even inside the unit.

She ran to Rafe's cabin and threw open the door. It banged against the wall, and Rafe sat straight up in bed.

"What?" he yelled.

"Rafe! I think I may have found the credits."

"Can't it wait until morning?" he said, clearly not awake.

"No. Come on. Wake up."

He had been in bed less than three hours, so it was not surprising that he was groggy and disoriented. She sat on the edge of the bunk and started talking. He did not understand about two refrigerator units. What difference could it possibly make? But as she talked, her theory got through.

"Coffee," he said. "Get me coffee."

Arden led him, dressed only in his underwear, to the salon and drew a cup of coffee. They sat at a table facing the refrigerator unit that had caused her so much excitement. The more she thought about the possibility, the surer she became that it made sense. She told him the line of thought that had brought her to this conclusion. She also described how she had checked the outside for any wires that would indicate a booby trap.

Rafe got himself a second cup of coffee, wanting to wake up as fully as possible before examining it. If there were explosives, he did not want to take any chances.

"There has to be some indication on the outside, some way of disarming the booby trap if there is one," he said. "Otherwise, how could they get inside and retrieve the credits themselves? If we find that there is a bomb . . ."

"What?" she prodded when he did not continue.

"You and Tahr will have to transfer to the *Starbourne*."

"No."

"Arden, if something goes wrong and the bomb goes off, this ship will be severely damaged. The salon is very near the environmental equipment. Near enough that it will most likely be damaged. It won't be safe."

"I'm sure that's all very true, but there is no way you can disarm such a bomb by yourself. Two hands just won't be enough. Tahr can go, but not me."

"I don't want any argument."

"Neither do I." She leaned over and kissed him on the cheek. "I'll go tell Tahr what we may be up against and have him notify Liel. I'm sure they'll want to keep their distance."

Rafe nodded and asked her to bring the tool box from the maintenance locker. On her way to the bridge, it occurred to her that he might lock up the salon and not let her back in, but that would be useless. If there was an explosion, the whole ship was at risk.

She reached the bridge and told Tahr what she suspected about the refrigerator and what Rafe was planning on doing. He agreed to notify the *Starbourne* but not to leave.

"I don't enjoy moving between ships in one of those dinky suits," he said. "I don't trust them."

And that was that. He was talking to Liel as she left the bridge and headed for the maintenance locker.

She breathed a small sigh of relief when she found the salon door still open. Rafe was crouched in front of the refrigerator, running his fingertips along the edge of the door. She shuffled her feet to let him know she was there, then stood quietly and watched as he checked the back edge. He moved slowly, stopping just short of the left corner.

"There you are," he said.

"The wire?"

"Yes." His hand probed a little farther. "Ah." He leaned back and looked up at her. "If we'd just moved it away from the bulkhead to check, it would have blown the bomb inside. A double booby trap."

"So. How do we proceed?"

"Assuming that they didn't have enough time to get real elaborate," he said with a devilish smile, "we disconnect the bomb from its source of power."

"How?"

"Either pull the plug, or cut that wire I just found."

"And if they did have time to get real elaborate?"

"Doing either of those two things will set off our bomb," he said.

"Oh."

"Last chance to abandon ship."

"No. No, I'll stay." She sighed. "Just tell me you have no intentions of committing suicide."

"None whatever."

"Thanks."

"Okay," he said. "Sit down here beside me and open that tool pouch."

She did as he said, and he started pulling out various

instruments. "Do you know what each of these is?" he asked at last. She did. "Hand me what I ask for, then. First, the wire cutters."

Arden handed him the cutters. He rose up on his knees and leaned over the top of the refrigerator. In a moment she heard the wire being cut. When nothing happened, she started breathing again and Rafe exhaled loudly.

He sat back on his heels. "One down."

He felt around the door again. Still finding nothing there, he checked around the latch release, then took hold of it. Slowly, he pushed it down, and the door popped open. He stopped it from opening widely and looked inside.

"Dammit!"

He threw the door wide, reached in with one hand, then hollered in pain.

"What is it?" Arden cried out.

She pushed the door aside so she could see inside. The device sat on the top shelf, a light shining right behind it. An envelope lay on the shelf under it. She would bet anything it held the credit transfer.

"It's light-activated," Rafe said from between gritted teeth.

Two of his fingers were caught in a spring device, and she realized that was all that prevented a connection that would blow them both to hell.

"Get something to shove between the two pieces," he said. "Nothing metal and at least as wide as my fingers."

Blood had begun dripping off his fingers onto the envelope. In an instant, she rejected everything in the tool pouch as unsuitable. Then she remembered the netsuke tied to her belt. It was a piece of ivory carved in the shape of a turtle, so she had been told. She grabbed hold of it and jerked, breaking the velvet ribbon. The figure felt cool in her hand. She reached inside and worked it between the two pieces of metal. She could feel them scraping against the figure's back and belly.

"Good," Rafe said. "Now, pull the two metal bars apart if you can. The spring is very strong."

She grabbed hold of each bar and tried to separate them enough for him to pull free, but they were strong, as he had said. Worse, the edges were serrated. That was what had cut Rafe's fingers and punctured hers in a few small places.

Well, she thought. *That was a test. Now I know how tight they are.*

Suddenly, she remembered the lifeweave square in her pants pocket. She took it out, folded it so that the picture could not be seen and the double layer would be more protective, then used it between her fingers and the serrated edges.

She closed her eyes and concentrated. Oh, so slowly, the bars moved minutely.

"I'm free!" Rafe shouted. "You can let go now."

Arden heard him but could not respond. He grabbed hold of her arms and pulled her away. Still she seemed to be a witness rather than a participant in what was happening. He shook her by the shoulders, and awareness started returning. When she finally saw him before her, his expression was one of deep concern.

"What the hell happened?" he asked.

"I don't know." She felt totally drained of energy. "It was as if I'd taken a drug."

She looked down at her hands resting in her lap. They still clutched the square of lifeweave. She raised her hands and studied the square. Blood stained the picture of Rafe.

"Do you always carry one of those around with you?" he asked.

"Just this one. And now it's ruined." She wondered what he thought about his own picture being on it.

He stood and pulled her to her feet.

"So are my fingers."

"Oh," she said, finally remembering his mangled hand. "I'll get the med kit."

"No, you sit. I'll get it."

He disappeared, and she sat down at one of the tables. She laid the lifeweave square flat in the middle of the table. The bloodstains seemed to have become a part of the colors of the fiber, as if being transformed somehow. The wounds in her own fingers still bled a bit.

Rafe returned with the med kit and started working on

her fingers. He wiped away the blood and daubed the wounds with antiseptic. Then he spread nuskin along each series of wounds.

"There, that should be better," he said.

He started working on his own fingers, but she took over, giving each the same treatment.

"They aren't broken, are they?" she asked. They were very swollen and already beginning to turn slightly purple.

"No, I can bend them. They'll be sore for a while, I'm sure." He leaned back in the chair and closed his eyes. He looked very tired.

"Want some coffee?" she asked.

"Yes, but I'll get it."

He got up and fixed two cups, setting one in front of her. He sat back down, but closed his eyes again for a few minutes.

"That was scary," she said, referring to the bomb. Disabling it had taken only a few minutes, yet it seemed like hours in retrospect.

"The bomb?" Rafe said. "Yes. But not as scary as what happened to you." He sat forward with his elbows on the table. "What was that all about?"

"I don't know. Nothing like that ever happened before."

She slid the square closer so they both could look at it. It was now almost impossible to discern the bloodstains.

"It's in my blood now," she said.

"What does that mean?"

"I don't know. But it can't be good."

After a little more work to ensure that it could be safely moved, and removing the envelope—which did contain the credit transfer—they jettisoned the refrigerator with the bomb inside. After distancing themselves from it, Rafe blew it up with a shot from the projectile cannon. For a moment, a new star blazed in the vacuum of space, then died quickly and silently.

The next few days they settled into a routine. When not working at some task set her by Rafe, Arden spent hours talking with Captain Alvarez on the comm and reviewing data he sent to the ship's computer. She and Rafe tried to eat their meals together, but that was not always possible.

They would have slept in the same cabin, but these were
not conducive to intimacy with their separate, narrow bunks
and small size. Their sleep cycles did not often match, either, but when they did, they would lie together, talking as
often as making love.

In spite of the hectic nature of the shifts on the bridge,
it was the quietest time she had spent in quite a few years.
She could almost see the wounds she had suffered on Baltha finish healing. The one thing she tried not to do was
think about Rafe and their relationship too much.

Once they were back on Glory, his job was done.

16

The seamstress and her three helpers fussed about their work. Two palace maids stood ready to assist them or their mistress whenever needed. Dressed only in elaborate undergarments intended to accent her figure, Jessa stood on a small round platform waiting for the first fitting of the actual wedding gown.

So far, she had been measured, pricked, draped with paper for making a pattern, and clucked over. She had put on a little weight since ascending the throne, and Madame Geneva had scolded her about that, suggesting a diet to "reduce the size" before the final fitting. That was of little import, and as long as she was not fat, Jessa had little intention of worrying about her waistline.

"There we are," Madame Geneva said.

Jessa brought her attention to the tall mirror, wondering at the same time why all seamstresses had pretentious names. And why they always looked like scrawny spinsters with their dark hair pulled back severely into a bun at the nape of the neck. Behind her, three women had hold of the gown and were carrying it toward her. They raised it as high as they could, handing it to Madame, who now stood on a ladder. The spindly woman lifted the bodice over the empress's head while the bulk of the skirt was lifted by the helpers. Jessa raised her arms.

"Yes, my empress," Madame said. "Your arms through there. That's good. Is it comfortable on the shoulders?" Jessa said it was. "That's good. Now we fasten the buttons in back. Spread the skirt out, girls," Madame said with a last tug at the bodice to straighten a seam. "There."

The effect was startling. Her reflection was almost unrecognizable. Her long, black hair was piled on top of her head to keep it out of the way. Her breasts were pushed up and toward the center of her chest to get the maximum cleavage above the very low, square-cut neckline. The long sleeves fit close but did not bind. The long train was being spread out behind her.

The lifeweave shimmered, its colors accentuating the paleness of her skin. From the front, it was very much a sheath dress with a slight split up the front center. However, yards and yards of material spread out on both sides and behind, beginning at the front hemline. A small bustle pushed the train away from her body in a graceful arc.

"Are you satisfied, my empress?" Madame asked.

The puckered mouth showed that the seamstress dreaded the answer, but she need not worry. It had been the right decision to not buy all new lifeweave material for the making of the gown. How many members of the court would realize where it came from?

"Yes, Madame, I am satisfied," Jessa said with a smile.

The older woman smiled in both relief and pleasure. Her work was acceptable and would not have to be undone.

"The veil, my girls, the veil," she urged.

She had been back a day, but the wedding was only six days away, and Arden felt overwhelmed. The scout ship had been turned over to General Hsing and his cohorts, who were actively engaged in reactivating some of the fleet for defensive purposes. It would take time, though, and the well-armed scout ship was most welcome.

The credits had been safely stored in the vault with very little pomp. Alvarez had kept everything for the wedding on schedule, but there were dozens of things that could not be taken care of until the last minute.

Now, she was on her way to see Jessa. The empress had

called her in the day after her return for an in-person report
on events. Putting her uniform on for the meeting had felt
odd, as if she had been gone a long time. Rafe, propped up
on pillows in her bed, had watched her dress with a smile
on his face. She leaned down and kissed him goodbye.

"Tell Jessa hello for me," he called after her.

"I will. Have fun," she called as she went out the door.

She was glad that he had decided to stay for the wedding,
although there would not be much time for just the two of
them. She had been allotted two apartments besides her
own for wedding guests. The smaller one had been refur-
nished to accommodate the crew from the *Starbourne* before they even got back. The larger had been readied for
Abbot Grayson and two monks who were coming with him.
She understood one of those was supposed to be Brother
Bryan, but Grayson could not decide on the other.

She looked forward to telling Bryan the use to which she
had put the netsuke in saving their lives and the scout ship
from the bomb's going off. Once Rafe had disconnected the
detonator, it had been tough work to free the small figure, but
she would not let him jettison the refrigerator and its contents
until it had been replaced with a wad of paper.

Going through messages, she saw that people she hardly
knew had been calling her, asking for rooms in the palace.
Somehow a few had gotten her private comm number. It
had chimed three times during the previous night before
she finally disconnected it. As yet, no one had her official
number except those who were supposed to. She reminded
herself to have the private number changed as she stopped
before the door to Jessa's apartment.

The computer recognized her, the door opened, and the
guard stepped aside. "Her majesty is in the conference
room," he told her. His being there was part of the increased security within the palace. She recognized him as
a longtime member of the guard, but could not quite remember his name.

Arden passed through the sitting room, then went down
the hall and started into the conference room. She stopped
short at the sight before her. The table and most of the
chairs had been removed, and a ladder stood off to one

side. The drapes were open to let in sunlight. Jessa stood
on a small platform in the center of the room, engulfed in
lifeweave. A spidery woman circled around the empress on
bare feet, stepping on the lifeweave while three others stood
poised for action. Two maids stood against the walls on
either side, apprehensive looks on their faces.

Jessa spotted her in the doorway and smiled.

"Arden, come in. I hope you don't mind if we talk while
Madame Geneva does the fitting."

"No," Arden said, unable to say much more. She took
three steps into the room and stopped. Never before had
she been so close to so much lifeweave fabric. It took her
breath away, made her head swim. The cuts on her fingers
throbbed beneath the bandages.

"Do you recognize it?" Jessa asked. "The cloth and
where it came from?"

"No, I don't think . . ."

"It's made from several pieces that my mother wove.
There are land maps and battle plans, star maps and troop
deployments." She fluttered the skirt on one side, and the
cloth rippled almost to the tip of the train. "This is to honor
my mother's memory." She turned back to the cheval mirror placed in front of her and cocked her head. "I wonder
how many will recognize it at the wedding."

Madame Geneva stood back and surveyed her work. "It
is done, your highness."

"Done?" An expression of sadness crossed her face.

"Yes, ma'am."

"Oh."

"Shall we help you out of the gown?"

The three helpers tensed as if to spring.

"Yes, of course." She still stared at her reflection as if
there was nothing of greater interest anywhere.

Two of the helpers carefully pulled the train aside and
moved the ladder close enough for the seamstress to reach
the buttons on the back of the gown. The cloth shimmered
with every touch, every movement of air. Colors flitted at
the edge of vision, and Arden tried to catch them. She could
almost smell them. She wanted to touch them.

"Arden, please wait for me in the sitting room. I'll only be a moment."

The words came through, but their meaning was lost. Were they important?

"Arden?"

Her name, spoken more loudly, brought her to the moment. She looked up at Jessa, realizing that she had moved farther into the room, drawn by the lifeweave.

"Yes, your highness," she mumbled, and turned to leave the room.

Lifeweave tugged at her, wanting her to stay, and she hurried her steps. She had to force herself to stop in the sitting room. Even there, the air was cloying and she still felt dizzy.

How could Jessa bear having that gown on, so much of it touching her skin? It was clearly having an effect on the empress—she had been more than distracted, and having to take it off saddened her.

Arden sat in one of the chairs, taking the weight off legs that were not too steady. It was distressing to realize that it was not just the weaving of lifeweave that had an effect on her. Cloth made from it now had a very strong effect.

"Would you like some tea?" Jessa asked.

Arden jumped to her feet, then had to rest a hand on the chair to steady herself.

"Yes, please," she managed to say.

Jessa gave the order to a maid who had followed her into the sitting room. She wore a dressing gown of silk, but still seemed distracted. She told Arden to return to her seat, then wandered around the room while they waited, seeming not to know exactly where she was, or at least refamiliarizing herself with the room's contents. She touched figures and antique pieces set on the mantle and tables. Smoothed the fabric on the back of her favorite chair. Looked into the cold fireplace as if something was missing.

"I thought lifeweave only had an effect if a person touched it," Arden said. She realized the sentence was from the middle of a conversation she had been having in her head.

"It bothered you in there?" Jessa asked.

"Yes. I thought I could smell it."

Jessa moved around her chair and sat down and leaned forward as if eager to discuss the subject. However, the tea arrived, and they were silent while the maid set the tray on the sideboard, poured, then placed their cups on the table between them. She left the room, but the guard remained near the door.

"Do you really think this gown is a good idea?" Arden asked.

She picked up her cup and took a sip, wondering if she should have asked the question. Jessa had become more and more unpredictable in her reactions the past few months, and the two of them talked as acquaintances less and less often. Sometimes Jessa was friendly; other times she was distant at best. However, her concern about the lifeweave was too real for Arden to ignore. That Jessa did not immediately chastise her seemed to show she might have been wondering the same thing.

"It's important to me," she said. "After the wedding, I will burn the gown and scatter the ashes over her grave. Then maybe I can go on with my own life."

Arden nodded, and they each took a sip of their tea.

"Now," Jessa said. "Let's hear about this latest adventure of yours."

Arden told her everything that had happened. As she talked, her head began to clear.

"The credits are in the vault," she finished.

"And how soon will you and General Hsing start building up the defenses around the city?"

"Within a week or so after the wedding. We hope to simultaneously start building facilities in the countryside. There are enough credits, and that will put a lot of the returned soldiers to work. The work is more important than the fortresses. We need to get these people out of the raiding bands before they get too used to it. Once it becomes ingrained in their lives, they might not want to return to a more normal way of life."

She picked up the cup, but just held it in both hands. The tea was cooling.

"That's true," Jessa said.

"Please be careful about the lifeweave, Jessa."

The empress looked at her, a slight smile on her lips.

"It has never had much effect on me," she said.

"I saw its effect in there." Arden motioned toward the conference room. "You were mesmerized or stupefied by it. There's so much in that gown."

"I know. I can handle it."

She stood, indicating that the interview was over. Arden set the cup down on the table.

"Good work with the lifeweave," Jessa said. "It is a shame that we still have General Radieux to contend with, though."

The words and the tone implied that Arden was to blame. Or was she being too sensitive?

"Yes, it is. But we'll be on the lookout for him."

Jessa paused at the back of her chair.

"Does it really seem logical to you that he and Don Vey will try something during the wedding? Everyone will be alert to anything out of the ordinary."

"That's one of the problems," Arden said. "There will be so many events out of the ordinary that things can slip through. We're going to be stretched pretty thin, too. If they don't try it then, they may try it right after."

She started toward the door, but turned back.

"You're still going to the summer palace for the honeymoon?"

"Yes. It's so much cooler there."

Arden nodded. "Security has been tightened there, too. That's part of what's spreading us so thin."

"Are you not up to the task?" Jessa asked.

The question caught Arden by surprise. In spite of the empress's occasional coolness toward her, her abilities had not been doubted before.

"Yes, ma'am, I am," she said. "However, I do think it's important that you know there are difficulties."

"I know there are, Commander. I also know there always will be."

She moved toward the hall in dismissal. Arden hesitated, then left the apartment and headed for her office in the basement. Lots of work awaited her there, but she thought of none of that. Jessa's behavior held her attention. When Arden went looking for her to bring her back to Glory, the then-princess had resented Arden's intrusion back into her life. She had not even expressed any regrets over the six years her former guard had spent in prison because of her escape.

Their relationship had eventually improved, and they had even been on friendly terms for quite some time. Especially since Jessa became empress, a position she had never sought. Only a sense of duty, maybe even a sense of spite, had convinced her to accept the crown. Arden could understand the spite, herself. They were both women who had been denied opportunities because of their sex.

The one thing she would have to accept after the wedding was that Jessa would probably turn to her husband for advice she now sought from Arden and other advisors. That was as it should be, as long as Jonas Belle had some sense about such things. From what she had heard about him, he was a competent, if pompous, man. That was only to be expected, given his family history. How he had become involved with a woman he thought was only an astronavigator was still a mystery. Even though he was only the second son, and not in line to inherit Weaver or much of the lifeweave fortune, she must still have seemed beneath him.

It could be that the terms of the promise to Pac Terhn were finally coming to an end. Until now, the only hope had been that Jessa might send her away one day. She had seen the future extending ahead along just one track.

Nearing the door to her office, she turned away from such speculations. Time to get back to work.

Dozens of decisions and tasks had to be taken care of. Alvarez had waited for her, and she thanked him once again for what he had accomplished while she was gone. One of the first tasks was to review the list of candidates for additional guard duty during the two weeks of festivities. At the end of that time, the bridal couple would move to the summer palace for the week-long honeymoon. It was a very large complex, and their entourage would include nearly one hundred guardsmen. Some were there already, activating security and watching over the staff that was getting everything else ready.

The bulk of planning for the new security posts had fallen on General Hsing. He had started plans into motion even before the actual sale of the lifeweave so that things could start as soon as the credits were in their possession. Several reports were already on her computer. He had surprised her with his new willingness to cooperate with her, but she was certainly very glad for it.

Also on her computer were surveillance reports on all incoming ships. Neither she nor Hsing doubted for a moment that General Radieux would try to return. Nor did they doubt, given his knowledge of their security, that he could slip through somehow. Hsing had put his most experienced men on that surveillance, and she hoped that might be at least enough to give them some advance warning.

She and Alvarez reviewed guard assignments, made a few changes, then turned to the guest list. The captain had gotten biographies on most of them, made requests for the rest, and listed where each person was quartered in the palace and surrounding hotels. Because of the years of war, most hotels had been closed and some work was ongoing there too, getting them cleaned and reopened.

Many of the guests were bringing small security coteries of their own. That could cause some problems in the area of authority, but everyone would be made to understand that Glorian security had precedence at all times.

When they finished that, it was well past the lunch hour. Arden sent the captain to get something to eat, and she located Rafe. He was on board the *Starbourne* along with most of his crew. She told the computer to comm him there.

"Have you had lunch?" she asked when he came on line.

He looked at his watch and frowned when he saw the time. "No, not yet."

"Well, give everyone a break and come on back here. I'll have something ready in my apartment when you get here."

He agreed and she headed out. This would probably be

her last chance to spend some time with him for a while, and she wanted to take advantage of it.

He appeared at the door shortly after she had the food set out. They sat on the sofa in the sitting room, eating cheese and fruit and bread, all of which were sent to her regularly from the monastery. She opened one of the special bottles of wine—an autumn zinfandel—and beamed at his praise of it. She asked him about his ship, and he described the work he and his crew were doing.

"Nothing serious," he said. "There was a bit of damage from Radieux's attack, and it's the first opportunity we've had to take care of some things since the refurbishment."

"You've kept busy, then."

"Yeah. Space can be a dangerous place. And there's always a war somewhere."

Arden found herself thinking that she could learn to live like that, always on the move, looking for treasure, but cut the thoughts short. Her promise to stay with Jessa made such a thing impossible for the time being, and he had not asked her to go with him. Even though they had talked about the possibility when he was on Glory before, he had never asked her.

"How go the security plans?" he asked.

"Very well," she answered, coming back to the present. "It's an ongoing thing, though. I just wish we had some idea of where Don Vey and his followers are. Rumors have reached the monastery, but nothing concrete. Nothing we can respond to."

"I reckon you'll find them eventually."

"You reckon? That sounds like something Abbot Grayson would say."

"I picked it up from my father. I think."

She chuckled. "Grayson says that such words and phrases always come back into use."

"Probably because of people like him and my father," Rafe said.

"You've never told me about your family," she said.

"Maybe one day I will."

"Yes, one day."

Arden poured a bit more wine for each of them, then started putting everything away.

"Do you have to get back right away?" Rafe asked.

"No, I planned on a long lunch," she said from the kitchen. "It might be my last chance for a while. Do you? Need to get back, I mean."

"No, they don't need me there to supervise right now."

She had everything put away and walked out of the kitchen area. She stood at a distance, looking down at him.

"Come here," he said, holding out his hand.

The day was typical of midsummer in the country. The temperature was warm, birds sang in the trees, and wild-flowers bloomed in the uncultivated fields. In the cultivated fields, monks weeded and picked ripe vegetables and fruits. And the smells . . .

Abbot Grayson strode into the reception room through the open French doors. He was in a very bad mood, and so far all of the monks had recognized that and stayed out of his way.

He hated leaving the monastery for any reason, but now was the worst possible time—because it was the best time to be there. He loved the summer. Just as he loved the winter. And the spring and autumn. Dammit! He just did not like to be anywhere else.

He was getting old, too. Too old to start gallivanting around the country. He would only be leaving because of Arden. Only she could drag him away.

His pace slowed as he thought of his goddaughter. The last time he had talked to her, she had sounded tired, even frustrated. She was coping with so many things to do for this wedding. And she would not admit it, but having Captain Raphael Semmes staying with her was another source of stress. She loved him, that was obvious, but the two of them came from different worlds, in every sense of the term.

He had reached his own rooms, and now he went into the bathroom to clean up for lunch. After that he would have to pack for the trip in the morning. He shook his head as he dried his hands. In the palace, he would be surrounded by so many people. Here, he was surrounded by monks.

Someone knocked on the main door that opened into his study. "Come in," he called, and Brother Farlow entered.

"A man from Mead is here to see you," the monk announced.

"That's the village southwest of here?"

"Yes. He says it's urgent. Something to do with the raiders."

"Where is he?"

"In the reception room."

"Go get Brother Bryan and have him meet me there."

Farlow acknowledged the order, and the two rushed off in different directions. After a lot of raids and other devilment, the raiders had been very quiet for nearly a month. Ever since that night Don Vey had appeared at the gates of the monastery.

Grayson had sent out several parties to various villages to check on rumors. Others had roamed the forest looking for any signs. But Lower Forest was only one-third of an overall forested area that occupied nearly the whole southern half of the continent. There had been signs of large groups moving from one place to another, but the trails always disappeared, sometimes after splitting into several smaller trails.

He had left word in every village that he should be notified if anything was heard or seen. Maybe there was some concrete news at last.

He entered the reception room, and a man sitting in one of the chairs jumped to his feet, holding his hat in both hands. He was dressed in typical clothes for a villager, bobbing his head as if he was overcome by his surroundings. His face was unfamiliar.

"You have news for me?" Grayson asked.

"Yes, sir," the man said. "There has been some large groups moving around our village, sir." He stepped closer in his eagerness. "We've also heard gunfire and heavy explosions. It must be them you was asking for information on."

"Sounds like it. No one has bothered your village?"

"Some men have come into Mead and told us no one

was to leave. It was very hard, sir, but I managed to sneak out last night. I traveled most of the night and all of this morning to get here.''

He came closer, seeming to have forgotten his shyness, his hands fiddling with the hat.

''We were in hopes that they would not miss me. I can't go back 'cause they'll know for sure I was gone.''

''We'll find you somewhere to stay,'' Grayson said, preoccupied now with what the man's information might mean.

If Vey and his forces were in the southwest area of Lower Forest, there was a good chance they were not planning on attacking the palace during the wedding celebration—unless they had lots of vehicles, but there had been not much to indicate that. The scout ship Radieux had bartered for might be fast, but it would not hold a large number of warriors.

The man suddenly lunged at Grayson, a knife in his upraised hand. The abbot raised his left arm, felt a pain just below the elbow. He stumbled backward, cursing himself for being unprepared. The man raised the knife again.

17

Rafe smiled up at her as Arden dressed in her uniform to go back to work. She leaned down and kissed him, and he grabbed her and pulled her down on the bed. She laughed and pulled away from him.

"Careful, you'll wrinkle my clothes," she said, and stood up again. She straightened her tunic. "Aren't we back where we started?"

"How so?"

"I mean this morning. Me getting out of bed, getting ready to go to work. You lying there, watching me . . ."

The comm chimed, interrupting her.

"See there," she called over her shoulder as she started into the sitting room. "You've made me late, and my subordinates are wondering where I am."

She keyed the comm on, using the speaker.

"This is Grenfell," she said.

"Arden, this is Bryan."

He spoke quickly, the words clipped.

"What's wrong?" She picked up the receiver so she could hear better.

"Everything is all right. Mostly. The abbot just wanted me to let you know that he was attacked about an hour ago."

"Attacked? Is he all right? Should I come down there?"

Rafe came into the room, a look of concern on his face.

"No! There's no need to come down. He will be up there tomorrow as planned."

"All right," she said with relief, knowing Bryan would tell her the truth, but still wondering why Grayson had not called himself. "Tell me what happened."

Grayson kept his arm raised to ward off another blow, in spite of the pain. He looked for an opening for a counter-attack.

"Halt!" a voice shouted from behind.

The assailant looked away, giving the abbot the time to recognize Bryan's voice and to strike. His right hand lashed out, palm forward, aiming for the man's nose. If the at-tacker had been taller, the blow would have forced the bones of the nose upward into the brain. As it was, it broke his nose, sending blood flying everywhere.

The man screamed, dropped the knife, and put both hands over his face. Bryan swept the man's legs from under him with his own leg, shouting at the same time for others to come. Monks appeared from everywhere. Two pinned the assailant to the floor while another raced off to find the physician. Bryan immediately took charge of Grayson, helping the abbot into a chair then checking the wound in his arm. Brother Marion appeared, looking from one wounded man to another. Although his wound seemed less threatening, he went to the abbot and began treating the cut.

The assailant writhed on the floor, fighting against the bonds that now secured his wrists behind him. Someone got a cold pack and applied it to the man's nose to stop the flow of blood. All that time, everyone talked at once.

Who was this man? How did he get into the monastery? Someone offered to kill the son of a bitch. The shock of those words silenced everyone, making it clear that they were getting a bit carried away. Brother Farlow looked cha-grined, but Bryan patted his shoulder, and everyone else acted as if the words were spoken by someone who had left the room already.

Grayson smiled, then shouted when Marion gave him a shot that stung.

"Dammit! Be careful!"

Now everyone was looking at him. He felt incredibly foolish, both for the outcry and for letting someone get the better of him right here in the monastery. Marion had finished applying nuskin and was turning his attention to the other patient.

"How is it?" Bryan asked the physician, referring to Grayson's wound.

"He'll be fine. I do wish he would use the other arm as a target once in a while."

He was referring to the wound the abbot had suffered in the same arm nearly two months earlier. Grayson smiled at both of them, then got serious.

"Once his nose is taken care of, find out as much as you can from him," he said to Bryan. "He's clearly not from Mead as he said. He also said that he saw signs of Vey and his people in the area around that village to the southwest. I suspect that means Vey is closer to the capital than that."

His last words were slightly slurred, and he realized that he was getting sleepy.

"What was that shot, Marion?"

"A muscle relaxer. He got you in the suprinator longus," he said, indicating the muscle in the upper arm, "and I want you to relax and not use that arm. You're probably getting sleepy about now."

"Yes, I am, dammit. And I've got too many things to do."

Marion turned back and walked up close to the abbot.

"Abbot Grayson, sir," he said. "You are not as young as you used to be. Healing now takes longer than when you were young. I'm the doctor here, and rest for the next twelve hours is what I prescribe."

He turned away and finally gave his other patient his full attention.

Grayson sputtered for a moment, not sure which was worse: being reminded of his age or being spoken to like that. Deciding that he was too sleepy to worry about either, and not wanting to fall on his face in front of everyone, he

started toward his rooms. Next thing he knew, Bryan and
Farlow were on either side, supporting him as he walked
down the hall.

"And that's why he could not call you himself," Bryan
finished.

Arden smiled at Rafe, who gave the high sign. He went
back into the bedroom to finish dressing.

"Tell him not to worry about getting here tomorrow if
he's too groggy or something. His room will be here for
him whenever he gets here."

"I will."

"Oh, and tell him I won't accept this as an excuse not
to come for the wedding."

"I am sure that will disappoint him." She could hear the
smile in his voice. "But he'll be there sometime tomorrow.
Marion says he should be alert in the morning."

"Good. And thanks for calling me, Bryan."

"You are welcome. See you tomorrow."

They said goodbye, and Arden hung up the receiver. She
stood worrying over what the attack meant.

Vey and his people might be trying to mislead everyone
about where they were. But trying to kill Grayson did not
make sense by itself. In fact, she agreed with the abbot's
assessment that the enemy was probably very close to the
capital. Had they hoped the attack would be enough of a
distraction for her to neglect her duties in the palace?

The comm chimed again. When she answered, Alvarez
was on the other end.

"There's been an attack on a village just south of here,"
he reported.

Was that the plan, then—to keep everyone off balance?

That thought recurred just over an hour later in her office.
A call came from General Hsing's headquarters that another
attack had been made to the northeast. She asked to speak
to the general, but the captain told her he was out inspecting
the city perimeter.

She disconnected and rang his wrist comm. When Hsing
answered, she could hear the strain in his voice and noises

in the background that indicated his vehicle was on the move.

"General, when you get a break can we talk about these attacks?" she asked.

"I should be able to get back to the palace in . . . ummm . . . say an hour."

"I'll see you about then. I'll be here in my office."

He agreed and hung up. She sat with the receiver in her hand for the space of several heartbeats. For a moment she wondered if she was up to this task, then slammed down the receiver, angry at her self-doubts. There was no time for such things, and she reminded herself that she was no longer a little girl, desperately seeking her father's approval.

Alvarez entered the office at that moment, distracting her from such thoughts. Wedding guests from off-world had been arriving for a day and a half. Security assignments had been made some time ago, but they would find that in the coming days, alterations were constantly needed. Those guests already present were not content to stay put very long, nor did they intend to notify anyone of their comings and goings in advance. These were people of wealth and power in their own worlds. Thank goodness most of them were bringing their own security groups with them.

One entire wing of the palace, used sparely in normal times, had been cleaned and aired out. Beds had been made and amenities laid out. The latter included fruit baskets, bottles of wine, and toiletries, where appropriate. Then there were the hotels outside the palace complex.

In the days ahead, in spite of parties and receptions held within the palace complex, many of the guests would insist on exploring night life in the city itself. Arden had almost forgotten there was such a thing. When originally attached to the imperial guard, she had been too busy being a superior warrior to go out. The others went to cafes, bars, theatres, and pleasure houses as often as they could, leaving her cleaning her weapons, studying one manual or another, or practicing in the gym.

Since her return and appointment as commander of the guard, there had been even less time to explore the night

life, although she had been tempted to visit one of the pleasure houses. Somehow, that had not seemed appropriate for
one of her rank, and she had stayed aloof and frustrated.

Perhaps that was why she had yielded so easily to the
temptation of loving Rafe again. Whatever the reason, she
had no regrets. Leave that to the time when he left Glory.

An hour and a half after Alvarez came into the office,
General Hsing appeared. The time had gone quickly and
unnoticed. Alvarez excused himself, and Hsing sat down in
the chair the captain vacated.

"You look tired," Arden observed.

"I am. These random attacks outside the city are just
that. I've called in the troops that have been trying to chase
down the raiders."

"Do you think that's wise?"

He nodded. "They're hit and run," he said. "I got a
report of another one just as I was coming in. I suspect
there are two or three groups out there moving as fast as
they can from one sector to another. With Jessa's intended
arriving in the morning, it's a crucial time and they hope
to distract us."

"Are they using the scout ship?"

"They would have to be to move this fast."

Arden shook her head, accepting that what she had
feared was happening.

"I sure hope we can keep Jonas Belle within the palace
complex while he's here," she said.

She went on to describe the problems with the guests the
guard was already experiencing.

"If he's smart, he'll stay put," the general said. "I do
hear he's pretty haughty, though. And willful."

Arden groaned inwardly. She had heard the same things
about the man who would be the empress's consort. In her
position she would have to deal with him on a daily basis,
a prospect she was not looking forward to. Especially given
Jessa's ever-changing attitude toward her. Things in the
palace could become very unpleasant, though she hoped
they would improve once the pressures of the wedding and
the threat from Don Vey were eliminated.

They discussed the current situation in the countryside

further and agreed they should not try to run down the
raiding parties. Troop presence was being strengthened in
the three cities on the coasts and in existing garrisons scattered about the continent. Hsing planned setting up something resembling a skirmish line around the capital. It was
not intended as a means of stopping any concentrated attack, but as a way to slow such an attack while the main
body of troops within the city could be notified.

The last thing was to finalize the security plans for
Belle's arrival the next morning. Remembering her own
arrival with Jessa and Rafe, under guard, all those months
ago, she suggested they have his ship stop in the same open
area. Any snipers or raiders would have to cross a lot of
open ground to get near him.

She pulled out a map of the port, and after some discussion, Hsing agreed to the landing place. They both knew
that many weapons could be used from a greater distance,
but only so much could be done.

"I guess that's all we can do tonight," he said, and stood
to leave.

"Thanks, General," Arden said. "I'm glad we're able
to work together on this."

He looked at her for a moment, then nodded. "Me, too,"
he said, and left.

She realized that it surprised him even more than it did
her that they were working together so well. She realized
further that she actually liked him, now that most of her
suspicions about him had been put to rest and he was
slowly losing his doubts about her. Not that he still did not
wish she were a man instead.

Alvarez returned and stood in the open doorway.

"You want to take that walkabout now or after dinner?"
he asked.

She looked at the clock on the wall. It was only four
o'clock.

"Let's do it now," she said. "And tell Lieutenant Garson I'll want her with me around ten tonight to make the
same circuit."

"I can do it," Alvarez said.

"I know you can, but she needs to become familiar with

the routine, too. And I want you rested and sharp in the morning when we go to the airport to pick up Belle.''

"Yes, ma'am." He looked as if he would like to argue further, but refrained.

She rose and slipped the sword belt over her head. Alvarez wore a sidearm and his own government-issue sword. She doubted that the enemy would have much use for the niceties of fighting with swords, and wondered one more time how many guns they had been able to get their hands on. Thank goodness they had lost some on Miga.

The midmorning sky was bright blue, and somewhere in the distance, birds sang. The surrounding fields were aglow with wildflowers, blooming as if wanting to participate in the festivities.

Belle's personal ship had landed and taxied to a stop in the most open area of the port. There had been some argument, but he and his captain had been convinced at last that it was the safest thing for him to do.

Talking Jessa into staying at the palace had been more difficult. She had wanted to greet him as he left the ship, the sooner the better. But Arden and General Hsing talked her into greeting him as he arrived at the palace instead, convincing her that she might be endangering her fiancé's life at the port. The longer he stays out in the open, the longer he could be a target for some assassin, they told her. Reluctantly, she accepted that, urging them to hurry back.

Not many besides Jessa had any real idea what the man looked like. If she had a picture, she had never shown it around. Arden had a photo, of course, that came with the profile, but it had been taken from a distance. He stepped out onto the ramp that had been pushed quickly into place. The bright sun blinded him, and he paused to let his eyes adjust. He started down the ramp at last.

Arden's heart thumped hard in her chest. Jonas Belle looked so much like Jessa's brother that it was uncanny. Oh, there were distinct differences, and she ticked them off in her mind: Jonas was dark, where Waran Parcq had been very fair. The prince had been tall and slender like a dancer, and the fiancé was shorter and muscular, as if he worked out regularly.

Given those very basic features, it was difficult to artic-ulate the similarities, but they were there. The haughtiness of expression. The self-confident way in which he moved. The slight smile, as if there were a joke only he heard. And the eyes. Most of all the eyes. They were the same blue color, the same look, the same shape. She knew all over again why she had been attracted to Waran.

She and General Hsing moved foward to greet the soon-to-be consort. He behaved pleasantly enough, allowing them to escort him to the waiting enclosed limousine. He climbed in first, settled into his seat, and the two escorts climbed in to sit opposite him. His own personal retinue, including five obvious bodyguards, climbed into another limousine that followed closely behind.

Jonas asked questions about the arrangements for the wedding, how Jessa was holding up, and what other plans might have been made relative to him. He had received an itinerary from Jessa's secretary, which he glanced at on the hand comm screen. Arden and the general had practically memorized it, and they were able to follow his recitation. Nothing had changed since the last transmission to him.

Their route had been blocked out, and they arrived at the palace in record time. The limousine pulled up in front of the main entrance. At that moment, the empress walked through the door and started down the steps. Arden and Hsing got out and stood on either side of the car door. The other vehicle disgorged its complement of bodyguards, who flanked them. Jonas moved to the bottom of the stairway, looking up at his beloved. He held out his hand as Jessa neared, and she took it. Her cheeks were flushed, her breathing was fast, and she could not smile any more broadly. This was a woman not just in love; she was ob-sessed with this man, and that was something that had never been made clear by her actions before.

Jonas very gallantly bowed and kissed her hand. At that moment, Arden knew he was not in love.

18

The hour was late when Arden returned to her apartment. She was too tired to even check the time. Rafe had left a light on in the sitting room for her, and she tiptoed around trying not to waken him. In the kitchen she poured a glass of wine, then went back into the sitting room and sat on the sofa. She pulled off her boots and curled her feet under her, took another sip, then took off the belt of her tunic.

She sighed as she stretched out, then curled around one of the large pillows. Gods, she was tired, but sleep would not come any time soon. Too many problems and possible problems rolled around in her head. More than anything, she wished she could know when Vey planned to attack the capital. She had no doubt that he would eventually.

She heard a soft tread and looked up to see Rafe coming into the sitting room. He smiled at her as he approached, and bent down to kiss her. He moved to the other end of the sofa, lifted her feet, sat down, and put her feet on his lap.

"So what were you so thoughtful about?" he asked.

"Oh . . ."

"I know," he interrupted.

He took a drink of her wine and handed back the glass. She wiggled her toes, and he started rubbing her right foot.

''Now that's a sure sign that we know each other too well,'' she said.

He smiled and nodded, but kept rubbing her feet, first right, then left.

''I'm sorry if I woke you,'' Arden said.

''You didn't. I hadn't been able to get to sleep yet.''

''Mmmm, sorry.''

Between the wine and his ministrations, she was starting to relax. He asked questions about security arrangements for Jason Belle's arrival and what he seemed like. She drifted from that to her frustration at not knowing what Don Vey might be planning or when he might be planning to do it.

''Don't you think where might be a good question, too?'' Rafe asked.

''Well, here, of course.''

''Not necessarily. You're assuming, first, that he plans to attack during the wedding festivities, while all of these visitors are here. That doesn't really make sense, does it? Your forces are going to be at full strength and completely alert. I'd think he might wait until after the festivities, when everyone is tired and your forces are divided.''

''Divided?''

''Between here and the summer palace in the mountains.''

''How did you know . . .''

''Everyone in the palace complex knows they're going to honeymoon there, and half the people at the port. It's not a well-kept secret.''

''Of course it wouldn't be,'' Arden said, and sat up. ''Just too many arrangements to be made.'' Rafe stopped rubbing her feet, and she wiggled her toes again. He smiled and resumed. ''With all the flights in and out of there, it's a wonder everyone doesn't know.''

''You can be sure Vey knows.''

''Yes, I'm sure he must.''

''If he has enough soldiers behind him, he might attack both places, especially if he thinks your forces are divided enough.''

''Damn!'' Arden said, and sat up. She swung her feet to

the floor. "There's no time to enlist more soldiers, either. We will be divided, as you say, especially if we prepare for the possibility of a dual attack."

She stood and started pacing.

"One of the problems is the amount of time we need to screen people before bringing them into the palace guard or the home guard. We're not even sure the new ones we have are totally loyal."

She sat down and faced him.

"We could bring a large troop from Baltha. It would take them two days to get here altogether. Then they'd need one more day to rest up, and off they go to the summer palace. It wouldn't be very tough for them to work with the soldiers already there to make sure it's secure while they wait for the wedding party to arrive. By the time that happens, everyone should be completely alert."

"And you feel pretty confident about their loyalty," Rafe said. He was lounging back into the corner of the sofa, his eyes looking into hers.

"Yes. They had their chance with Radieux if they were going to rebel."

"One question," he said. "Are you that sure the armory won't be attacked? Radieux lost his opportunity to get a large supply of guns on Miga. Might he not aim for those instead?"

"First you say the summer palace. Now Baltha. Make up your mind."

She jumped to her feet again and started pacing. Finally throwing up her hands, she sat back down. If she was not so tired, it would be easier to think calmly. At the moment her mind was having difficulty sorting everything.

"It could be any of the three possibilities, I would think," he said. "Talk it over with Hsing in the morning. You need some sleep right now."

"You're right. But I don't know if I can sleep."

"I'll help," he said, and leered at her.

"Sure you will."

She smiled back and leaned over to kiss him. When they parted, he took her by the hand and led her into the bedroom. As he helped her undress, she thought of the half-

full glass of wine sitting on the little table where she had
set it, but decided not to get it.

Rafe kissed her tenderly, made her lie down on the bed
on her stomach, and started rubbing her back. In spite of
the torrent of questions their discussion had brought to
mind, she was asleep in a few minutes.

Pac Terhn came to her dreams that night. He taunted her,
laughing at her inability to cope with the problems at hand.
She argued with him, citing her strengths and the strengths
of the people she worked with. He laughed until tears came
to his eyes, and she jerked awake to escape.

Her guide's appearance in her dreams was a new devel-
opment. Was it her subconscious trying to tell her where
to look for answers? Or was her bloodstream so full of
lifeweave now that she need not weave to slip into his
realm? The fact that the lifeweave in her bloodstream made
her react even to woven cloth certainly indicated greater
susceptibility. Whichever it was, her questions could be answered there.

Arden slipped out of bed and saw that the time was only
five in the morning. She had been asleep all of two hours
and would have gotten up in an hour or so anyway.

She grabbed up her clothes and carried them into the
sitting room. She dressed quickly, grabbed the cloth bag
from its hiding place, and slipped into the hall. The elevator
took her up one floor, where she moved quietly through a
matching hallway. Farther down than her own apartment
just below, she knocked on a door. It opened more quickly
than she expected.

"Well, daughter, you've come to welcome me at last."

Brothers Bryan and Farlow slept quietly in one bedroom.
The second bedroom was the abbot's, but he had not been
to bed. When Arden apologized for having caused his
sleeplessness, Grayson hastened to explain that he had trouble sleeping these days and she was not the cause this time.

"Although I was a bit concerned that you didn't come
by," he added. "I knew you were going to be very busy
for the foreseeable future, but felt sure that you would come
as soon as you could."

"Well, here I am," she said, shrugging her shoulders and smiling. "I have to confess that there's a reason for my being here, though."

Grayson smiled broadly. "If you think that comes as a surprise, you have another think coming." His smile faded. "And I think the reason will not come as a surprise either."

Arden pulled the pouch from her tunic pocket. The abbot frowned and nodded.

"I must have some idea of where Vey will strike, or at least what his main target will be."

"And this is the only way?"

"Yes."

She went on to explain that there were three likely targets: the armory on Baltha, the palace complex in the capital, and the summer palace in the northern mountains.

"It's possible that he has enough soldiers to attack two of the three, but not all three," she said. "I feel sure about that. The scout ship he traded for on Miga makes the armory possible. If we had managed to prevent his dealing there, or disabled the ship when he attacked us on the return trip, there would only be two options. For now, we think he's using the scout to move small raiding groups around the countryside."

"Don't get bogged down in 'ifs.' You know the current situation, and you must deal with what exists."

"Yes, I know." Arden looked down at the pouch. "I don't want to do this alone. Not after what happened."

"What happened?"

His brows arched upward, and she realized that she had not yet told him about the lifeweave getting into her bloodstream. She told him quickly, and he expressed graver doubts about her using it now.

"I have no choice," she said.

They discussed the situation, even though he knew all along there were no other options. He agreed reluctantly to oversee her trek into the other world. Arden emptied the contents of the pouch into her lap, picked up the hand loom, and began.

• • •

Fire raced through her body. Sweat stood out on every inch of her skin.

"It burns!" she cried.

She struggled against arms that held her from behind. She could scarcely breathe from the heat and the tightness of that hold. She screamed and fought harder.

"Easy now," a familiar voice whispered in her ear. "Mustn't injure yourself."

She kicked backward without impacting on anything, as if Pac Terhn were mere smoke himself. She panted until her mouth became too dry, swallowed, and panted more. Her hair was completely wet.

"Please make it stop," she whimpered.

"Yes," Pac Terhn whispered. "What will you give?"

"Anything. Please. It burns."

He loosened his hold slightly, but her breathing came only slightly easier. Somewhere in the distance, someone kept calling her name. The fire within was the same throughout her body, along her limbs, inside her head, as if she were going to spontaneously combust.

"Lie down," Pac Terhn said.

He supported her as she lowered herself to the ground. She tried to open her eyes to see him but they burned and teared so badly she could not. Suddenly, cold water was thrown over her. She screamed at the extreme shock. A sizzling sound rose from her body, like that from a piece of hot metal plunged into cold water. She imagined steam rising from her. It helped some. The fire within cooled, but not to a normal level.

"You said you would give anything," he said from above her.

"I'm still burning up."

"Not my problem. I cooled you off. You can at least breathe now."

"Yes, I can." Arden was still panting. "So what do you want?"

"Jessa."

"How do you mean?"

"Her and lifeweave," he said. He squatted down beside

her. "The wedding dress is bringing her to us, but she may give it up afterward. We want to keep her."

"We?"

He smiled but said nothing. However, she sensed that Jessa's mother was part of this. It was she who had helped find Jessa after she was kidnapped by the feminist/peace group who wanted to place her on the throne. She had also sent the message to the princess that convinced her she could, and should, accept the crown. Were Lyona and Pac Terhn working together to protect Jessa, or were they working against her? Whichever was the case, it was clear they intended to influence dynastic events on Glory.

"Is that why you wanted me to stay with her? And why you wanted me to use lifeweave more often? So I could help bring her to you?" She sat up, realizing how weak she was from the fever.

"Of course."

"I can't do that. I don't want her to end up like her mother." The heat inside was building up again.

"Appolyona was an extremely satisfied woman—until the lifeweave ran out. And she did not die young."

Arden wondered why they wanted the empress and not her. Not that she wasn't glad of that, since she herself was more vulnerable than ever.

"I can't," she said. "It's a decision she must make on her own."

"Then I cannot help you."

Arden lowered her head, fighting against dizziness. He started to turn away, then paused.

"Everything that has happened led us to this moment," he said, sounding more serious than she had ever heard him. "Saving Glory and Jessa depends on her being insulated from events to come."

Suddenly, she knew what they hoped to do. "You want to protect her from her husband?" He smiled. "What do I get if I agree to help you?" she asked.

"Information about Don Vey's plans of attack: where, when, even the size of his forces. Everything."

"You never tell me everything."

"That's true. However, I will tell you something about everything. Perhaps you can deduce the rest."

"I suppose that will have to do," she said.

The fire within her body was mounting, and it was difficult to think. Difficult to breathe. Again she heard a voice calling her name from a great distance.

Not yet. Not yet, she thought. *I must be sure I get what I need, as much as I can. Am I weaving, back in that other world? Will the picture in the square be of help?*

"Well?" Pac Terhn asked.

"Was this always your plan?" she asked, gasping now. "Did you always intend drawing Jessa under your influence?"

"We knew she was born with the same talents as her mother. She just had to want it."

"And the lifeweave in the wedding dress—that's your entrance into her life?" He nodded. "How did you make her want to do that?"

"We didn't. She had to want it herself. Anger over her mother's death was nearly enough. Yearning for her beloved Jonas Belle pushed her along."

"But she only wears it. She doesn't weave it."

"Her mother's blood is in those pieces. Her soul, if you will."

He paused and offered her a drink of water from a cup that appeared in his hand. She took it gratefully. The water was cool in her throat. It helped lessen the heat overall and the dizziness that made her want to lie back down.

"Then you should have no trouble in keeping her tied to the lifeweave," she said when she had drained every drop from the cup. "You don't need my help."

"We may not. We just don't want to take any chances."

"Is Lyona in on this?"

He smiled. "She is here" was all he would say.

"All right," Arden said. "I will help you."

Surely her own mother would not cause Jessa harm. And maybe this would be the answer to both of their problems.

"Good," Pac Terhn said, and her body rose from the ground.

The distant voice called her name over and over, coming nearer and nearer. She opened her eyes to find Grayson's face right above her own.

"At last!" he said. "Are you all right?"

"I think so," she said.

"Here." He helped her sit up and handed her a glass of water. "You have been burning up. And you cried out so loudly that the others woke up and rushed in to see what was wrong. We were afraid we were going to lose you this time."

She emptied the glass and relaxed against his arm.

"I had the same fear," she said. "I was sure Pac Terhn was going to let me burn up."

He touched her forehead, her cheek, and her hand in turn.

"Well, you've cooled down considerably," the abbot said. "Did you get what you needed?"

He held up the hand loom with a completed square still attached. At least she did weave one. How much help it might be she did not yet know. Arden remembered the argument with Pac Terhn, but nothing of what he had shown her.

"What's in the picture?" she asked.

Grayson turned it so she could see the square. At first, she could see nothing. He tipped it a little from side to side, the movement making the colors shimmer even in the dim light. There it was—or there they were. A picture of the palace complex in the foreground, with the summer palace to the right behind it, and the arsenal to the left behind it.

That could not be. She could not believe that Vey and Radieux had enough soldiers to attack all three places. Unless one attack was a feint, like the attacks that had been occurring around the countryside.

She looked at the picture again. The most prominent of the three places was the palace complex. Did that mean it was the least likely to receive a full attack? Or that the main attack would come there, while the other two would be feints?

One way to eliminate part of the problem would be to simply blow up what was left of the armory. No one would have access to those arms then, and the troops there could be brought home to guard and protect both palaces and the empress. However, neither Hsing nor any of the other army leaders would agree to destroying so much materiel. And there certainly wasn't enough time to ship the weapons somewhere else.

It had occurred to her several times to ask Jessa to stay in the palace until the threat had passed, but that could be months, maybe even a year or more. No way would she agree to that.

Arden realized that she had just been sitting there thinking while Grayson waited patiently. It must be near midmorning, and she needed to get to her office. She looked at her watch, and was surprised to find that only an hour had passed. She stood, and the abbot stood beside her. He handed her the hand loom, and she slipped it into the bag.

"Thanks," she said, and gave him a hug.

"You're welcome. Let me know if I can be of any further help."

"I will."

They parted, and she turned to leave. She waved goodbye at the door, shut it, and headed for the elevator.

She and Hsing needed to commit to a plan of defense and stick to it until events dictated otherwise. The armory would probably have to stand on its own with the forces already there. Of the three sites, it was the most easily defended. The elevator door opened, and she stepped in.

Five days until the wedding. That was the height of events, and anything subsequent would be downhill. It might be dangerous to think that way, though.

She got out of the elevator when it reached the basement and headed for her office. Once there she called General Hsing, but had to leave a message for him. She described in detail the possibilities of a three-pronged attack and some suggestions on what they should consider doing to counter them. The rest of the morning she read through reports, made changes in assignments as necessary, and toured the palace complex twice with Alvarez.

The guests were proving as difficult as expected. Her inclination was to leave them on their own when they went into town or traveled elsewhere, but the big danger was the

possibility of their being kidnapped. They must not allow
Vey that kind of trump card to use against them.

She ate lunch at her desk, talking to Rafe by comm. He
was back at the *Starbourne*. Afterward, she prepared to
meet with Jessa and Hsing. Full Council meetings had been
suspended until after the honeymoon, although each coun-
cilor was submitting reports to the empress through her
secretary.

When Arden came face to face with Jessa in her sitting
room, she wondered how much attention the empress was
paying to the reports or any other matters. Her manner was
distracted, she fidgeted constantly, and her face was very
pale. That probably was not unusual behavior for a woman
soon to be married, but the lifeweave wedding dress kept
coming to mind.

The general tried several times to discuss the security
situation and the decisions that needed to be made, but
Jessa showed no interest at all.

"I've hardly seen Jonas since he arrived," she said suddenly. "Apparently that is the custom on Weaver."

Was that the source of her distractedness rather than the
lifeweave?

"I had looked forward to spending time together," Jessa
continued. "I've missed him so much."

"There is the prenuptial party tonight," Arden said.

"And what if his traditions don't allow him to be there?"

"He'll just have to follow our traditions for a change.
The wedding is taking place here and not on Weaver, your
highness. And I believe it's usually the traditions of the
bride's world that are followed anyway."

Hsing nodded agreement.

"Insist on your own traditions being honored," Arden
said. "You are the bride, after all!"

Jessa perked up at that.

"I will. And I am the empress." She smiled, and even
her complexion got a bit rosier. "You will both be at the
party tonight?"

"Yes, ma'am," they answered almost in unison.

"Good." Jessa stood. "Oh, and do what you think best
regarding the troop placements. However, I do want a

strong force nearby at all times. Nothing is to happen to spoil my wedding, or my honeymoon.''

Hsing bowed and Arden nodded as their empress left the room. They immediately went out into the hall.

''I wonder what that last bit meant,'' Hsing said.

''For one thing, I suppose it meant that she was listening, at least halfway.''

''I suppose.''

They started toward Arden's office.

''Is this distraction common for a bride?'' Hsing asked.

''I suppose.''

''Could it be the lifeweave? I've heard about her gown.''

''That's possible, too. And that's what scares me. Whatever is the cause, the outcome may be her subervience to Belle. How do you feel about taking orders from him?''

Hsing shook his head. ''I don't think I'd like that very much.''

They had reached her office where they settled in to spend the afternoon debating troop dispositions. Around five, they ordered sandwiches and she called Rafe, finding him in her apartment. She told him she would meet him there in another hour and they would go to the party together, even though she would be on duty.

''I like your idea about possibly blowing up the armory,'' Hsing said around a mouthful of food when she hung up the receiver. ''With some modifications,'' he said hurriedly.

''Oh?'' She could not hide her surprise.

''We can have the soldiers there ready the underground facility so they can get down there at a moment's notice,'' he said. ''Those explosives that were placed around were disarmed but not removed. Right?''

Arden nodded. ''There wasn't enough time.''

''We rearm those bombs so they can be set off. If Radieux or whoever attacks the armory with a force large enough to capture it, our men set off the explosives, destroy the arms, and wait it out below ground.''

She pondered his proposal a moment. ''That would make it easier to bring some of our forces back here for duty at the summer palace.''

"Well, I don't know about that."

"The number of soldiers at the armory right now could be overrun by how large a force?"

"It would take a pretty big one to get through those defenses," Hsing said.

"But if we're willing to write it off . . ." She leaned forward in her chair.

"I didn't say we were going to write it off."

She sat back, trying to relax. "We would rather lose it than let it fall into Vey's and Radieux's hands, right?" He nodded. "We cannot afford to send any reinforcements to Baltha, correct?" He nodded again. "Think about it to-night. Let's talk about it in the morning. We'll need to start moving the troops right away if we decide to go that route."

"All right." He looked at his watch. "I need to go so I can get ready for the party."

It was only five-thirty, but Hsing's headquarters were not in the palace complex and he would need time to get there and back. They exchanged goodbyes, and he left. With half an hour left before Rafe expected her, Arden tried to do another bit of paperwork. It was impossible to concentrate, though, and she gave it up. Grabbing the bag she had thrown in the desk drawer earlier, she headed upstairs.

When she walked in, the sitting room was empty. Sounds came from the bedroom, where Rafe must be getting ready. Arden went into the kitchen and poured herself a glass of wine, then went back into the sitting room and sat down on the sofa. She listened to Rafe, enjoying his presence, thinking how empty the place would feel once he was gone.

Another feeling crept in, unnoticed at first, but it grew stronger, demanding her attention. She took another swal-low of the wine, wanting to ignore this new presence. *No, old presence*, she thought. It had been here before her. Why was it coming back now?

There had been a hint of it during the argument with Pac Terhn, as if it were an additional threat. She remembered the room the first time she had seen it, with the old loom taking up most of the space, darkened by heavy drapes at the windows. The room was smaller now, part of the space having been taken by the kitchen that had been added for her.

She felt herself drawn to the hand loom and lifeweave in the bag lying beside her. She felt compelled to pick them up, to feel the lifeweave between her fingers. The memory of the fire that had engulfed her earlier came back, and she pushed the bag to the other end of the sofa.

The room was darkening with the setting of the sun, suddenly seeming ominous in the gloom. Light would drive away the fear that flickered in her mind. Fear brought by Lyona, whose presence had returned to her rooms.

Arden turned on the lights with the control panel on the table beside her. That was better.

"Arden?" Rafe called from the bedroom.

In a moment he appeared, half dressed, smiling. He came close, then stopped.

"What's wrong?"

She looked up and smiled, wanting to bring the smile back to his face.

"Nothing," she said. "I'm tired and I think maybe imagining things."

"These rooms bringing back memories?"

"Yes, in a way. Sometimes Lyona is still here."

"Have you been using the lifeweave again?"

This was one of those times when his powers of perception surprised her.

"Yes, just this morning."

"It's drawing you in tighter and tighter," he said, concern in his voice.

"There are times when I need it," she said, then added hurriedly, "not because I'm addicted to it. I'm not trained for the kinds of things I need to do in this position. I'm a warrior, not an administrator or a planner. I have no head for strategy, per se, for guessing the next step someone else will take. And Jessa is so very vulnerable right now. Maybe she will never be secure on the throne, but she will never be as insecure as she is right now."

"I know," he said. He sat down beside her and took her

left hand in both of his. "I know that you're pledged to her, to protect her and her government. But you can't do that if you aren't strong enough."

"That's true."

"Promise me you will stay away from that stuff for a while at least. You're under a strain right now, and that makes you vulnerable."

She patted his hand with her free one and kissed him on the cheek. "I will be careful," she said.

He frowned. That was not what he had asked of her.

"I promise," she said.

He sighed, then smiled at her.

"Come on, you need to get dressed." He stood up, pulling her to her feet. "I don't have much in the way of dress suits. I've been trying on everything I have, and I think this suit will probably have to do."

She led him into the bedroom. "Let's see the whole thing," she said.

He put on the shirt and jacket, and she pretended to appraise the effect. Actually, his clothes always fit him well and were quite handsome. Even in the grey dress suit, he looked somewhat casual. It was just his manner, and she loved it, because it was part of his self-confidence. In spite of his nervousness over his appearance for this occasion, in most ways he did not care how others perceived him.

"You look beautiful," she told him, and started undressing. He stuck out his tongue at her, and she laughed. "Are the others coming?"

She had made sure that the whole crew of the *Starbourne* was invited.

"I don't think so," he answered as he put on his shoes. "They had better excuses than I did."

She stuck her tongue out at him. He jumped to his feet, grabbed her, and kissed her. She pushed him away, laughing, and finished undressing.

"I have to take a shower and get dressed," she said. "You'll make us late."

"But for a very good reason," he said. "Besides, you should have told me you were going to shower. I could have joined you."

"Well you're all dressed now."

"I can get undressed and . . ."

"No, you don't. We get in that shower together, and we'll be forever getting ready. Just bring my glass of wine."

She showered quickly and ended up having to banish Rafe to the living room. As she dressed, she finished off the glass of wine. She had decided to wear her dress uniform, since she was on duty. Most of the military types would probably do the same. It was maroon too, but stiffer and with gold braid around the standing collar and cuffs. The insignia of her rank of commander was part of that braid. A hat went with it, but she almost never wore hats, finding them attractive but uncomfortable to wear. It was one of the few privileges she insisted on due to her rank.

Rafe whistled when she went into the sitting room. "Now I know you're a soldier," he said with a wide grin.

She kissed him lightly, sat on the sofa, and pulled on the dark grey boots. A glance at her watch told her she had to leave.

"Do you want to go with me now?" she asked. "I have to check that all of our men are in place before the guests begin arriving."

"Sure," he said. "Will you be in the receiving line?"

"No, there won't be one, thank goodness."

"Good. Let me know if I can be of any help during the night. Should I take my sword?"

"No, that would not be a good idea," she said as she settled her own katana in place across her back. "Only the guardsmen are supposed to be armed, but I'll show you where extra weapons have been stashed."

"All right."

They smiled at one another and started down to the second floor, where the Sunset Ballroom was. Captain Alvarez met them as they walked in. A chamber orchestra played classical terran music from a dais at the right.

"Where in the world did they get those instruments?" Rafe asked softly. "I learned to play some of those."

"Which ones?" Arden asked.

"The piano. And the bass." He had to tell her which

was the bass. "You still see pianos sometimes, but not that kind of bass. It's wonderful."

She took his hand and led him back to their tour. Round tables were set up around the room with a long table near the wall across from the main doorway. That was where Jessa and Jonas Belle and members of their families would sit. These included Jessa's maternal aunt and paternal great-aunt. Belle had invited several relatives with him, including a younger brother and assorted aunts and uncles.

The tables were set with the best china, crystal, and silver the imperial family owned. Small but beautiful floral bouquets were placed as centerpieces. Garlands of flowers were draped across the front of the main table, around the walls, and from the three crystal chandeliers. Their scent was strong and sweet, and Arden wondered if it might become too heavy to bear later in the evening.

"The staff is ready for your inspection," Alvarez said.

Arden nodded and followed as the captain led the way into the pantry. Rafe followed close behind. The waiters who would serve the food were grouped together, being actual palace staff. She scanned their faces as she walked along their ranks, greeting some by name. They stood stiffly, self-conscious because of her scrutiny and the work that lay ahead of them. She recognized every face and moved on to the other group of waiters.

These had been recruited from the ranks of the imperial guard and trained extensively in carrying trays of drinks and being attentive to the needs of the partygoers. Most of them would spend the evening standing against walls in the ballroom, watching and waiting, ready to pour a glass of water or fight with one of the swords that had been stashed away.

After inspecting the waiters, Alvarez led the way into the kitchen, where there was a flurry of activity. Chefs shouted, cooks sped from one work station to another, and pots and pans banged as part of the general background noise always found in a large kitchen. The smells made Arden's mouth water. The three visitors walked the aisles between stoves and counters, trying to stay out of the way as best they could. Here the faces were not quite as familiar, but not one was that of a stranger, since she had made it a point to meet every one of them early on.

She spoke to only a few, not wanting to interrupt their concentration any more than she had already. Overall, they managed to ignore her and her escort.

In the corners and the other few places that were out of the way, guardsmen stood watching. These were armed with both rifles and swords. They had orders not to leave their posts until relieved by replacements; the rotation was planned for every half hour.

Arden checked her watch. Time to be in the ballroom. She led Rafe off to one side while Alvarez started his rounds.

"See this panel?" she said, pointing at the nearest one in the wall. Rafe nodded.

The walls had chair rails three feet up from the floor. Below the chair rails, the walls were divided by trim into panels. Some of the panels had decorative rosettes in the center, some had fleur-de-lis decorations, and others were plain. The one she indicated bore a rosette.

"Press the center of the rosette," she instructed.

He did, and after a click, the panel sprung outward. He grabbed the edge and pulled it wider. Inside were shelves, some bearing swords, some bearing rifles.

"We hope that if there is an attack, they will be using swords," she explained. "We certainly don't want any civilians hit, and I don't think they do either. If they do use only swords, we will do likewise. But we can't fight guns with swords."

Rafe nodded.

"Are there arms behind every panel?" he asked.

"No, only the center ones with rosettes in the wall opposite and this one." Across the way she noticed that General Hsing had arrived and was making his own inspection. She turned back to Rafe and indicated the nearest table. "That's where you and I will be seated. If something happens, arm yourself as quickly as you can. Hand out the weapons to the waiters, too, if you get there first."

He did not need to ask where she would be. With her

own sword at hand, she would be one of the first in the thick of it.

A detail of ten guardsmen entered the ballroom, lining up on either side of the entry. Almost immediately, guests began arriving in a dazzling array of costumes and jewels. Everyone was supposed to be there by seven or shortly after, ready to greet the happy couple at seven-thirty.

"We're on," Arden said, straightening her tunic.

"Shall I just mingle?" Rafe asked.

"Yes, please. Keep an eye out for anything that looks suspicious, but don't try to handle it yourself. Find me or Alvarez or Hsing if you can. If you can't, look for one of the uniformed guards."

"Yes, ma'am."

She looked from the cluster of guests to him, and he smiled mischievously. "Behave yourself," she said, and poked him in the ribs. He grabbed at his ribs and grunted, feigning pain.

"Yes, ma'am." They smiled at each other. "Good luck to us," he said, and winked. She winked back and moved off.

Guests arrived continuously. Arden greeted those she knew and nodded to those she did not. She stood and talked with Abbot Grayson and the two brothers for a time. Their table was near the center of the room, but she told them where the weapons were hidden, just in case. Even the abbot was in a festive mood, and the noise level rose rapidly in spite of the acoustic dampening features of the room.

The waiters began circulating with trays of drinks: alcoholic, nonalcoholic, fancy, and plain. Many of the revelers would be drunk before the night was over. She remembered the Calderan brandy she had grown to like even in the short time she was on Caldera and wondered if there might be any. Not that it mattered. She could not drink anything tonight.

At exactly seven-thirty, trumpets sounded. Everyone grew quiet, and a path was cleared from the door to the center of the ballroom. In the hush, the swish of a skirt and the tap of several feet were clearly heard. The orchestra waited with instruments poised.

With another trumpet flourish, the empress appeared with
Belle on her right. They were followed by family members
and a few of the most important guests. Everyone was ex-
travagantly dressed, but Jessa stood out. Her black hair
hung loose to her waist, contrasting sharply with the silver
lamé dress. Like the wedding dress, the bodice was low-
cut, accentuating her breasts, but the train was shorter. It
shimmered with each step, each breath, she took. The jew-
elry she wore was all silver with onyx and jet stones. Her
smile was as genuine as the stones. She was happy with
her love beside her.

In contrast, Belle appeared stolid in his black suit with
a silver-grey shirt under the jacket. His brown hair was
slicked back, and an earring sparkled in his left ear. He
wore black cufflinks, and a black pin in his lapel. They had
coordinated their costumes well.

Everyone in their entourage wore bright jewel colors,
each seeking to outdo the rest. They walked behind the
betrothed couple, smiling their own smiles, enjoying the
attention.

The guests on either side bowed and curtsied, and Arden
followed suit. Across the path, Hsing stood at attention and
saluted. Arden looked for Rafe, but could not spot him in
the crowd. She was disappointed that none of his crew had
yet appeared, but understood their reluctance.

The orchestra had started playing again right after the
trumpets had sounded. Belle led Jessa to the dance floor in
front of the orchestra, and they danced. Seeing them glide
around the floor, Arden wondered if she had been wrong
about his feelings for his bride-to-be, and hoped that was
the case. When the tune was half over, others joined in the
dance, while some held back as if not wanting to crowd
the floor.

The dancing and drinking lasted until eight o'clock when
the trumpets sounded again. Everyone took their seats at
their assigned tables and dinner was served. The wonderful
smells in the kitchen had not been false—the food was
superb, course after course. Arden fought the strong desire
to relax and enjoy the event. She realized that the warmth

of the room, the music from the orchestra, and the buzz of voices were having a dulling effect on her senses.

She leaned over and whispered to Rafe that she was going to take a tour around, then excused herself and rose from the table. She walked around the perimeter of the ballroom, reminding the guards to stay alert. Those still circulating with drink trays were more alert by virtue of their moving around, but she stopped a couple of them and talked a moment.

Finished there, she started into the kitchen. She pushed through the outer doors and headed for the inner ones. Noises continued to come from that inner sanctum, but there was a subtle difference. She drew her sword, took a deep breath, and barged in.

19

In an instant, Arden took in the chaos. Several of the waiters were fighting against overwhelming odds. Even a couple of the cooks were fighting. The intruders all wore brown jumpsuits.

She started forward, but someone grabbed her from behind, wrapping his arms around her chest and pinning her arms. She stomped down with her right foot, the boot heel catching the man's foot squarely. He yelled in pain and she ground down, breaking his hold with her arms. She took one step forward and turned, slashing horizontally with the katana. The man grunted and collapsed.

She turned to join the fight and found the odds were about three to two against. However, her guardsmen were holding their own. It was gratifying to know that all of the drill and practice she had insisted on were paying off.

Stepping into the fray, she assisted rather than taking over. Part of her wanted to rush back into the ballroom and notify Hsing of what was happening, but she knew he was alert and would be ready for any attack that might come there. She hoped that his soldiers surrounding the ballroom and the palace might deter any further intrusion, but it clearly had not worked all around.

One of her guardsmen cried out in pain, and she looked around in time to see him stumble. Just before his adversary could deliver a killing blow, she intervened, beat him back against one of the stoves, and thrust her sword into his abdomen. He put his hand down to keep from falling, but it landed on a hot burner. He screamed, pulled up his hand, and fell to the floor.

Looking around again, she saw that the fight was nearly over. The sounds of metal striking metal had been replaced by moans. One of the cooks, holding a large skillet, looked down in surprise at the intruder lying at his feet. The last two of the enemy still standing threw down their swords and raised their hands in surrender. She waited a moment, letting everyone catch their breath a bit, then picked out the waiter who looked the least disheveled and sent him into the ballroom to find Alvarez and Hsing.

The two were there in seconds. Hsing took one look, asked her if she was all right, then hastened out to check on his own men. Alvarez began the cleanup: dead sent to be identified, then buried; living sent to the cells in the basement for medical attention first, and later transport to the prison.

She straightened her uniform and returned to the ballroom. She sat down next to Rafe and took a drink of water from her glass.

"What happened?" he asked.

"Intruders in the kitchen."

His eyebrows rose slightly. "Everything taken care of?"

"So far. Hsing has gone to check on how they got in. We have to keep any further problems outside of here if we can."

She looked around the room. Everyone was eating dessert, talking and laughing, the orchestra still playing. No one had a clue. Her own dessert sat untouched in front of her.

"Do you really think there might be more?" he asked.

"It's a possibility. If they could get into the kitchen . . ." She shrugged.

The others at their table looked at them for a moment. Arden smiled, and they went back to their food and conversations. Rafe fluttered the fingers on his left hand, and she wished there was something she could give him to do.

At that moment, there was not much to be done by anyone.

"Stay alert," she whispered to him, and stood.

The toasts would begin soon. After that, more dancing and drinking. The party would go on as long as Jessa and Jonas stayed, maybe even after they left. If not here, then in town.

The waiters had started clearing the dishes while she headed for the door. Hsing had not yet returned, and she wanted to find out if everything appeared secure. She stopped and asked a guard in the hall where the general had gone, but all he knew was that Hsing was going to inspect the perimeter.

She went farther from the ballroom and activated her wrist comm. The general answered almost immediately.

"Everything looks all right," he said. "I suspect those men got into the complex earlier. How and when I don't know. However, only military people and guests entered since late this morning. All other security people stayed outside the gates."

"Could they have been disguised in our uniforms?" she asked.

"None have been found anywhere. I'd have to say no."

"The toasts will be starting soon in the ballroom," she said. "Did you want to be here for that?"

"I should be, I guess. It will only take me two minutes to get back."

They disconnected, and she returned to the ballroom doors, stepping just inside as the guards closed them behind her. Waiters scurried around, making sure every person had a glass of something to toast with. The first person to propose a toast, Jessa's aunt, looked around, waiting to rise. The doors opened partway, and Hsing entered. Arden motioned to one of the waiters, and he brought his tray. They each took a glass of wine, but stayed where they were. It was easier to see most of the ballroom from that vantage point.

At last, the old woman rose shakily to her feet. Her name was Matilda, Arden thought, and she was Appolyona's older sister by some fifteen years. She held a glass in a hand that shook, threatening to splash its contents all over the table any moment.

"Friends, relatives, and guests," she began. The murmur that had blanketed the room died down. "It is my honor to raise my glass in the first toast to her majesty, my niece, Jessa Parcq."

She went on for nearly two minutes, wishing the couple well in their upcoming life together. When the end came, everyone rose and raised their glasses. "Here, here," "Good wishes," and other words were spoken by all. Two more toasts were planned, one from a member of the Belle family, and one from a representative chosen by the guests.

All the while, Arden and Hsing scanned the guests and the windows behind the orchestra, watching and listening for anything that might even hint at trouble. The second toast, given by Jonas's brother Thomas, lasted about the same length of time as Matilda's. Ambassador Qualen, from Nolyn, a large lifeweave customer, spoke last. Since he was a politician, his toast lasted quite a bit longer. Arden resisted the temptation to check her watch and breathed a small sigh of relief when he finished.

Everyone raised their glasses. Something crashed through a window behind the orchestra. Beyond, sporadic gunfire came from the courtyard below.

People screamed and ran toward the other end of the room. Arden signaled two of her guardsmen to check the window and the rest to stay where they were. Hsing had already bolted for the door, and she followed quickly. She ran behind him through hallways and down stairs until they both stood panting under the arcade on the edge of the courtyard.

Three of his soldiers wrestled with three intruders. No one else was in sight. A captain spotted his superior and trotted over.

"That's all there were," he reported after saluting. "We're doing a sweep to make sure."

"There's nothing more we can do here," Arden said.

"I'm going to stay another moment," Hsing said. "Go on back and keep an eye on things in the ballroom." Before she could bristle, he grinned. "If that's all right with you."

She nodded and smiled back. He must be feeling frustrated since he had checked for any other invaders and found none, just prior to this attack. "I suppose one of us should be there," she said. "Be careful." He nodded and turned to the captain. They were in deep conversation as she sped away.

These were little skirmishes meant to disrupt the festivities and keep everyone off balance. And they were working.

Back in the ballroom, frightened people still huddled together, their voices loud. Jonas was surrounded by his people and Jessa by hers, but she looked to him longingly. From his attitude, he cared nothing about protecting the empress.

Arden walked up to the main table, bowed to the empress, and said, "May I, your highness?"

"Of course," Jessa answered.

She turned to face the guests. "May I have your attention, please," she said loudly. Only the nearest people heard her. Jessa put two fingers in her mouth and whistled. The sound startled everyone, and by the time they turned their eyes in her direction, they could not have told who had made it. Arden smiled. She had forgotten the empress could do that.

"May I have your attention, please," Arden called again, and everyone quieted. "I apologize for your having been frightened, but . . . Some people from the town and off-duty palace personnel were celebrating and got a little carried away. There is no danger to any of us. There were just too many for the guards to control at first, but we have remedied that and there should be no more such incidents."

She turned back toward Jessa, who motioned for Arden to come nearer and leaned across the table

"Is that true?" she asked.

"No, your highness, not entirely. However, it should put your guests' fears to rest."

The empress nodded. "Then we have nothing to fear?"

"Nothing at all. The situation is in hand."

Jessa nodded again and straightened. The conversation was over. Arden made her way to the bandstand and told the orchestra leader to begin playing again. Staff members were cleaning up the broken glass from the floor, but it had been decided not to worry about sealing off the window. The cool night air coming in was mild and diluted the smell of the flowers.

Next, she found Rafe and told him what had happened in the courtyard.

"Looks like you might have a busy night," he said sympathetically.

"The next several days, I'd say."

"More than likely. I think I'll check with the *Starbourne* and make sure everything is all right at the port."

She agreed that it was a good idea, and had one of the guardsmen show him to the nearest comm station. In spite of the early hour and the assurances that everything was under control, the empress, Jonas, and their entourage left shortly after. Most of the guests began drifting away. By the time General Hsing returned, the ballroom was nearly empty.

"Everything okay?" he asked.

"Yes. The hullabaloo just seemed to dampen everyone's spirits." She sat down at one of the empty tables. Waiters were clearing the tables all around them. "Do you think we ought to close and lock all the gates and doors? We know many of the guests will be heading for town if they can, but we just aren't going to be able to control this situation if we don't."

"There will be hell to pay," he said. "It would be ideal if we could, but I don't think we can."

"Well," she said, and levered herself to her feet. "I'm off to check security around the imperial apartments. Care to join me later for a cup of coffee?"

"I'll call you."

He headed off to check the perimeter again, and she started off on her own errand. Lieutenant Garson appeared, prepared to accompany her on the rounds. They met Rafe in the hall. Arden decided to send Garson to check the surveillance room and asked Rafe if he would like to go along. The guard outside Jessa's apartments opened the door for her.

"Her highness is in the conference room," the servant informed them.

Another guard stood inside the door, two stood in the sitting room, and another in the hall, all alert. She and Rafe made their way to the conference room, each step nearer increasing the fear in Arden's mind of what they would find there. When they first entered, she could not see Jessa. However, the wedding dress was impossible to miss. It was on a dress dummy placed on the little dais. It was reflected in the mirror, and the two views almost filled the room.

"Beautiful, isn't it?" Jessa's voice said. She appeared from the other side. "My mother did wonderful work."

She sounded either tired or mesmerized, perhaps even a little sad. The sadness could come from memories of her mother or from her fears involving Jonas Belle, or both. How many parallels were there between her mother's relationship with the emperor and her own with the son of Weaver's owner?

Jessa reached out a hand as if to touch the skirt of the dress, but did not quite. Arden thought she could almost see rays emanate from the fabric and engulf her hand. Rays of what, she was not quite sure. The sudden thought that it might be empathy came to her, but that was not possible.

Two guards stood on either side of the room, noticing nothing to all appearances, but in reality they noticed everything. Two more waited in the bedroom, making sure no one sneaked in before the empress retired for the night.

"Do you hope to marry one day, Commander?" Jessa asked.

"I never thought about it, your highness."

"Perhaps you and Rafe."

Arden felt the heat of a blush move up her neck, to her face. Rafe changed his stance, and the fingers on his hand fluttered again.

"Jessa . . ." he said. "Your highness, I want to congratulate you on your coming marriage and wish you much happiness."

"Happiness?" Jessa said. "There should be happiness in marriage, shouldn't there? No, that's not true. I was happy when I was an insignificant astronavigator. The only time

I was happy. Except perhaps when I was a very little girl and my mother was still with me. But as an adult, I was happy on the *Starbourne*."

Guilt rushed through Arden. What could she say in response? If it had not been for her, Jessa would still be on Rafe's ship. It was her fault that Jessa was now empress of Glory and would soon marry a man who did not love her. Was she beginning to realize that?

Was that why Pac Terhn wanted Jessa? Lyona was there, too, somewhere within the world entered through lifeweave. Did they intend to protect her from an unhappy marriage? But it was her mother who told Jessa that she could marry Belle, that it would be all right. She was also the one who found her own happiness within that addiction, and her sanctuary away from an unhappy relationship.

Their motives might never be clear. How could they, if no one would tell the truth?

"I look forward to wearing this dress," Jessa said, pulling Arden from her reverie. "It is so beautiful." She did reach out and touch the skirt then. A shiver went through her. "Arden."

"Yes, your highness?"

"After the wedding and once everything else has been taken care of, you will need to find other employment."

"What?"

"There's no discussion," Jessa said. "You are a constant reminder of what I have lost, and I don't want you here anymore."

Alvarez opened the door, but looked back before he left. Concern wrinkled his forehead.

"Give me a holler if you need anything," he said.

"I will."

He walked out, closing the door softly behind him. The sound of his footsteps faded away, and aloneness settled over her.

Arden had tried to act as if nothing untoward had occurred, but clearly she had not been successful if Alvarez had noticed something was wrong. Concentrating on busi-

ness while making the rest of the tour around the palace
had been very hard.

Why now? she wondered. Why would Jessa wait so long?

Rafe had expressed his own amazement after they left
the imperial apartments. He had walked down to her office
with her and sat talking for a while before heading to the
third floor and bed.

"It doesn't make sense, Arden," he said. "After everything you have done for her. And after all this time. Why
would she wait until now to decide she doesn't need you
around?"

He echoed her own thoughts and questions, and so far
she had not been able to get any further than that. Had
Jessa's friendliness been a sham all along? If so, it was a
cruel trick.

"I wonder if she kept me around intending to use me as
a punching bag."

"I would think that even an empress wouldn't be that
cruel," Rafe had said.

Arden shrugged. "Who knows? I suppose she could
change her mind when it comes right down to it. I had
expected some changes once she was married." She hit the
desktop with the palm of her hand. "Dammit! I never expected this. I feel as if I was set up."

"Maybe you were."

"Well, if it was planned, she did a good job of it."

They sat in silence for a moment, then Rafe had stood
up to leave. "I'm going off to bed unless you'd like me to
stick around."

She shook her head. "I may just catch a nap here later.
I had planned to hang around anyway and keep an eye on
things. Now this . . . I'm too keyed up to sleep anytime
soon."

He leaned down and kissed her tenderly.

"I'm sorry this happened," he said. "But who knows?
Maybe something good will come of it."

She smiled. "I suppose."

Captain Alvarez appeared shortly after Rafe left, and
they went over and over security assignments. They discussed views on how the intruders had made it inside

the palace in spite of tight security, but there were just too many possibilities. Especially with the wedding guests coming and going at all hours.

"Could it be that they were here all along?" Alvarez had asked at one point.

"What do you mean?" His question seemed to echo Hsing's earlier observation.

"We have added a few new guardsmen, and Hsing added some soldiers over the past few weeks. We know that it's impossible to tell how loyal someone might actually be. Hell, they could have been here all the time, just waiting for a certain moment."

"Did any of our people recognize any of them?"

"I haven't heard."

"Check it out. Go look at them yourself. See if you recognize even one of them."

That was just prior to his leaving. Now she sat wondering about it, using that worry to chase away other concerns.

A knock came on the door, distracting her from even that.

"Come in."

The door opened, and General Hsing entered. He looked tired and in bad need of that coffee they had discussed earlier.

"I thought you were going to get in touch with me," he said a bit peevishly.

"No, you were going to call me."

"I was?" She nodded.

"Sorry."

"Alvarez just left a few minutes ago," she said. "I was thinking about something he said."

While she poured coffee from the machine, she told him of the captain's suspicion, although it was hardly that strong. A thought, really, she explained. Hsing did not dismiss the possibility out of hand.

"Maybe I should send someone to look over the bodies, too," he said. "Can't hurt anything."

They discussed reasons why no one would have said anything at this point even if they had recognized one of the intruders. They agreed that it had not been very long since the fight and everyone had been pretty busy.

The coffee was hot and much needed by both of them.
They went down to the surveillance room and checked the
monitors together for fifteen minutes. Lieutenant Garson
looked beat, and Arden sent her to her quarters. Back in
her office, she drew two more mugs of coffee and they sat
back down.

"I guess I should head home and get some sleep," Hsing
said.

"Good idea."

"Who am I kidding? I couldn't sleep now if I had to."

"Me neither. If you want to sack out anytime tonight,
though, we can find you a cot or something here in the
palace."

"What? Every room must be full."

"True, but we could set you up a cot here in the basement somewhere. And there are plenty of beds in the
cells."

He grinned. "I don't think that's a good idea, considering the men already detained there."

They talked about the fight in the kitchen and how surprised they both were that the intruders managed to get
inside. The talk turned to what might come next, what to
expect during the wedding and honeymoon. Hsing had decided to go with her plan relating to the armory and had
arranged to bring a good part of those soldiers to the summer palace.

Arden realized that she had no idea what to expect after
that, and she found herself telling him about her last conversation with Jessa.

"You won't have to worry about working with me after
that, I guess," she finished.

"I can't believe she could be so ungrateful," he said
angrily. "After all you've done for her."

"What I did was bring her home where she didn't want
to be, help her take a throne she didn't want, and helped
keep her there for the past year and a half."

"You also saved her life."

"She must figure that debt is paid."

He shook his head. "The worst part is pretending to be

your friend when all the time she hated you. If that's where this is coming from.''

Arden shrugged. ''She's unhappy and needs someone to blame. I'm not only handy, but an easy target. I'm pledged to her. There is no way I can strike back.''

''She's a coward, then,'' he said firmly. ''Women . . .''

''Don't blame this on her being a woman,'' Arden broke in quickly. ''The problem could be that two women can't work together, but women are not inherently dishonest. When you find one that is, she'll be worse than any man.''

He took a drink of coffee and made a face. It had cooled. He got up and dropped the mug into the recycler, drew both of them fresh ones, and sat back down.

''What will you do?'' he asked.

''I don't know. I could go back to the monastery, but I don't think I would be happy there all the time. I could travel . . .''

''With Captain Semmes?''

''Maybe. If he asks me to.''

''You could ask him?''

''I could, but I won't. I need to know that he wants me with him.''

Sudden embarrassment silenced her. She had not talked to anyone except Abbot Grayson about her feelings for Rafe. She had never had a female confidante with whom to discuss personal issues, and only the one male friend, although she could talk to some of the monks about other things.

A deep longing to go back to the monastery, to things known and familiar, descended on her.

''You've never married?'' she asked, changing the subject.

He smiled. ''No, I've always been married to my career. An old and familiar story.''

''And you've never thought highly of women, as I recall.'' She smiled to let him know it was not a criticism.

''Oh, I've always thought very highly of women. Just not when they want to do a man's job.'' He winked at her. ''I have to admit that you've done it well, though. I'll miss working with you.''

Arden was surprised that those words meant something to her. She felt immensely flattered, but it went deeper than that, too. His opinion mattered. She hoped that he would never disappoint her.

She yawned. ''Guess I'm finally getting sleepy,'' she said.

He stood. ''I'll let you get to bed, then. You sleeping here''—he motioned to the sofa—''or in your own bed?''

''Here tonight. Maybe every night until this is all over.''

''All right.'' He stood. ''I'll see you in the morning. Later this morning, rather.''

''Want me to get you a cot?''

''No, I'll find someplace if I decide to take a nap. Good-night.''

He was gone quickly, and there was a momentary feeling of loneliness. Rafe was here for her, but the general's presence was more satisfying—in a professional sense.

20

Rain fell hard, running down the windows in sheets. Fog plunged against the palace walls, dispersed in its wild rush to tear down the stone that was too hard for it.

Arden stepped away from the window and studied her image against the darkness outside.

"That uniform sure is getting a workout," Rafe had said before she left the apartment.

She had several dress uniforms and had worn nothing but them to the parties and soirees. During the regular hours, she had worn the uniform of the day. And suddenly she was very tired of both. Wearing a beautiful dress to the wedding would be wonderful. However, the uniform would actually make her stand out from the crowd, since all the other women would be gowned and coifed formally.

"I've never known a woman to look better in one, though," Rafe had continued.

She bent down and kissed him and realized that the compliment was not added to soften his first comment. He meant what he said and was totally unconscious of any criticism the first might have implied.

When she left, the bedroom was a shambles from her frantic attempts to find everything she needed and Rafe's search for the same suit he had worn to the prenuptial party, only to find he had hung it on the wrong side of the closet.

Next, he had to search for his invitation to the wedding which was not in the jacket pocket where he had expected it to be. The maids would have a busy day cleaning up here and would probably face the same disasters elsewhere.

The rain fell harder. Did tradition say it was lucky or unlucky for a wedding to be held on a rainy day? There were probably superstitions that went both ways. She could only count her blessings that the wedding was to be held in the chapel within the palace. It had been little used during the past months, Jessa not being a particularly religious woman. She had observed the requisite holidays and observances, and that was about all.

The priests and others had managed to keep it in good shape, however, and many had worked the past week or so getting it in pristine condition. From brief conversations over the past few days, Arden knew that Abbot Grayson had even supervised some of that work, to the chagrin of the priest who officiated there.

In spite of being raised in a monastery, Arden had little of the religious in her. She did not even know what god was supposed to be worshipped in the chapel, although she suspected that didn't matter. Worship on Glory was a mixed bag at best. In the monastery, the monks were allowed to pray to whomever they chose as long as they did pray at the appointed times. It was the contemplative, cooperative, and communal life that Grayson thought important.

Arden smiled when she realized that the descriptive words all began with the letter "C." The smile turned to a frown at her own reflection. There had been no time to do anything special with her hair. It had grown even with her jawline again and just hung there straight, as did the tunic. Food had been the least of her worries for several weeks, and she had lost weight.

She sighed. Hers was not a glamorous occupation, after all, and no one expected her to look pretty. And today, it would be best if she was not the center of attention. Today, it was the bride who was and should be. Arden tried to imagine the gasps of surprise and pleasure when everyone saw Jessa's wedding gown.

Time to get to the chapel and see what was going on.

She hoped for a moment that Rafe had found his invitation. No one would be admitted without one.

She reached up and touched the pommel of the katana. Below that, she had attached the netsuke by its velvet cord. She had always considered the small figure a lucky charm, but felt even more strongly since the incident with the bomb on the scout ship. It was going to be a long day, and she had gotten only three hours sleep last night. She was going to need all the luck she could find. Getting by with little sleep was becoming a habit, though it was one she would like to break soon.

The wedding was scheduled for three, and she would spend the rest of the morning hours and the early afternoon checking on security. Again. Everyone was getting tense and jumpy, partly because there had been no attacks since the prenuptial party five days ago. But that had kept them expectant, waiting for the next, knowing it was sure to come, and tensed for action. The waiting was wearing on everyone's nerves more than another fight would have.

Something was bound to happen today. But as memory of her last search with the lifeweave had slowly returned, Arden was convinced that this would not be the major attack. That would come at the summer palace.

The rest of the time was spent routinely. Complaints came from some guests about the tightened security, but they would just have to complain. This was no time to worry about hurt feelings, even if it was the hurt feelings of some of the most powerful people in the sector.

Jonas Belle also complained, but in some ways he had more cause. He was one of the most closely guarded, and after several days of little privacy, it must be wearing. Even so, he had been remarkably quiet overall.

At two she entered the chapel for her last inspection. It was empty except for her and Captain Alvarez. She carried several swords, and he followed with the guns. She headed straight for the altar, found the spring catch, and opened the door. Behind it was a small chamber, the one in which she had hidden her own katana before being arrested years ago. She slid the swords inside and then stood back, holding the door open, so that Alvarez could put the guns with the swords.

She closed the door, making sure it had latched; then the two of them proceeded to check every nook and cranny within the sanctuary. A detail of guards entered. Arden gave them their final instructions, and they took their places. Two smaller guard details appeared. One was placed in the vestry to oversee the safety of the priests who would conduct the service. The second was positioned in the balcony above the entrance with the chamber orchestra.

Just outside the chapel she found Hsing overseeing the placement of his guards there. He drew her aside.

"I understand that the priest is raising a fuss about weapons in the chapel," he said. "I hope her highness does not order us to disarm."

"I can't believe that she would!" Arden said. "She knows the dangers. He should, too."

Hsing shook his head. "Priests rarely understand such things. In fact, we haven't exactly been explaining the threats against the empress and her regime. If she orders us to disarm, though, I suspect it will be more at the whim of that man of hers."

"Belle wants us to disarm?"

"Yes, it seems that he has some very strong religious views. One of those uncles he brought with him is a priest of the old kind."

"I knew Belle was going to be trouble. If worse comes to worst, there is at least one hiding place inside if they say we can't wear our weapons. I'm sure we could find others."

She explained about the spring door in the altar, and they decided to set one of her guards to seeking out another hiding place in the short time remaining. Just as they started to separate, a messenger came running up. He handed Arden a folded piece of paper. She unfolded it, read the message written in Jessa's own hand, and gave it to Hsing.

"You were right," she said. "We had better move fast."

According to the order, no armed personnel were to be inside the chapel. It had said nothing about the vestry, and Arden decided not to disarm the men there. Her own assigned place was on the left side, which would put a lot of people between her and the altar.

"Let's find those hiding places," the general said.

Music played softly and guests arrived quietly. No one was wearing lifeweave, seeming to confirm the rumor that Jessa had *requested* they not do so. How many were out a great deal of money for a great lot of the fabric they now could not use? Except perhaps at the next wedding. Arden spotted Rafe in a crowd that had just entered the chapel. She worked her way to him.

"I see you found your invitation," she said.

"I'd put it in my other jacket pocket." He looked at her more closely. "Where's your sword?"

"That's another story."

She smiled but kept her eye on those still arriving and looking for their assigned seats in the pews. Slowly, she drew him to one side.

"Your place is there, pew seventeen, right side."

"Oh, lord," he complained. "I'm right next to Belle's cousin."

"It could be worse, my dear."

"How?"

She chuckled. "I'll think of something. I will be standing against this wall with half of the honor guard. The other half will be against the opposite wall with Alvarez in command."

She went on to tell him where all of the arms had been stashed. Her own katana was under one of the pews near where she would be standing. She and Hsing had discovered that although the pews were enclosed from the seat to the floor, the end panels lifted on hinges, providing a perfect place to slide a sword into. They considered moving the rest of the weapons, placing them around the sanctuary under all of the pews, but it was too late. Guests had started to arrive by then.

Rafe went to his seat. Everyone sat quietly. Those still arriving went to their seats almost as quietly, until finally everyone was in place. Arden went into the hall outside the main entrance where the honor guard had formed up. The

banners and flags they carried on long staffs hung limply.
The squad would escort the groom and his brother to the
altar, then divide in two, taking their places on either side.
Once they were in place, the empress's aunt would enter
and stand as the representative of her family. The priest
would enter from the vestry, and that would be the signal
for the bride to make her appearance.

The program had been written down and a copy given
to all participants, which more than likely meant that Vey
or his underlings also knew about it. Arden prayed over
and over that nothing would happen, at least until the ceremony was concluded. Which meant, of course, that any
disruption would come at the worst possible moment.

The groom arrived with his own entourage, and the music changed at some signal that she missed. Arden checked
her watch: almost ten minutes behind schedule.

All of Belle's followers went into the chapel and found
their seats. He and his brother stepped into the center of
the honor guard and, when the music changed again, the
guards moved inside as a body. The cadence was slow.
Arden was expected to keep her eyes to the front, but she
checked to each side as surreptitiously as she could. General Hsing was seated within the crowd; she spotted both
him and Rafe.

They reached the altar, and as the two lines of the honor
guard peeled away to either side, Belle and his brother
moved a little to the right and stopped. The members of
the honor guard reached their positions, wheeled to face the
front of the chapel, and stopped. Arden faced the crowd.
What a collection of color, elegance, and gaudiness they
were, even without lifeweave.

The music stopped, and perfect silence filled the room.
The sense of expectation was palpable. The imperial aunt
entered. Softly, the music resumed. It rose in volume so
subtly that Arden did not notice at first. When she did, she
caught her first glimpse of the bride. There was an immediate intake of breath from the crowd, sounding as if the
chapel itself had sighed with envy.

Within the white and gold chapel and against the dark
red carpet, the lifeweave appeared to be in its own best

environment. It shimmered so that Arden expected it to sing
out at any moment. It was more than it had been during
the final fitting, overpowering the senses.

Jessa's long black hair hung straight down her back, and
a large tiara encrusted with opals shone on her head. The
end of her train took forever to appear, and when she
stopped beside her beloved at last, it was half the length of
the aisle.

Jonas held out his left arm, and Jessa rested her hand on
top of his. She smiled up at him, and for the first time that
Arden had seen, he smiled at her. They turned toward the
priest, and the ceremony began. Except for his voice and
the music playing softly in the background, the chapel was
totally quiet. Arden looked to see if everyone was holding
their breath.

She felt like holding her own breath. Maybe that would
guarantee a quiet, uninterrupted ceremony. At least, she
might hear any movement outside of the expected.

Across the way, Alvarez and his group held perfectly
still. The muscles in his jaw twitched, and his eyes shifted
around the room, trying to take everything in. She could
almost glimpse Abbot Grayson sitting on the other side of
the ambassador from Luthe. Rafe sat next to the cousin,
seemingly engrossed in what was happening.

She heard Jonas say, "I do." Soon, it would be time to
move the detail forward to escort the newlyweds from the
chapel.

The priest continued with the litany, and Arden tensed
even more. She had been so sure something would happen,
and time was running out.

Jessa said, "I do."

The two exchanged rings, then were blessed, and the
music swelled. Two attendants rushed forward to hold the
train while Jessa turned to walk up the aisle and leave
the chapel. A reception was already set up in the ballroom.
The two details moved forward to follow them out.

The two lines had just turned into the main aisle when
a commotion erupted in the outer hall. Jessa had almost
reached the last pew when the doors burst open. Rafe leapt
from his seat, grabbed hold of the empress, and pulled her

out of the way. Jonas, unencumbered by a long gown, turned and ran. The two lines of the detail separated to let him pass. Guests were screaming as Arden reached down to gather up the train of the gown so that the guards could get past.

They dashed forward to meet the rush of warriors coming through the doorway. Unarmed as they were, the guards had to rely on their skill in hand-to-hand combat, using agility and skill to counter swords and knives.

A gun fired, a projectile type, wisps of smoke rising from where it was fired. Arden tried to fight her way back to the altar where the nearest cache of weapons was hidden. Guests poured from their seats into the aisle, many going in the same direction, fighting the ones ahead of them. People screamed and cried out, and she could not tell if any of her men had been hurt. She had to get their weapons to them. This time, they would need the guns, and she feared many more people would be hurt.

More gunfire, and a woman fell in front of her. No time to see how badly she was hurt. She stepped over, fighting now to move ahead, pushing people aside, ignoring their indignation and fear.

Her progress was stopped by a man in a brown jumpsuit. He swung his sword horizontally and she jumped back, knocking over a smaller woman and nearly stumbling over her. The tip of his sword caught the arm of a man dressed in purple. His scream was lost in the overwhelming noise that filled the chapel.

Arden gained her balance and kicked out while the sword wielder was off balance. The blow knocked the wind out of him and he fell sideways, then caught his balance with the sword point against the floor. She caught his chin with a right cross, and he stumbled backward and fell to the floor.

She stepped up beside him, stooped down, and grabbed up his sword. Surrounded by the surging crowd as she was, she could neither see any more of the enemy, nor be seen by them. However, as she neared the altar the crowd thinned while everyone worked their way toward the vestry, since the main exit was blocked by intruders. The spring door opened at her touch. She grabbed a pistol and shoved it in her belt. After grabbing two more swords and pistols, she closed the door and headed toward Rafe. Most of the guests had either gotten through to the vestry or were pressed against that wall. Two of her men lay in the aisle at the far end. She could see Rafe now, standing between the empress and two men in brown.

Arden ran down the aisle, shouted Rafe's name, and threw him a pistol. She raised another and fired at one of the men menacing him. The beam caught his left arm. He shouted and nearly went down. Rafe juggled the pistol for a moment, got control of it, and fired at the second man. That man had been distracted by his companion's distress, and he was caught by Rafe's shot. He collapsed to the floor, and the man Arden had shot ran away.

She ran toward Alvarez, who fought hand to hand with someone, getting the better of the struggle in spite of favoring his right arm a little. Those in imperial uniforms outnumbered those in brown jumpsuits, but the latter were armed. The battle was even.

She closed in on Alvarez, raised the pistol, shot the man he fought with, and then threw the gun to the captain. A shot cracked behind her. She crouched and turned. The shot came from an enemy soldier near the vestry entrance. Those civilians still there screamed. She could not fire for fear of hitting a guest. He fired again just as she dropped to the floor. The shot whizzed overhead.

Arden crawled down the aisle and turned between the pews. She had to get into a position to be able to aim before firing. At the end of the pews, she looked around. The man still stood among the civilians, who could not get through that exit for some reason. The way they milled around, it was difficult to get a clear shot. She raised the pistol, waiting. Suddenly, he was in the open and she fired. The beam caught him in the thigh, and he went down. One of the guards near him stepped on his arm and took the pistol out of his hand. Arden stood and saluted the man.

She looked around the chapel, seeking the next hot spot, only to find it was quiet. Shouts and screams still came from the vestry. She started in that direction, only to be stopped by Lieutenant Garson working her way into the chapel.

"We have it under control," the lieutenant said. "We'll have everyone out of the vestry soon."

Arden nodded and patted her on the shoulder. "Any injuries in there?"

"One of the civilians was trampled. One of our men is dead. Several of us are wounded, civilians and guardsmen. I don't think any of the intruders escaped."

"Good. Get back in there and get the civilians back to their rooms. Bring me an updated report when things have settled down a bit."

She looked around. Alvarez was sitting on one of the pews, looking pale and grimacing in pain. Jessa sat farther back, clinging to Rafe, who seemed unhurt. Abbot Grayson stood near them looking grim. Several intruders lay on the floor, some looking quite dead, others moaning in pain.

"Anyone know where the groom got to?" she asked Garson.

"He got out pretty quickly." The woman's tone was tinged with contempt. "I think his own guards surrounded him outside the other entrance to the vestry and hurried him out of here."

Arden sighed. Belle was not the man she had hoped he would be. Too bad. She wondered again if Pac Terhn and Lyona knew what kind of man he was and if that was the reason behind their wanting Jessa to take up lifeweave.

"All right," she said. "Off with you."

Garson saluted and hurried back the way she had come. One more crisis overcome. How many more would there be?

"You deliberately disobeyed my orders!"

Jessa's face was flushed, and her hands clenched the corner of a shawl she wore made of lifeweave. She stood with her back to the fire in the fireplace in her sitting room. Arden and Hsing stood before her, listening to the tirade that had gone on for two minutes or more. It definitely seemed longer.

"If your highness pleases, we did not disobey your order,'' the general said calmly. ''None of our guards was armed. The arms that we used were placed in storage areas around the chapel.''

''Will I have to relieve you of your command, too?'' Jessa said, glaring at him. ''The attack came because there were weapons within the chapel. That was sacrilegious at best. Direct disobedience at worst.''

''I serve at your highness's pleasure,'' he responded with a bow.

She continued railing at them about disobeying her and defiling the chapel. She was clearly delusional and Arden could think of half a dozen reasons why she would be. After a time, she dismissed both of them.

''This is not finished,'' she hurled at them as they left.

The two of them started toward Arden's office in the basement. They walked silently at first. Hsing was the first to speak.

''Those words weren't hers,'' he said.

''No, I'd guess all of that came from Belle. You said that he was religious, but I suspect now that doesn't even begin to cover it.''

''I'm beginning to be afraid of this marriage.''

Arden nodded. ''I know. On top of everything else . . .''
She looked around making sure no one was within earshot.
''He's a coward.'' She shook her heard. ''I'm very much afraid for Glory. I have the feeling that the next few years may be worse for us than all of those years of the war.''

''You may be right.''

They entered her office, and she got them each a mug of coffee. They sipped the brew and talked further about the next few days and weeks, avoiding long-term considerations. When he left to check on preparations for the imperial couple's trip to the summer palace, she went in search of her old mentor. Grayson had some knowledge of religious fanatics, and she was in dire need of his advice.

21

The comm unit sat on the corner of the desk, silent and worrisome. The honeymooners had been gone three days, and not a word had come back to the main palace except the initial report that everything was all right.

Arden could not help checking to make sure the line was clear every so often. Since the earlier small attack on the chapel during the wedding, she had been so sure that the main attack would come during the honeymoon at the other palace that this silence wore on her nerves.

In some ways, she regretted agreeing to remain behind with the majority of her guards as reinforcements. General Hsing had been convincing when he pointed out that her smaller force might be more easily overcome than his larger one. And being smaller, they were much more mobile. She had also agreed that a joint attack could also come on the main palace. If that did not happen, she and the imperial guard would be available to come to his assistance.

The additional guards taken from the armory for duty in the mountain retreat were also a good reason for staying behind. She had asked Rafe to make sure that the scout ship they had picked up on Miga was ready at all times. He had offered the *Starbourne*, but there was not enough of a clearing for the salvage ship to land in the mountains. The smaller ship was also faster, and since he and Tahr had

manned it on the trip back to Glory and were the most
familiar with it, she had also asked them if they would pilot
it if they needed to get to the mountains in a hurry. His
whole crew had agreed to help in any way they could.

Jessa had avoided contact with the commander of her
imperial guard during the short time before leaving for the
mountains. That lack of contact had its good points and bad
ones. Off and on, Arden considered the question of what
she would do once her dismissal became official.

Since the wedding party had left the capital, she had not
been idle. The parties planned for that night and the next
day and night were canceled out of respect for those who
had been killed in the attack on the chapel. No one had
wanted to hang around anyway. Most of the guests had left
shortly after the wedding. The dangers were not to their
liking, and the weather had stayed wet and gloomy. Su-
pervising their departures had taken up much of her time.

In her spare time, what little there was, she had investi-
gated those intruders who were caught and killed. It turned
out that many of them had entered the palace among the
additional cooks and staff hired to handle the influx of wedding guests. Several others were members of General
Hsing's home guard, some having been under his command
for months, driving home again that there was just no way
to ensure loyalty among the forces. General Radieux's de-
fection was sufficient proof of that. Still, it was frustrating.

She had talked several times with Grayson about that
problem, and he had not come up with any suggestions.
Then he went back to the monastery, promising to give it
more consideration. The abbot had suggested she come
home and rest a bit while deciding what to do with the rest
of her life.

Home. The monastery was the only home she had had
for most of her life. It would be good to rest there for a
while.

The comm unit chimed, and when she answered, General
Hsing was on the other end.

"We have word of a large force moving toward the summer palace," he said without preamble. "We still can't be

sure that this is the main target, but I think we need to act as though it is."

"I agree. But I don't like the idea of Jessa sitting there like a target."

"Where would you suggest she go?"

They had talked about this several times before, knowing all along that it was not their decision to make. Jessa would not hear of going off world for her honeymoon, no matter how much safer it might be.

"Just be ready to come," he said. "I'll be in touch."

"Of course. Good luck."

"Thanks."

The connection ended, and she sat for a moment with the handset against her ear. She wanted to be there, in the thick of it. For some time now, action had become an unacknowledged addiction. She had thought she could settle into the routine of commanding the palace guards, but there had always been an underlying restlessness. Although being fired by Jessa—and that was what it amounted to—hurt her pride, it was probably the best thing that could happen to her.

She went back to studying the usual reports and analyses, trying hard to concentrate on them. After an hour, the comm chimed again.

"It looks like it's about to happen," Hsing said. "Are your people ready?"

"Yes. We can be there in less than an hour."

"Good. I'll get back to you."

He was gone. She called the hangar at the port where the guardsmen awaited orders, and gave Rafe the information she had gotten from Hsing. He reported that the scout ship was ready. They had taken all unnecessary equipment out to lighten the load so it could carry more people than it was built for. The guardsmen kept checking their weapons. Everyone wanted to get in on the fray.

"It won't be much longer now," she told him.

"We're ready," he said.

"Thank you for doing this."

"Didn't have anything else to do today," he said, and she could hear the grin in his voice.

An awkward silence fell between them. There was so much to say, but neither of them knew the right words. They rang off. Almost immediately, the door to her office opened and Alvarez came in.

"I have . . ." he began, but the comm cut him off.

Arden pushed the speaker button as her captain handed her some papers.

"Commander Grenfell," a familiar voice said. The papers slipped from her hand. She looked at Alvarez, then back at the comm.

"This is she."

"General Radieux here."

"I know. Where are you?"

"That's what I am calling about. I am visiting a friend of yours."

"A friend?"

She immediately thought of the monastery. Alvarez moved to hover close to the comm unit.

"It's very quiet here," he said. "I think I might stay a while."

"Where is here?"

"I think you know, but just in case you have not worked it out, I will let the man who was formerly in charge tell you."

Some rustling noises came over the speaker, and then another voice spoke.

"Daughter, we seem to have a problem," Abbot Grayson said. Anger strained his voice.

"Are you all right?"

"At the moment, I am. Unfortunately, we were overcome by force."

"Any casualties?"

"Yes . . ." he began, followed by a grunt.

Alvarez's eyes widened, and Arden clenched her right hand into a fist. If Radieux hurt the abbot, he would pay with more than his life.

"Your friend is all right," Radieux said. "I am sure you would like for him to stay that way."

"Of course."

"You may have been contacted by someone in the summer palace," he continued. "We know that your imperial guards are poised for transport there. We suggest that you do not order them to move. We outnumber your friends here by at least two to one, and we will kill them all if you do anything foolish."

"I understand."

"Good. For now, you will sit there and we will sit here. We will stay out of the bad weather and wait until . . . Well, you know."

"Yes, I know."

"I will be back in touch," he said, and the connection ended with a click.

Alvarez dropped into a chair, a horrified expression on his face. There was also a hint of curiosity. He wondered what she was going to do. So did she.

The noise in the hangar was deafening. Everyone checked and rechecked weapons and loads again and again. A new factor had just been inserted, and a division of personnel and arms added to the overall bustle.

Rafe had sent Liel to ready the *Starbourne* in case it was needed. He suspected it would be.

The door was flung open across the way, and he looked over. Arden stalked into the hangar with Captain Alvarez right behind her. She carried a small bag and had her katana strapped across her back and a pistol holstered at her waist. She spotted Rafe and headed in his direction. He had never seen her look so grim, and he suddenly pitied General Radieux. There would be no mercy if he fell to her sword.

"How are things proceeding?" she asked when she stopped in front of him.

"Rapidly," he said. "Liel is getting the *Starbourne* prepared, and the guards are just about ready. Are you sure that fifteen will be enough at the monastery?"

"No, I'm not sure of anything. I have only an idea of how many men Radieux has there, and no idea of how many of the monks are able to fight. The greatest problem is going to be the shuttle. We'll have to land farther away from the monastery than I like, since we'll have to make about four trips."

"That many trips would make us very noticeable," he said. We'll need that distance if we're going to take them by surprise."

"I know. I only . . ."

Her wrist comm buzzed, and she answered. Her expression became even grimmer, which he had not thought possible. She listened, then talked and listened again.

"We're on," she said when she disconnected. "The attack has begun at the palace. We'll take off in the *Starbourne* as soon as we can, and the rest will take off in the scout ship an hour later. I just hope that gives us the lead time we need."

"You know that Radieux will be expecting you to try something like this," Rafe said.

"Maybe, maybe not. We'll have to do everything we can to make it look like we're all going to the same place. You've made sure that no one has left the hangar since I called?" He nodded. "And I made sure there's been a total communications blackout within the city. No one should be able to notify Vey or Radieux of our movement until it's too late." She put her hands on her hips and took a deep breath. "I hope."

Arden called Alvarez over and gave him last-minute instructions. He would lead the guards in their attack on the rear of Vey's forces. From everything Arden had said, she had confidence in the captain, but Rafe knew it was difficult for her not to be in charge there, too.

She returned to Rafe, and they watched the flurry of preparations around them. The noise level had gotten louder, if that was possible. When Arden spoke again, she had to step even closer than before.

"I spread the word that you and your crew were leaving Glory and that you would come back when the danger had passed. Hopefully, if anyone does see people boarding the *Starbourne*, it will be assumed . . . Well, you know."

He shrugged. She knew, of course, that could be construed to mean that he was not brave enough to stick around. This was a time when that did not bother him.

"Don't worry about it," he said, and put his hand on

her shoulder and squeezed slightly. "Anything I can do to help."

She smiled at him, and he resisted the impulse to hug her. It was neither the right time nor the right place.

"I'd better get out of this uniform," she said, looking around for a secluded place to change. He pointed out a corner hidden by crates from most of the hangar, and she moved over there.

The torment Arden went through in deciding what to do showed in her eyes, the tight set of her jaw. She was pledged to Jessa—in several ways, he guessed, since the empress's plan to replace her had not lessened Arden's loyalty. However, her loyalty to the monastery and its occupants was older and more binding. It was an obligation of the heart. There was ample justification for her going to their rescue rather than speeding off to the palace with the major force: General Radieux was as much an enemy of the empire as Vey and his forces threatening in the mountains.

Rafe was glad he had not needed to make that choice himself. Everyone might still be waiting for him.

Arden returned, dressed in grey tunic and tights, her uniform neatly folded away in the bag. She wore the holster and pistol, but carried her katana. She handed it to him.

"I can't carry that on board," she said. "It's pretty noticeable. But I do want it with me."

"I'll put it with some of the other things," he said. "Ready to go?"

She nodded and put on a bulky jacket that hid the gun. He went to a covered stack of arms and slipped the katana under the tarp. Then he led the way outside and to a waiting truck, also covered. The vehicle was pulled up close to the door in hopes that no one would see the soldiers as they slipped from the building and into the truck. They had also traded their uniforms for more civilian-style garb. If they were spotted and their ruse discovered, the communications blackout had better work.

Once everyone was on board the truck, it moved off toward the *Starbourne*. Behind them, the other guardsmen began boarding the scout ship. For a moment, Rafe wondered what the hell he was doing there. He was no soldier, nor were any of his crew. He should leave this kind of work to the professionals. But Jessa had been a member of his crew, and they had always stuck together. He had helped put her on the throne in the first place. And Arden needed all the help she could get, especially someone to watch her back.

Radieux put down the handset and leaned back in the desk chair. The leather creaked, and he took pleasure in the sound and feel. These monks knew how to live well, although he could do without some of the aged pieces of furniture they seemed to like so much.

Outside the monastery walls, some of their number were busy digging graves for their own dead and a few of his men. He had heard that some of these monks were trained in martial arts, but had not dreamed they would put up such a fight. No wonder Commander Grenfell was such a skilled fighter. Even so, he preferred training in the military schools to the religious-based training in places like this. Lotus-trained, indeed. Even the name sounded weak.

The door of the study opened, and Captain Djinn entered. His face was red, and he moved with barely controlled rage.

"Those damned monks won't give up," he said without waiting for leave to speak.

"Calm down, Captain," Radieux said. "And address me properly."

"Yes, sir. Sorry, sir. It's this abbot and his monks. They keep demanding things."

"Like what?"

"They want to send their cooks into the kitchen to fix their meals. They say they need their physician for their wounded. Don't they know that they're prisoners of war?"

"I suppose we will have to teach them that, won't we? However, it might not be a bad idea to set the cooks to work in the kitchen. We could all use something to eat."

He stood up and went to the French doors. Outside were gardens and outbuildings. In the distance, he could see the main wall of the complex. Beyond that were the cultivated fields and vineyards. Quite a little world of their own. It was about time they learned they could not isolate themselves.

"As for the physician," he continued, "tell them he will come to them when he has finished treating our men. That's the price they must pay for resisting us."

"Yes, sir."

Radieux turned back around in time to return Djinn's salute and watch him leave the room. *Civilians!* he thought. It was bad enough to have to deal with people like Don Vey and Arden. They at least had a certain amount of discipline.

He opened the French doors and stepped outside. A multitude of fragrances and the sounds of birds seemed to fill the air. The general, having spent much of the past few years in the filtered air of the armory and on spaceships of one kind or another, felt nauseated at the sweetness of both. He went back inside and closed the doors. He would be glad to get out of this place as soon as possible. He was equally glad that the imperials appeared to be following his instructions.

From the top of the desk, he picked up a large piece of cloth. It shimmered in the light. Having found it in what turned out to be Arden Grenfell's room in the monastery, Radieux had kept it close. It was another piece of the puzzle that was the woman warrior.

22

Arden peered through bushes and undergrowth at the monastery wall. So far their landing seemed to have gone undetected. On the ship, she had told Rafe about the hidden gate in the wall and how there was a hidden path once they got inside. As far as she knew, neither had been used for years.

Off to her right, a burial party worked in the monastery's cemetery. The rain had stopped, but the ground was saturated, and it was heavy work. The monks doing the digging were guarded by five men in brown jumpsuits and carrying rifles. General Radieux must have increased his command with men from Vey's raiders. The small force he must have been left with after Miga would not have been enough to overcome the monks.

She turned to Rafe, crouched beside her.

"We'll have to take those men," she said, referring to those guarding the five monks digging graves. "There is no way we can get inside without their seeing us. And it looks like they will be there for a while. We can't afford to wait."

Rafe nodded. "We'll have to be quiet about it."

"Can you take some of the men around to the other side? There is more cover there. Once you rush them, we'll head for the gate and get inside."

"Where is the gate?" he asked.

"See that lilac bush?" she said, pointing. He looked puzzled. "The one with the purple flowers just ahead of us."

"Oh, yeah, that one."

She smiled. She had been raised among the flowers and bushes and trees and knew the names of each. Sometimes she forgot that others did not.

He smiled back then pointed to five of their soldiers, including Liel, and led them through the brush and trees until they were out of sight. She watched with the rest of her group as time stretched out. It had been proved to her over and over recently that she was not made for waiting. However, this was a time for patience.

Her patience was rewarded a moment later when she spotted Rafe on the far side. He peered out, then led the others into the open. They covered more than half of the open area before one of Radieux's men spotted them. With a shout, he raised his rifle. The others started to turn. Rafe reached the first man before he got the rifle to his shoulder and dispatched him with a thrust of his sword.

"Let's go," Arden said.

She led the way across open ground. The latch for the gate was embedded in a brick at the bottom. She pressed it with the toe of her boot, and the gate swung open. The hinges squealed. She slipped inside and directed her guards toward a path shielded from the main building by hedges and bushes. They made their way into that shelter and waited for her. She took one last look toward the cemetery. The monks were taking care of the intruders, now prone on the ground, and waving Rafe and his men toward the wall.

They came at a run, still crouching low. Soon, everyone was inside. Arden made her way to the front and led them in single file around the perimeter, working closer to the main building. Halfway there, they had to stop and wait for a soldier patrolling the gardens to pass in the opposite direction.

When it was clear, they moved on. Arden cringed at every sound they made, but it seemed that the sounds either blended in with natural sounds or were not as loud as they

seemed to her. Nearer the main house, more guards pa-
trolled and they moved more slowly.

During the ride in the *Starbourne*, she and Rafe had discussed a plan for retaking the monastery. Everything was
very nebulous, since they had little idea of the actual placement of the enemy or their numbers. However, she knew
the buildings and the grounds intimately, and what they
would most likely find, not only because of the territory
being held, but also because she knew the general. Not that
there was much room for creativity on such a limited field.

She also knew the abbot and hoped that he had some
influence on what was happening. Given the personalities
of both men, she would guess that most of the monks were
being held in the main reception room. It was the largest
in the whole complex. That way there was no need for
Radieux to split up his force to guard several rooms. It also
gave Grayson ample opportunity to calm his monks and
keep them prepared for action.

Based on all of that supposition, their first target was the
reception room. When they were as near the building as
they could get under cover, Arden called a halt. Everyone
squatted close around her in an enclosure almost surrounded by boxwoods.

"See the French doors near the center of that wing?"
she asked, pointing at them. They craned their necks, peer-
ing through and between the bushes, then nodded. "That's
where the monks are most likely being held, as we discussed. Behind the French doors nearer the end"—they all
looked again—"is the abbot's study. I suspect that Radieux
has headquartered there."

She raised up slightly to look over their heads. She could
see five guards patrolling outside the building on this side.
The roof pitched too steeply for anyone to be posted up
there, but she suspected someone was up in the bell tower
above the entrance to the main building. Two men could
reach there undetected if they were careful.

"Liel, you and Harris make your way to the main entrance and up into the bell tower, there." She pointed, repeating instructions given earlier. "There is a path through
those hedges, the ones with the green and yellow leaves.

Radieux may have someone up there, so be careful. When you have secured it, signal from the window. We'll stay right here until we know you've succeeded. Stay there and give us covering fire if we need it.''

Liel nodded, and he and Harris moved off, each armed with rifle, sword, and pistol. It started to drizzle, and Arden pulled her hat out of her waist pouch. The bill kept the rain out of her eyes.

Here she was, waiting again. Why was it so difficult for her to delegate? That was supposed to be a sign of a good leader.

As she watched, she caught occasional glimpses of the two moving carefully away. The grounds were not actually designed for sneaking in, and they weren't ideal for that purpose. If Radieux was confident that she would not come, however, no one would be expecting anything and probably would not see the occasional flashes of solid green.

She wished that the rain had brought fog, as it often did in the forest, but that could work against them as well. And it did tend to carry sounds we well as hide figures.

Suddenly, Liel appeared, dashing across the open space to the main door. Harris followed once the exec was inside. So far, so good. A moment later, a guard passed the doorway, seemingly oblivious to everything.

The comm unit chimed, and Radieux picked up the handset. After a moment, he slammed it back down. He jumped to his feet, slamming the chair backward.

"Djinn!" he yelled into his wrist comm. "Djinn, get in here."

The captain burst into the study, panting.

"What is it, sir?"

"We've been double-crossed. It looks like Grenfell has sent her guards to the summer palace after all."

"She's not coming here?"

"No!" Radieux said, and began pacing. He shrugged. "I was so sure she would come here to rescue her precious abbot." He stopped and looked at Djinn. "The *Starbourne* did take off, too," he said reflectively. "It is possible that was a ruse." He rubbed both hands across his face. "Tell the men to be alert. Any sign of her or any of her guards, start shooting the monks.''

''Sir?''

''You heard me. I warned her what would happen if she didn't do as I said. And, by god, that's exactly what I'll do.''

''Yes, sir.''

The captain looked worried as he departed, but Radieux knew he would obey. He was a good soldier.

The signal came from the tower. Arden stood, cursing under her breath because crouching in the damp had tightened her joints a bit. She led the way to the hedge, holding her pistol. As she burst into the open, a guard shouted just ahead. A shot from behind brought him down. She and two others veered toward the study while the bulk of her command raced toward the reception room.

Another guard appeared from around the corner to the right. She fired just after he did. His shot went awry, but hers hit the mark and he crumpled.

Shots were being fired rapidly. Some were coming from the tower, now. Arden reached the French doors and fired a burst at the lock. The two glass doors quivered and opened slightly. She pushed one open and burst into the room. A shot whizzed past her ear, and she dropped and rolled. Another shot, and one of her companions yelled in pain.

A soldier in brown burst into the room from the hall, and her other companion continued his rush forward to grapple with him. Still in a crouch, she peered around the familiar overstuffed chair at the massive desk. Behind it stood the general, pistol in hand, pointed right at her. He smiled.

''Hear that?'' he said. Gunfire rattled in the other part of the wing. ''Your friends are being slaughtered because you could not follow orders.''

''Perhaps,'' she said, trying not to visualize such a slaughter. ''But you and I are here, and I'm going to teach you a lesson.''

He laughed. ''I think I have the advantage,'' he said.

"If your shot will go through the chair, so will mine."

His smug smile faded a bit. He had a projectile-type pistol and she held a laser-type. The chair was thick with padding. It might be a toss-up as to which would penetrate better.

"Then why don't we settle this like gentlemen?" he said mockingly. "You have your sword. I have mine."

His offer surprised her a bit, but he did have a reputation as a great swordsman. He spread his hands wide apart, letting the pistol dangle from the right one.

"All right," she said, and stood up, still keeping the chair between them.

He set the pistol on the desktop, and she let hers drop onto the chair seat. He pulled his saber from its scabbard where it lay across the desk. She pulled the katana and scabbard over her head, drew the sword, and laid the scabbard down with the pistol.

"A nice sword, that katana," he said, and moved from behind the desk. "I would like to try it out."

"You had your chance on Baltha," she said.

That brought a frown to his face.

"And you missed your chance on Miga," she added.

He picked up a piece of cloth from the top of the desk. She saw with a start that it was lifeweave.

"I found this in your room," he said. "At least it looked like your things were in there."

He grabbed one edge of the cloth, letting it unfold, then swung it so that it wrapped around his left hand.

With a yell, he raised the saber and charged. No niceties here, not even a chance to get some of the furniture out of the way. It was a big room, but Grayson had filled it.

Arden blocked his overhead blow, turning his blade aside. He attacked again, clearly wanting to take the fight to her and keep her on the defensive. There was little room to move backward in a straight line, and she had to maneuver around chairs and tables and lamps. She ducked one blow completely, and his blade cut through a floor lamp. Electrical sparks sizzled. He threw up his arms to protect his face and moved aside.

Arden attacked, raining blow after blow on him. He was

slightly off balance, and his defense was somewhat awkward. Still, he kept her blade at bay. Their swords locked and they pressed against each other, jockeying for position. An edge of the lifeweave fell loose, covering her right hand and the handle of the katana.

The cloth burned her hand. The room swirled around her, images elongating. She sensed the presence of Pac Terhn and, surprisingly, that of Lyona. The only sound she heard was her own breathing, loud in her ears. She struggled to get her balance as she and Radieux continued pressing against each other. She took a step back, and then another, slowly retreating as he kept pressing. For a moment, she could see in his eyes that he sensed victory; then her vision blurred. She had to get free of the lifeweave. But she did not have enough strength to move away from him.

She dropped to all fours, freeing her hand from the lifeweave. She scrambled to one side on hands and knees, gaining some distance from the general. His surprise at her sudden movement slowed him just long enough for her to get clear. She rose unsteadily to her feet. Radieux closed in, but he had dropped the lifeweave.

As they had moved back and forth around the room, she worked to keep furniture between them. Her arms grew tired, but she knew that with a vagueness that surprised her. She was beyond caring, beyond knowing, and she began to sense when and where he would move next.

With that she noted that everything had taken on a red hue. Sound became a part of that haze, movement slowed slightly, and she felt more like an observer than a participant.

Exhaustion showed in Radieux's eyes now, and in the panting breaths he took. He moved in a more flat-footed way, as if his legs had become too heavy. The red haze deepened without blurring her vision. If anything, she saw more clearly. Yet she saw nothing but the two blades and her opponent.

Suddenly he took a wide, horizontal swing. She dropped to one knee and thrust upward. The tip of her blade penetrated just below the sternum and moved upward. Radieux stumbled backward as if to pull himself free, but she pushed herself forward on both knees now. The sword handle pulsed in her hand as if transmitting his heartbeat. Pain twisted his mouth and veiled his eyes. She almost felt it in an abstract way.

The general dropped slowly to his knees. One hand left the handle of his saber and gripped the blade of the katana. She pulled the sword free, slicing the palm of his hand, reached over, and took the saber from his limp hand.

"I'll get the physician," she said, and started to stand.

"No need," he said, his voice husky. "It's good that it ends this way."

"It doesn't have to."

"Would you have me die in prison, then?"

He grimaced in pain, and blood oozed between the fingers of the hand he held against the wound. He sat back on his heels. His face was grey.

"I misjudged you," he said, and attempted to smile. "You're better with a sword than I thought a woman could be."

"I'll take that as a compliment."

He nodded, and his eyes closed. He looked tired, and she expected him to collapse any moment. He chuckled, then grimaced in pain again.

"What?" Arden asked. She sat back and continued to watch him, feeling that someone should witness his death.

"I'm just sorry I've no more tricks up my sleeve."

"You mean like the charges you had placed around the armory?"

"Yes. It never occurred to me that I would need anything here."

"You couldn't help underestimating me."

There was the sound of movement behind her, but she did not turn around. Even if it was one of Radieux's men, he must see that it was over.

"I should have gotten to know you when I had the chance," he said.

A sigh escaped his lips, his eyes closed, and he slipped sideways to lie curled up on the floor. Arden knew at that moment that he had fought for what he believed in, and although some of his tactics seemed less than honorable, she could still admire that.

A figure came to stand beside her, and when she felt strong enough, she looked up. Through her tears, she saw that it was Brother Bryan.

"Are you all right?" he asked.

"Yes." She reached up a hand, and he helped her to her feet. "I finally did it, Bryan," she said. "The red haze. It happened. I think it was the lifeweave."

For a moment he looked dubious; then he nodded.

"I knew it would happen. One day."

A tear rolled down her right cheek. She had been a warrior for years, and this was the first time the red haze had come. Most lotus-trained warriors experienced it earlier—the color that tinted everything they saw and slowed movement, allowing them to react to an adversary's actions almost before he moved. It was a step forward in their experience

"I wish it could have happened differently."

A large figure burst into the room, and she had to focus to see Grayson clearly. She was so very tired, and sadness overwhelmed her. He put his arms around her and pulled her against his large bulk.

"Thank goodness you're all right, daughter."

"Yes. And you, father." She shook her head. "I have to contact Hsing. Or Alvarez. See how things are going at the summer palace."

"Sit," Grayson ordered. "I'll make the connection."

She let herself be led to one of the overstuffed chairs. Someone spread a sheet over the general's still form. Rafe stood in the doorway, looking as if he was not sure what to do or where to go. She smiled at him, and he came in. He reached down and took her hand in his. Arden looked down at her sword lying on the carpet. Radieux's blood was still on the blade, but she had no desire to wipe it clean on his clothes. That brought an overwhelming feeling that everything had somehow changed—and not for the better.

EPILOGUE

"In honor of service to the imperial house, we present this award to Commander Arden Grenfell."

Jessa moved forward and placed the ribbon around Arden's neck. The medal lay heavily on her chest, but not as heavily as her heart felt inside. This was her farewell present, her grand hurrah, and Jessa seemed untouched by any feelings regarding it. Or was she hiding them?

The premonition she had back in Abbot Grayson's study had been right. Everything had changed.

Within a day after his forces repelled and captured most of the rebels who attacked the summer palace, General Hsing turned in his resignation. The empress accepted it, but no one could tell if she was glad he was leaving or not. The imperial consort was bringing religion to Glory, and his empress wife was fully under his sway. Rafe and his crew boarded the *Starbourne* just yesterday and took off for parts unknown. Arden had gone to the port to see them off.

"I will be back," Rafe had said. "I know I said that the last time, but I realize now that's what I want to do."

"Me too," she said. "The only thing I have left here is Grayson and the monastery. I love them both, but that will never be enough. Still, I need these next few months there."

"I know, and that's all right. I have some things to take care of, then I'll come back for you. We'll do some salvaging together, see if that is what what we want to do for the rest of our lives. If not ..." He shrugged. "It can be very exciting sometimes."

"I'm sure it can," she said with a little laugh.

Within her own experience, salvaging had been very exciting. And profitable, although Rafe was set for life financially unless they got very careless.

One more kiss, and he had turned toward the ship. At the hatchway, he paused, waved, then disappeared inside. Arden had not waited to see the *Starbourne* lift off. She had some packing left to do.

Regret washed through her, as heavy as the medal against her chest, but it was not their time. Not yet. They had not said it aloud, but they both needed time to get used to the idea of giving up some measure of their freedom and changing their lives so drastically.

The empress stood back, and Arden got to her feet, bowed, and backed away. In another moment the ceremony was over. As people moved out of the throne room, Arden watched guests and guards alike. How many of them were truly loyal to Jessa? Probably they were not the greatest danger, though. That lay much closer to home, in the person of the imperial consort.

Pac Terhn told her what she should have seen for herself: as the younger son, Jonas Belle would not inherit much of the lifeweave fortune. He had embraced religion as could only a man with nothing else in his life to care about. As Jessa's consort, he would bring ruin to her world. There was already talk that he intended to use Glory's resources to try to take Weaver from his elder brother.

She shook her head. It was not her problem any more, and Arden tried to tell herself she was well out of it. Let Pac Terhn and Lyona cope with it now.

She made her way to the basement to finish cleaning out her office. After that she would gather up her things in the apartment. She had spent her last night in the palace, something that brought both relief and regret.

As she sat at the desk, sorting through things, the door

opened. General Hsing walked in and sat down. She had never seen him out of uniform until now, but his civvies had a military look to them.

"How about some coffee?" he said.

"Help yourself."

He smiled and got up and did just that, bringing her a cup, as he had so often in the past few weeks. He sat back down and put his feet up on her desk, crossed at the ankles. She grinned at him, sat back in her chair, and sipped at the coffee.

"What are you planning to do?" she asked.

"Relax for a while. It's been a long time since I had some time off. I'll decide later where I'm going. You?"

"I'm heading back to the monastery for a couple of months. I need to do some thinking, too."

"Are you sure you did the right thing, not going with Captain Semmes? I know he cares about you. And you care about him, but waiting can be dangerous."

"That's true," she said, somehow not surprised that he was asking that particular question. "He's coming back in a couple of months, and we will be off together. We'll see if we can actually make a life for ourselves."

"Well, you've had two chances."

"Yep. And not likely to get a third."

She sipped her coffee again, and they sat in silence for a while.

"You should have gotten that medal," she said, pointing at it where it lay. "You saved Jessa and the summer palace."

He shrugged and stared into his coffee. "She probably thought she should give you something after treating you so badly." He looked up. "Would you mind if I come see you at the monastery?" he asked without looking at her.

That question did surprise her, but she liked the idea.

"Not a bit. Maybe we could train together some."

"Well, maybe something like that." He looked at her then, and she realized he was an attractive man. She had never been able to see beyond the uniform before.

"Just as friends," she said.

He got up, threw the cup in the recycler, and walked to the door. He turned and smiled at her as he opened the door.

"I'll be in touch," he said. "That's a promise."

He walked out, and she listened as the sound of his foot-steps receded toward the elevator for the last time.

Change isn't always a bad thing, she thought, and turned to finish packing.